A DUKE WILL NEVER DO

DARCY BURKE

A DUKE WILL NEVER DO

After failing on the Marriage Mart, Jane Pemberton has two choices: submit to her parents' edict to marry their boring neighbor or become a self-declared spinster and take up residence in the official headquarters of the Spitfire Society. It's really no choice at all, and Jane is eager to embrace her newfound independence. She soon finds an unconscious viscount on her doorstep and nurses him back to health. When he offers to compensate her, she requests payment in the form of private instruction of a scandalous and intimate kind.

Having spiraled into a self-destructive abyss following the murder of his parents, Anthony, Viscount Colton, physically recovers under the care of an alluring spitfire. But it is her charm and flirtatiousness that soothes his soul and arouses his desire—until an extortion scheme forces him to face the sins of his past. Now, to save the woman who's given him everything he lost and more, he'll have to pay the ultimate price: his heart.

A Duke Will Never Do
Copyright © 2020 Darcy Burke
All rights reserved.

ISBN: 9781944576752

Book design: © Darcy Burke.
Book Cover Design © Hang Le.
Cover image © Period Images.
Darcy Burke Font Design © Carrie Divine/Seductive Designs
Editing: Linda Ingmanson.

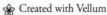 Created with Vellum

For the three funny and lovely humans and four sweet and cuddly cats who make staying at home a pretty great place to be.

This is book #41.

"I'm only this far
And only tomorrow leads the way"
-David J. Matthews

CHAPTER 1

London, May 1819

*J*ane Pemberton hummed to herself as she tied the ribbons of her bonnet beneath her chin. "I'm just going for a quick walk around the square before the meeting, Culpepper."

The butler, a thoroughly capable and unflappable man in his late thirties with thick sandy-brown hair and sherry-brown eyes, inclined his head. "Enjoy your walk, Miss Pemberton."

"Thank you." Jane smiled at him as he reached for the door. Though she'd only moved to the house just over a fortnight ago, she felt completely at home, and that was due in large part to Culpepper's kindness and support. It was most welcome considering the disaster she'd caused by taking up residence here in her friend Phoebe Lennox's house.

No, not Phoebe Lennox. She was Marchioness of Ripley now, after marrying the marquess a fortnight before. Today would be the first time Jane had seen her since the wedding.

Culpepper opened the door, and Jane stepped

toward the threshold. Where she stopped short before tripping over a...

"Good heavens! There's a man on the doorstep!" Jane squatted down and moved his hat, which was sitting askew and covering most of his face. At least she thought it was a face. His eye was so swollen, she doubted he could open it, and a cut, coated with dried blood, marred his upper cheek. Dried blood also covered the space between his nose and mouth, and his lower lip was split. Whoever he was, he'd been in a terrible fight.

"Is he alive?" Culpepper asked.

Jane leaned over him, lowering her cheek to his mouth and nose. His breath, reeking of alcohol, told her he was. "Yes. Let's take him inside."

"I'll fetch Jones." Culpepper referred to one of the footmen.

While the butler was gone, Jane brushed the stranger's dark, wavy hair back from his battered face. Who was he, and why was he on her doorstep?

Culpepper and Jones arrived and hefted him into the entry hall. The stranger moaned but didn't open his eyes.

"Take him up to the front bedchamber." It was the room Jane had used when she'd first arrived, but Phoebe had insisted she take her chamber, which was larger and boasted an adjoining sitting room. Since Phoebe now resided with her husband just down the street in Hanover Square, Jane hadn't refused.

"Yes, Miss Pemberton," Culpepper answered as he led the way, carrying the man's shoulders, going backward up the stairs.

Jane untied her bonnet and removed her gloves as she followed them. Depositing the items on a table at the top of the stairs, she trailed them to the bedchamber, where they placed the man on the bed.

Culpepper turned to her in question.

"Please fetch cloths and water so we can clean him up," Jane said, moving to the bed.

The butler and footman left, and Jane studied the stranger. She could see the other side of his face now, and it was a bit less damaged than the other. "Who are you?" she murmured, gently touching his forehead, which seemed the only unhurt part of his face.

Simultaneously, his hand curled around her wrist, and his lids opened to reveal stunning cobalt eyes. She gasped as recognition finally shot through her. "Lord Colton!"

His eyes narrowed briefly, then his features relaxed into a lazy smile. "Good evening, my lady."

"It is neither evening nor am I a 'my lady.' Don't you know who I am?"

He struggled to sit up and loosened his grip on her wrist, but didn't let go. Instead, he caressed her forearm up to her elbow. "Sorry, love, I've forgotten your name. It's no longer evening, you say? We must have had a lovely time."

Jane stared at him, thinking he had to have lost his senses in the fight. "You don't remember?"

He winced. "It seems not. Ah well, all the reason to begin again." He released her elbow and snaked his arm around her waist, pulling her down.

Surprised by his maneuver, Jane lost her balance and landed against his chest.

He let out a howl of pain that ended in a groan. "Bloody hell, that hurts." He let her go and lifted his hand to his head. "Everything hurts."

"I should think so," Jane said, working to push herself off him without causing him more discomfort. Given how he'd reacted, she assumed his body was also injured.

A maid entered at that moment with towels as well as fresh water, which she brought to the table beside the bed. Jane turned to her. "Thank you. Did you happen to bring some salve?"

The maid glanced toward the viscount and flinched. "No, but I will." She turned to go.

"And Cook's headache tonic," Jane called after her.

"Yes, Miss Pemberton."

Jane turned back to the bed and saw that the viscount's eyes were closed once more, and he appeared to be asleep again. Dipping a cloth into the warm water, she applied it to the cut on his cheek, wiping away the blood. When it was clean, she set about cleaning the rest of the blood from his face. But he was so swollen and his flesh so reddened, she didn't feel as if she was helping all that much.

Leaning toward him slightly, she studied his features for the man she knew. Anthony, Viscount Colton, was a very handsome gentleman, buried somewhere beneath the injuries he'd suffered. He was also the brother of a good friend, Sarah, the Countess of Ware, who was currently in the country preparing to give birth to her first child any day.

What on earth had happened to him? And why was he on Jane's doorstep, of all places?

"Miss Pemberton?"

Jane turned her head to see Culpepper stepping into the bedchamber. "Should we send for a doctor? I think his injuries may go beyond his face."

"Do you know a discreet physician?" he asked.

No, she did not. And discretion would be vital. Jane might have shunned society's rules when she'd declared herself a spinster and moved away from her parents' house, but she didn't wish to add fuel to her smoldering reputation.

"Let us just take care of him for now," Jane said. "We'll see how he is later."

"Should you notify Bow Street to perhaps find out who he is?"

"Oh, I know who he is." Jane glanced down at his almost-unrecognizable face. "He's Lord Colton."

Culpepper's eyes flickered with surprise. "I see. My apologies, Miss Pemberton, but I came to tell you Lady Gresham and Miss Whitford have arrived."

"Thank you, Culpepper. Will you have Meg come up and tend to Lord Colton?"

"Right away."

Jane sent one last lingering look toward the unconscious man on the bed and hastened from the room. She rushed downstairs to the garden room, situated at the back of the house. A bright, cheerful chamber, Phoebe had refurbished it to feel as if it were part of the garden that lay just outside the doors that led outside.

Phoebe was, in fact, also there, along with Lady Gresham and Miss Whitford. Seated in what had been her favorite chair when she'd lived there, Phoebe smiled at Jane in greeting. She looked incredibly happy, her green eyes sparkling.

Jane took the empty chair near Phoebe's, which was opposite a settee where the sisters, Lady Gresham and Miss Whitford, were seated. "Welcome, ladies. I'm so glad you could come to our first official meeting of the Spitfire Society."

"We're delighted to be invited," Lady Gresham said. Tall and slender with a delicate bone structure and glossy, honey-brown hair, she was the epitome of elegance—at least to Jane.

"What is the purpose of this meeting?" Miss Whitford asked without preamble.

Lady Gresham looked toward her younger sister, and it seemed she was going to speak, but Phoebe got there first.

"Before we get into the meeting, Lady Gresham

and Miss Whitford found a gentleman's hat on your doorstep." Phoebe stood and went to a table near the door where she picked up a black hat and brought it back to where they were seated. "Do you know to whom it belongs?"

Jane's mind scrambled as she took it from her. If it was just Phoebe here, Jane would tell the truth of it, but she didn't know Lady Gresham and Miss Whitford well enough to disclose that there was an unconscious man upstairs in the guest chamber. "I don't. Perhaps it blew there from the square."

"Surely a gentleman would know if he'd lost his hat," Phoebe said.

"Maybe someone left it there on purpose," Miss Whitford suggested as a maid entered with a tray of refreshments, which she arranged on a low table situated between the settee and chairs.

"Would you pour the lemonade, please?" Jane asked.

"Thank you, Laura," Phoebe said warmly to the maid, who smiled in response.

"It's nice to see you, my lady," Laura said to Phoebe while pouring.

Miss Whitford appeared to be a few years younger than her sister. With blonde hair, light hazel eyes, and a shorter, more curvaceous frame, she and Lady Gresham did not look very much like sisters.

"That's right, this is your house, isn't it?" Miss Whitford asked.

"Yes, but it's Jane's home now." Phoebe inclined her head toward Jane.

Miss Whitford reached for her glass while glancing toward Jane. "And how is it that you find yourself living here alone?"

"Beatrix," Lady Gresham said quietly before sending an apologetic glance toward Jane and Phoebe. "Pardon my sister. Sometimes she speaks a bit recklessly. Having come from the country, we are not used to polite society."

"Please don't concern yourself, Lady Gresham. I find Miss Whitford's demeanor refreshing, for you see, I am quite weary of Society myself." Jane smiled encouragingly at Miss Whitford. "That is why I am living here alone. I don't wish to participate in the rituals required of unmarried women of my age. Furthermore, the purpose of the Spitfire Society is to celebrate womanhood and whatever independence we can claim."

Miss Whitford blinked, her lashes sweeping briefly over her hazel eyes. "Fascinating. We came to town so I could have a Season. I must say, independence sounds rather lovely." She cast a glance toward her sister, who, as a wealthy widow, enjoyed as much independence as a woman could probably hope to.

"Marriage is also lovely," Lady Gresham said, eyeing Phoebe, who was, of course, very recently— and blissfully—wed. To a consummate rake, no less. Rather, former rake.

Phoebe picked up her lemonade. "I certainly can't complain. And I daresay if any of you are lucky enough to find a man like Marcus, you wouldn't either. Not that there are any other men like him." A faint blush stained her cheeks as she sipped her drink.

"So what do spitfires do?" Miss Whitford asked.

"That's up to us," Jane said. "We support each other, obviously, but perhaps we can also do something meaningful for other women."

"What a marvelous idea," Lady Gresham said, perhaps with a hint of surprise to her tone. "Do you have anything specific in mind?"

"No, but I'm sure we can come up with something." As Jane plucked a biscuit from the tray, a loud crash upstairs made her drop it. Her gaze shot toward the ceiling as her pulse picked up.

Phoebe frowned. "My goodness, what was that?"

"My, er, kitten!" Jane said quickly. "I just brought him home yesterday."

Surprise flashed across Phoebe's face. "You have a kitten?"

"Yes, I hope that's all right. I should have asked you first, but the poor thing needed a home." Jane realized she could have been talking about Lord Colton. He was in desperate need—not for a home, but for care. And she'd tell Phoebe about him too —later.

Culpepper appeared in the doorway, his forehead rippled with concern. "Miss Pemberton, might I have a word?"

Alarm spread through Jane as she rose from the chair. "Please excuse me a moment," she managed to say calmly before walking sedately from the room just as a second noise sounded from upstairs.

She followed Culpepper into the hall and spoke in a frantic whisper. "What the devil is going on?"

Culpepper's brows pitched low with a mixture of frustration and annoyance. "I'm afraid his lordship has awakened and is being rather...disruptive. Meg and Jones are trying to keep him quiet, but I don't know if they will be successful." The sound of something breaking carried down the stairs, and Jane prayed her guests, especially Phoebe, couldn't hear it.

"Clearly not," Jane said. "I'll go right up—after I adjourn the meeting. Will you please show them out with alacrity?" She bustled back into the garden room with a wide, artificial smile. "I beg your pardon, friends, but I'm afraid the kitten is having some difficulty. Might we postpone the meeting? I do thank you for coming today and am sorry to shorten our time together." Jane turned and hurried from the room before another noise further stretched the believability of her kitten story.

Rushing into the bedchamber where she'd left Lord Colton unconscious, Jane stopped short at the sight before her. A broken vase cluttered the floor, a table lay overturned, and Jones, the strong, young footman who'd helped carry Lord Colton upstairs, massaged his jaw while frowning at the viscount. Who was currently on the opposite side of the bed, holding Meg's hand and smiling at her.

"What is going on here?" Jane demanded. She walked past Jones and threw him an apologetic look as she made her way to Colton and Meg.

"I was just telling this beautiful creature how beautiful she is," Colton slurred.

Meg's lip curled, and she snatched her hand away.

Jane touched the maid's arm. "I'm so sorry, Meg." Then she put herself in between them and glared at the viscount. "You're drunk. And injured. Why are you even out of bed?"

He winced, his blue eyes squinting briefly. "How injured am I? I don't recall—"

Jane pushed him against the side of the bed, her hands briefly connecting with his chest. He yelped in pain, and she felt a moment's regret. But only a moment. He was behaving horribly. Perhaps she should throw him into a coach and send him home. Yes, that would be best.

Lord Colton pulled his coat off and dropped it to the floor, then began unbuttoning his waistcoat.

"What are you doing?"

"I fear my ribs are bruised. Or broken." He winced again as he drew the waistcoat off. Then he tugged away his cravat and tried to peer down the open neckline of his shirt. Holding the linen away from his chest, he scowled. Muttering a curse, he pulled the shirt over his head with a groan. "That's better," he said as he surveyed his chest once more.

A faint bruise already colored the left side between his breast and abdomen. A rather muscular breast and abdomen.

Jane pivoted from him as she realized she'd been staring. Perhaps he should rest before she threw him out.

"I think I should rest," he mumbled, giving voice to her thoughts. He fell backward onto the bed, gasping. "Ow." He gingerly touched his face.

Jane looked toward the table on the other side of the bed and realized that was the one that had been overturned. "Where is the salve?" she asked.

"Somewhere," Meg said. "I'll find it." The maid went to the other side of the chamber in search of the ointment.

"Jones, will you remove his lordship's boots?" Jane asked. She felt bad asking him and Meg to help the viscount when he'd behaved so reprehensibly, but she knew his mind was altered by drink and likely pain. Yes, perhaps it was best that he stay. For now. She turned her attention back to him to see that he was staring up at her in consternation.

"Do I know you?" he asked.

She ignored the question. "You're going to stay here for now."

His lips spread into a leer—albeit a rather charming one. "Only if you promise to stay with me."

Jane rolled her eyes. "You need sleep."

Lord Colton stared down the bed as Jones pulled off his second boot. "Or him." He waggled his brows suggestively.

Shaking her head, she sent another apologetic look to Jones. "Perhaps you should help him back to unconsciousness."

The footman smirked. "I'd be delighted to."

Jane smiled in return. "Just stay outside near the door, if you don't mind. I daresay he will have tired himself out after all that nonsense." In answer to her prognostication, the viscount's snores filled the room.

Meg came around to her side of the bed with the jar of salve. "Found it."

Jane took the medicine. "Thank you. Will you bring fresh water?" The cut on his cheek had started bleeding again. She wondered if it needed stitching, which would require a physician.

Meg took herself off, and Jane stared down at her patient. Yes, he was now in her care. At least for the time being. "You are a mess," she said softly as she removed the lid from the salve.

Dipping her fingers into the thick unguent, she spread it along the redness of his jaw where another bruise was beginning to form. Then on his cheek, careful not to disturb the cut too much. She moved up to his swollen eye and then the other side of his face, which, while less battered, was beginning to show colors that said it had not been ignored during the tussle.

And what tussle was that? What had he done to warrant such a beating? She flinched inwardly, thinking of the violence that must have transpired even as she recalled seeing him fight at the masquerade ball at Brixton Park last month. Had this behavior become the norm for him? She couldn't quite reconcile that with the gentleman she'd met a few years ago. But then that had been before he'd taken up with Phoebe's husband, the Marquess of Ripley. Ripley was an inveterate rake with little concern for Society's rules. Or he had been before he'd met Phoebe. Now he was hopelessly in love and quite reformed.

As far as Jane knew, Ripley hadn't ever been a

fighter. In fact, he was the one who'd put a stop to Colton's altercation at the ball. Was he aware of what Colton had been up to? Perhaps Ripley could help.

Jane shook her head. Of course he wasn't aware —he was enjoying his newly wedded bliss with Phoebe, as he should. Jane would not trouble him, or Phoebe, with this. Not for now, anyway.

Finished with his face, Jane looked at the bruising on his chest. Had it spread just since he'd first removed his shirt?

She swallowed as she covered her fingers with more salve and contemplated the inappropriateness of massaging a man's naked chest. A man who wasn't her husband and who was residing in her home. A home in which she lived by herself in flagrant disregard of Society's rules. Oh dear, was she now, somehow, a female version of Ripley?

The thought brought a smile to her lips. Since Phoebe had done this before Jane, perhaps it was that Phoebe was the female version of Ripley and that was how they'd come to find each other.

But no, Phoebe hadn't been rakish at all. On the contrary, she'd wanted nothing to do with men for reasons that were entirely understandable and unassailable.

Jane, however, was not the same as Phoebe. She was rather...interested in men. In fact, she'd never been more aware of that until this moment as her fingertips caressed the hard, muscular plane of Lord Colton's rather estimable chest.

Moving quickly, her cheeks flaming, she finished her task. What on earth was she doing? She'd left her parents and declared her spinsterhood, moving here just to avoid a marriage they were pushing her into.

Not wanting Mr. Brinkley doesn't mean you don't want any *man.*

Jane exhaled. That was true. Indeed, since her

friend Arabella and then Phoebe had both recently wed—and quite happily—Jane was feeling...unsettled. Not because she desperately wanted a husband. No, she wanted what a husband could give her—that secret smile of satisfaction that both her friends now wore when they spoke of their husbands or looked in their direction. The way their eyes lit with heat and...desire. Jane wanted that.

How ironic since she'd now put herself in a position so as to make that happening even less likely than it was before. Ironic and frustrating.

Frowning, she put the top back on the salve. Her gaze traveled down Lord Colton's body until she saw his stockings. Those should probably come off too.

She set the salve on the edge of the bed and then moved down to tug the stockings from his feet. As she exposed his calves and the dark hair covering them, her belly fluttered. Inappropriate didn't begin to cover this situation.

Now that his feet were bare, she wondered if the rest of him should be too. Surely he'd be more comfortable. And shouldn't she check for further injuries?

No. She'd let the discreet physician—assuming they could find one—take care of that.

Scoffing, she stepped away from the bed. She had no business taking any pleasure from caring for Lord Colton. Especially when he'd hit her footman and flirted with her maid.

Meg returned just then with the water. She glanced around, clearly to see where to place it.

"Here, let me." Jane rushed to right the table and positioned it next to the bed so Meg could place the ewer on it. Then Meg fetched the basin and the towels, which she set beside the ewer.

Jane turned to her. "Did Lord Colton hurt you in any way?"

"No, miss. I don't think he even realized who I

was. He asked me to dance, then suggested we could find a dark corner in the garden afterward." She laughed. "I think he thought I was a lady."

Jane shook her head. "I'm relieved to hear it was nothing more than that. Thank you for your help. Will you see if Culpepper is free?"

"I am here, miss," the butler said, stepping into the room, his gaze falling on the broken pottery. "Meg, will you tidy this up, please?"

"Right away." Meg took herself off, probably to fetch a broom.

Culpepper approached the bed with a frown. "I see he's fallen back asleep."

"Yes, after stripping off his clothing," Jane said. "He said his ribs may be broken. And his face is bleeding again." She frowned. "We may not know of a discreet physician, but we need to find one." She looked at Culpepper, and he met her gaze. "Can you do that?"

The butler gave her a single nod. "I will."

Jane's lips curled into an appreciative smile. "How lovely. Thank you, Culpepper."

"Will there be anything else, miss?"

She'd been about to say no, but then realized there *was* something else. "Yes, in fact there is. I need a kitten."

CHAPTER 2

*A*nthony Colton tried to roll to his side, but pain shot from his abdomen, forcing a moan from his parched throat. Blinking his eyes open—rather, one eye since the other seemed to not want to cooperate—he struggled to sit up. Though he could only see from one eye, one thing was plainly apparent: this was not his bedchamber.

He brought his hand to his face and winced, letting out a hiss of pain.

Two things, actually. Someone had beaten him to a pulp. God, his head felt as if it might explode. Perhaps that would be for the best.

He let his hand fall back down to the bed beside him, then winced once more as his knuckles brushed the bedclothes. He brought his hand back up and squinted at the back of it. Judging from the scabs and reddened flesh, he'd maybe beaten the other man to an equal state of collapse.

Anthony tried again to sit up, gritting his teeth through the agony shooting through him. Once he was upright, he had to stop to catch his breath. He took the opportunity to look around the room, a medium-sized bedchamber scarcely lit by a candle beside the bed and the coals in the fireplace. Where the bloody hell was he?

He didn't recognize a thing. Not the green up-holstered chair near the hearth, not the landscape painting hanging over the mantel, nor the ivory draperies cloaking the window. And while he didn't recall the bedside table to his left, the pitcher and cup atop it were most welcome.

It took considerable pain-filled effort to turn his body and swing his legs over the side of the bed. The room tilted, and he had to sit still for a moment for the world to right itself. His hand shaking, he reached for the pitcher and managed to bring it to-ward him so he could view the contents. Water. Splendid.

Wrapping his hand around the cup to hold it steady, which seemed laughable given how uncertain his entire body felt, he managed to pour water into the cup and only sloshed a small amount onto his hand and the table.

"Well done, Anthony," he murmured.

Then he drank. A spot of gin might go down better, but he wouldn't complain. It just felt good to get his throat wet. He poured a second cup and downed it, only a bit more slowly than the first.

Feeling slightly refreshed, he braced his feet on the floor to stand. With an exhalation, he pushed the bedclothes away and then realized something he should have known since awakening.

He was bloody naked.

Where the hell were his clothes? Was he in a brothel? If so, he didn't recognize it, and he was fairly certain he'd been in every single room at Mrs. Al-ban's, his bawdy house of choice.

He tried to stand and immediately regretted the movement as the room pitched again. After he was settled once more, he scooted down toward the end of the bed and wrapped his hand around the post. Clutching tightly, he brought himself to a standing position and was again winded by the act.

"Christ," he muttered in irritation. Whoever had pummeled him had done a bang-up job. The unintended pun made him smile, and then flinch as his sore lips and cheeks rebelled against the action.

Who *had* beaten him? Anthony tried to think back to the events of the evening. Was it still evening? He had no notion of the time.

He'd gone to a gaming hell where he'd drunk to excess, as he did most nights. The drinking, not the gaming. He didn't gamble anymore. He merely watched, and every time he felt the urge to join, he drank. Which explained the excess.

Someone had tried to coerce him into gambling, he suddenly recalled. The man had been looking for a fight, and Anthony had been more than happy to give it to him. He vaguely remembered another man —or several men—breaking them apart, and then Anthony had stumbled out of the hell. The rest was blackness. Had some benevolent soul found him and given him care?

There was only one way to find out. He saw his clothing on a chair tucked into the corner. Hell, that was incredibly far away. Clenching his jaw, he gathered the energy to make the journey. His steps were more like shuffles as he inched his way to the corner. Halfway there, he had to stop and draw several breaths to continue. He closed his eyes as the floor seemed to move beneath him. He was well used to the aftereffects of drinking too much, but this bout was particularly nasty.

At last, he reached the chair. And he promptly sat, his body slouching in exhaustion and defeat. Perhaps he should just climb back into the bed until he was more recovered.

Except, he wanted to know where he was. Turning at the waist, he rifled through the pile of clothing until he found his shirt. Pulling it over his head took a great deal of exertion. So much that he decided that was all he could manage.

After mustering the ability to stand once more, he did so slowly, bracing his hands on the arms of the chair until he felt steady. Or at least somewhat steady.

The shirt reached to the bottom of his backside, which was good enough for him. And since he was likely in a brothel, no one would care.

It took several long minutes to reach the door, but by then, he was starting to feel a little more like a man and not a pile of rubbish. Opening the door, he peered outside into an empty corridor.

Summoning what little strength he possessed, Anthony haltingly made his way along the corridor. He still recognized absolutely nothing. A wave of unease rolled through him, and he put his hand on the wall to brace himself. When the queasiness passed, he continued on until he encountered a door.

He pushed it open and found himself in a sitting room. It was quite feminine, decorated in pink and ivory, but disappointingly devoid of people. Where was everyone?

Another door on the opposite side caught his eye. He strode quickly—as quickly as he'd yet dared —and nearly collapsed against it when he arrived. Breathing heavily, he pushed it open and stumbled into what was clearly a bedchamber.

Also decorated in pink and ivory, it was obviously the domain of a woman. A brothel owner, perhaps.

Anthony pushed himself to walk to the bed, where a shape was visible beneath the bedclothes. At last, he'd found someone who could tell him what the bloody hell was going on.

He reached down and touched the form. "I beg your pardon."

The woman started, her body twitching before she rolled over and shrieked.

Her reaction pushed him off-balance, and he teetered. She gasped and leapt up to her knees, then grabbed his forearms before he went down. "I've got you."

In fact, she did have him, quite forcefully. He pitched forward onto the bed, barely missing her as he landed atop the mattress.

"My goodness," she said. "You're, ah, not wearing breeches."

The cold air on his arse told him that his shirt had come up to reveal his naked backside. "No," he said into the bedclothes, which made the word come out garbled and likely unintelligible. He turned his head so he could speak more clearly. "I don't think I can get up." In fact, his body was screaming with pain and exhaustion, as if he'd consumed every bit of energy he possessed.

She moved off the bed. "Can you at least get under the covers?"

Anthony started to move, then groaned as agony burned through him. "Maybe."

"I'll help you." She pushed the covers down as far as she could. "Can you roll under them or something?"

"I can try." He closed his eyes and pushed himself over, letting out a moan.

"Oh! Your shirt." She'd turned away from the bed.

"This isn't a brothel, is it?"

"Of course not!" She sounded scandalized.

And here he was, half-naked. More than half, actually. Anthony worked to shift himself under the coverlet and pulled the bedclothes up to his waist. "I'm covered."

She turned toward the bed, and his eye was drawn to the rise and fall of her breasts, clearly visible beneath the thin lawn of her night rail. Despite his pathetic state, he felt a rush of desire. A long, blond plait grazed her nipple. Anthony swallowed as he raised his gaze to her face. She looked familiar…

"Lord Colton—"

"You know me, but I'm afraid—" He stopped short as recognition flooded him. "Miss…Pemberton?"

"Yes. This is most assuredly *not* a brothel."

Christ. She was an unmarried young woman! What the hell was he doing in her bedchamber? He bolted up and instantly regretted it as pain careened through him. Groaning, he fell back. "What happened? Why am I here? *Where are your parents?*"

Miss Pemberton's brow creased as she moved closer to the edge of the bed, her light brown eyes surveying him. "You mustn't cause yourself further injury. I don't know what happened, but I found you yesterday on my doorstep."

"*I paid a call like this?*"

"No, nothing like that. You were unconscious. And you looked like, well, hell."

"I feel like hell," he muttered.

"You may rest easy—while this is not a brothel, it is also not my parents' house. You're at Phoebe Lennox's house in Cavendish Square." She shook her head. "I mean the Marchioness of Ripley's house. Someday, I will remember that."

Anthony knew her, and he definitely knew Ripley. The man was one of his closest friends. Rather, he had been until he'd gotten married a fortnight ago and instantly transformed into a managing mama.

Anthony hadn't seen him since the wedding breakfast.

"I still don't understand why I'm here, of all places."

"I don't know why either," she said. "I did consider sending you home. However, you were in a rather bad state."

He had to admit the thought of a coach ride in his current condition was about as alluring as spending a night on a torture rack. And would probably feel just about the same.

"I do appreciate your compassion and good sense. And I apologize for assuming this was a brothel. When I awakened nude in an unfamiliar place, it was the only thing that made sense."

She narrowed her eyes at him, her head tilting. "This has happened to you before?"

"No, not *this*. Of course not. But if I wasn't at a brothel, why would I be nude in a strange bed?"

"Because you were beaten almost beyond recognition and you were completely soused to boot."

Unfortunately, none of that was unlikely, and he was, at least, clearly injured. He had to have been completely inebriated to have fought in the first place and then to end up here in Cavendish Square. How had that come about? He tried to recall what had happened, but only managed to make his head hurt worse.

He raised his hand to the vicinity of his temple. "Do you have anything for my head?"

"There's a tonic in the other bedchamber. I don't suppose you should move back there just now. You look quite pale, at least what parts of you aren't red or bruised. There's also salve for your injuries. You really are a mess." She pursed her lips, and he knew she was judging him. As everyone did.

Anthony fought a wave of irritation. "Thank you."

"We sent for a doctor, and he examined you last night—that's why you weren't wearing any clothes."

"Were you there?" The question leapt from his mouth without thought. His brain really was addled, and he was frustratingly sober.

"I waited outside." Was that a faint hint of color in her cheeks? It was hard to tell in the dim light from the hearth and due to the fact that he currently had but one functioning eye. "He confirmed that you have injuries to your ribs and instructed strict bed rest for at least a week."

That explained the horrible pain in his chest and abdomen.

"He said your face would clear up—nothing was broken, and the cut on your cheek did not require stitching."

"You've gone to a great deal of effort for me."

One of her blond brows arched. "You've no idea," she said dryly.

He flinched inwardly. "Do I want to know all that happened yesterday?"

"Probably not, but I'm going to tell you anyway." She perched on the edge of the bed, and her thigh pressed against his. The contact sent a rush of awareness through him.

Presumably it did the same for her, because she jumped right back up as if she'd been burned. Well, this was bloody inconvenient given his current useless state. Never mind that she was untouchable—a proper, unmarried miss.

Whose bed he was currently in. Naked. Well, not naked anymore, but did the shirt really count? Hell, his cock was stirring in spite of all that.

She looked away from him, and this time, he was certain of the blush spreading through her face. "We tended to your injuries despite your inebriated state. You were rather insensible—flirting with me, my maid and, I think, the footman."

Anthony closed his one good eye and groaned.

"Are you all right?" Her voice lowered with concern.

He opened his eye again and lied. "Just a pain in my ribs." Along with his pride for causing this perfectly respectable young woman to have to deal with his bad behavior. "My apologies, Miss Pemberton. I deeply regret that I've caused you such difficulty."

She studied him a moment in silence. "Once I realized who you were, I became quite worried. I was concerned to find a wounded man on my doorstep, but once I discovered I knew you... Well, I couldn't *not* help you."

"You're an angel, obviously."

She scoffed. "My parents would debate you about that." Her tone was wry once more.

"You've a sarcastic streak. I like it." He grinned and immediately winced. "I'm afraid I can't smile without causing an enormous amount of agony."

"Your lip was split in the fight. Have you any idea what happened?"

"I was in a gaming hell. I do remember fighting, but I don't know with whom. And I don't recall how I ended up here in your house." That was truly bothering him.

"Well, you're here now, and I think you should remain. For a week, at least, until your ribs have begun to heal, as the doctor said."

A week in Miss Pemberton's care... He could think of far worse things. And yet, it was wholly scandalous. "I don't think that's wise. What are you even doing here, anyway? At Phoebe's house, I mean."

"Perhaps you are not aware, but I've declared

myself a spinster. I moved out of my parents' house. This is my home now."

She'd bloody ruined herself. Probably. And Anthony considered himself an expert on self-ruin. "Why would you do that?" he asked.

She lifted her shoulder, moving the plait so that the end grazed her nipple. Already somewhat parched, Anthony's throat took on the landscape of a veritable desert.

"I was weary of the Marriage Mart and Society's rules for unmarried misses. I saw that Phoebe was quite happy living independently and decided I wanted that for myself. While it's true I am socially ruined, I can't say I really care, since being socially acceptable wasn't exactly providing any benefit. My friends remain my friends, and that's all that matters in the end."

Anthony found her honesty and self-awareness utterly refreshing, albeit strange in someone such as her. "Then I must congratulate you."

"Thank you."

"I would still prefer not to contribute to your ruination," Anthony said. "I'm sure I can get home without exacerbating my injuries." He wasn't sure at all, but decided injury to his body was better than to her reputation.

"We'll keep your presence secret. No one need know you're here." She smiled. "It's not as if I'll be entertaining." Her smile faded.

"What?"

"I did yesterday, actually. I hosted a meeting of the Spitfire Society. Phoebe was here, as were two sisters who are somewhat new to town."

His one eye widened, and despite the injury to his other eye, it tried to do the same. The resulting pain drew a soft groan from his throat. "Did they know I was here?"

Miss Pemberton shook her head, sending the braid moving against her breast again. God, she was going to send him the rest of the way to his grave. And she had no idea. Unless she cared to glance down and notice the tent he was likely creating with the bedclothes.

"They did not," she said. "I did, however, have to make up an excuse for all the racket you made. You overturned a table and broke a vase. I hope it wasn't dear to Phoebe."

He winced again. "I'm a menace," he said softly but with as much self-loathing as he could manage. Which was quite a lot.

"You aren't."

He looked at her with great doubt.

"All right, perhaps a little." The smile appeared once more, and he was tempted to return one of his own but knew it would be at considerable cost to his comfort.

"You are definitely an angel."

"Then it's settled," she said. "You're staying here."

"Here…in your bed?" Again, words tumbled from his mouth without thought. Flirtatious, provocative, seductive words. Words he ought to apologize for but didn't.

He'd expected another blush or perhaps surprise or even admonition. None of those things happened. When she spoke, her words were measured. "When you are feeling better—tomorrow perhaps—you can return to the other chamber. In the meantime, yes, you'll stay *here*. In my bed."

"How delicious." He really needed to stop talking. "And where will you go?"

"The other chamber. I'll go there now to fetch the headache tonic and the salve." She started to turn, but he reached up and grabbed her hand. Her skin was soft and warm, and gave him a comfort that sank into his very soul.

"Thank you."

She curled her hand around his briefly, then let go. "I'll be right back."

He watched as she donned slippers and a robe, then departed. Casting his head back against the pillow, he stared up at the ceiling. He was very lucky things had not turned out far worse. He could have ended up on anyone's doorstep instead of that of a beautiful angel bent on saving him.

The image of that made him uncomfortable. He didn't want saving. But he'd accept her care, since he was clearly in need of that. Furthermore, she hadn't offered to save him.

Exhaustion rolled through him, pulling his eye shut. Her scent surrounded him—a light, fruity but seductive aroma that lulled him into a sense of blissful safety.

Yes, his brain was well and truly addled. But that was better than the alternative, which was probably death.

Is it, though?

As he drifted off, he pictured Miss Pemberton with white wings and a halo of light around her head. It illuminated the beauty of her face, which he recalled from having met her several times before—elegant brows with a natural arch, intelligent tawny-brown eyes, a pert nose, sculpted cheekbones, a heart-shaped mouth that smiled often with genuine humor.

She represented kindness and generosity, beauty and truth.

And he had no business being around her.

CHAPTER 3

*J*ane climbed the stairs after dinner that evening, intent on visiting her patient. She hadn't checked on him during the afternoon as he'd been sleeping, which he'd spent most of the day doing, according to Meg and the other maids who'd cared for him.

She opened the door to her chamber, thinking it was odd that someone else was inhabiting her bed. Perhaps tomorrow, he'd feel strong enough to move back to the other bedroom.

"Good evening, Miss Pemberton," he greeted her from the bed, with a smile in his voice if not on his face. "I was hoping you'd pay me a visit."

Jane took in the tray perched on the bed beside him. "You ate dinner?"

"I was famished, and it was delicious. Please give my compliments to your cook."

"I will." Jane rounded the bed and picked up the tray to transfer it to a small table near the door. She had to remove a figurine to make room for the tray. Looking down at the ceramic maiden, she wondered if Phoebe planned to fetch it. There were many things in the house that she would probably like to have, particularly the Gainsborough in the garden room.

Setting the figurine on the narrow mantel, Jane turned back toward the man in her bed. He sat up against the headboard, wearing a fresh nightshirt, which she'd sent one of the maids to purchase that morning. She wanted to say he looked better, but the bruising on his face had darkened to a rather horrid degree. He actually looked worse.

"I look hideous," he said, again sounding as if he were grinning. "Meg gave me a mirror before dinner so I could verify what I already suspected. I do feel a trifle better thanks to your cook's headache tonic. I daresay I may steal your cook when I leave here."

"She's not my cook. She's Phoebe's."

"But isn't this your house now? The marchioness will surely reside in Hanover Square with Ripley. I can't imagine him giving that house up."

Neither could Jane. While this house was one of the nicest in Cavendish Square, it couldn't compare to the opulence and grandeur of the marquess's residence. Or so it seemed from the outside—and Phoebe had confirmed the interior was just as impressive.

"Well, I'd rather you didn't filch the cook in any case," Jane said.

"I'll consider your kind request. " His face seemed to spasm. "I can't wink."

Concerned, she walked to the bed. "Why not?"

"That's my bad eye."

"You can't wink with your other eye?"

"I don't know. Let me try." He scrunched his face up. "Ow."

She held up her hand. "Stop, don't hurt yourself."

"Everything hurts. But what kind of rogue am I if I can't wink?" He tried again, and the effort it took to affect a rather sad-looking wink drove Jane to laugh.

"If you are trying to appear roguish, I'm afraid it looks more like you're attempting to stave off a fit of apoplexy."

"Well, we don't want that," he said in mock horror. Then he actually smiled, and despite the damage to his face, Jane recalled he was quite handsome.

"You shouldn't smile if it hurts."

"As I said, *everything* hurts. And you are far too diverting. I can't seem to help myself. Anyway, speaking of when I leave, we should probably discuss that."

She thought they'd already decided that the night before. But perhaps he didn't remember. "Discuss what?"

"My departure. I should go. My servants will be horrified by my appearance, but they likely won't be shocked. They already fuss over me too much."

Because he'd fought before? "You're not leaving. I told you last night, but perhaps you don't recall our conversation, that the doctor said you should rest for at least a week. I won't let you return home until that time has elapsed. Perhaps even a fortnight."

"You are far too kind." He looked her straight in the eye, his gaze vulnerable. "What did I do to deserve your generosity?"

"It's not like that. I would have done the same for anyone."

Really? Anyone who'd appeared in his state on her doorstep?

He shifted slightly toward her. "How can I ever repay you?"

She waved a hand. "That isn't necessary."

"It *is* necessary. We'll come up with something."

She had no notion what that could be. She certainly wasn't going to accept payment. To avoid further discussion, she reverted to their previous topic. "I sent a message to your butler today saying you were fine."

He stared at her. "You did? He knows I'm here?"

"No. I didn't tell him where you were. I just said you were safe and would be home in a week. Or a fortnight. And I signed your name."

"Bloody hell," he breathed. "You've quite taken care of everything. You are *surely* an angel sent to watch over me."

She laughed. "Hardly. I'm just glad you showed up on my doorstep and not somewhere worse."

"Indeed," he agreed with vigor. "I can think of plenty of terrible places."

One of his brows arched, and she was surprised he didn't flinch. "Such as?"

"The door of the man who did this to me."

She nearly laughed again. "Yes, that *would* be worse."

"Or the doorstep of one of the patronesses of Almack's."

She did chuckle then. "Most definitely. Carlton House?"

He grinned again. "Yes, that. Or Westminster."

"Oh dear, you're going to miss your duties in the Lords, aren't you?"

He did wince then. "They won't miss me. I've been a bit, ah, remiss this session."

Because of his drinking and reckless behavior, probably.

"Is there wine?" he asked. "My dinner came with ale and nothing else."

Because she'd told the maid and cook to only serve him ale. "I thought it best you keep a clearer head whilst you recover."

His eye narrowed briefly. "How in the devil am I

supposed to endure the pain without the assistance of alcohol?"

"The salve should help, and you said the headache tonic was working well." She hesitated before adding, "You were awfully inebriated when you arrived. In fact, it seemed as though you imbibed enough to keep yourself drunk for a week. Why aren't you still soused?"

"Ha-ha," he said, clearly unamused and perhaps even a bit annoyed.

His irritation rankled because of everything she'd done. Maybe she did expect some sort of payment— or appreciation at least. "You seem to be inebriated much of the time. Perhaps your altercation was a warning for you to behave with more care."

He scowled at her, but she continued, "You seem to be having…difficulty of late."

"Why do you care?"

She heard the edge of anger in his voice but didn't heed it. "You always seemed like a nice gentleman, and I like Sarah very much." Jane counted his sister as a friend. She cocked her head to the side and studied his wounded face. "This is not your first brawl. I saw you fighting at the Brixton Park masquerade. Perhaps you should refrain from spirits for a while."

"You think I fight because I drink?" He snorted. "You know nothing about me."

Perhaps she didn't. "I still care," she said softly. "About you…and your reputation."

"And that's taken as much of a beating as my face recently," he said.

"We are kindred spirits, then, for mine has also suffered damage due to my behavior."

His gaze snapped to hers. "Are you speaking of moving from your parents' house, or that other rumor?"

Jane froze. "What other rumor?"

His eye widened almost imperceptibly, but she caught it. "Oh, it was years ago. I'm not sure I remember exactly—"

She didn't believe him for a moment. "Of course you remember. Otherwise, you wouldn't have mentioned it. What was the rumor?" She saw him hesitate. "You owe me."

He exhaled and pressed his lips together, his gaze softening with sympathy. "That I do. Very well. I'd heard you were unchaste, that you'd resorted to… seductive measures to try to attain a husband."

Her belly flipped, then tensed, and her pulse sped. Turning from the bed, Jane paced to the fireplace. She didn't know what she'd been expecting, but it wasn't *that*. Years ago? As in five years, when she'd had her first Season? She'd been eager to conquer London, to make a match. And she'd failed. That Season and every Season after, until she'd grown utterly jaded. Whipping around toward the bed, she demanded, "Who started this awful—and *false*—rumor?"

"I've no idea. I'd quite forgotten about it until you said we were kindred spirits. In fact, can we pretend I never said anything?" He looked at her hopefully.

Hot anger sizzled through her. "The damage is done, I'm afraid." She was livid. And hurt. To think she'd thought she'd been to blame for her failure. Her parents certainly thought so. How had she gone this long without knowing this rumor existed? "Who knows about this rumor?"

He lifted a shoulder. "It was well known amongst the young bucks." He winced, and she didn't think it was due to physical pain this time. "I'm sorry, Miss Pemberton. I never would have said anything if I thought you didn't know."

She appreciated his sympathy. And the fact that he would have spared her this information. Except he'd apparently believed it? She stalked back to the bedside and narrowed her eyes at him. "You thought it was true."

He opened his mouth, then closed it. He stared at her, then averted his gaze. "As I said, I didn't think of it. I'd forgotten. It's ancient history." He tried to smile, but she could tell it wasn't genuine, that he was trying to make her feel better.

"It hardly signifies. It likely ruined me as effectively—more effectively, even—than moving out of my parents' house." Groaning in frustration, she spun about and strode to the corner, where she flopped into a chair and leaned back, stretching her legs before her in a most unladylike fashion. But dammit, if people were going to say she wasn't a lady, why should she behave like one? "Do you want to know what's most enraging?"

"What?"

"The fact that I have a scandalous reputation without even the benefit of enjoying it. You're a rake and a rogue. But at least it's true, and you've claimed the rewards." Scowling, she clasped the arms of the chair and squeezed. "What's more, I will likely never get the chance now."

"What do you mean?" he asked slowly.

She riveted her gaze to his across the room. "I won't ever have the opportunity to experience physical pleasure."

"Ah, I think I can safely assure you that you will not have difficulty attracting any gentleman you choose for the purposes of experiencing physical pleasure."

She glowered at him. "What the hell does that mean?"

"You're   attractive,   alluring,   and   many

other...*things*." His voice cracked a bit. "Any man would be glad—and *fortunate*—to tup you."

She launched out of the chair and walked to the other side of the bed. Lowering herself to the mattress, she sat on the edge. "Does that include you?" It was a daring question, and she hadn't thought too much about it before saying it aloud. In fact, she hadn't considered it at all.

"I—" He stared at her, his jaw clenching as his Adam's apple bobbed in his throat. "Yes, of course." His gaze remained steady with hers, and something deep in her core kindled to life.

"I know how you can repay me," she said with a certainty that surprised her almost as much as what she said next. "You can relieve me of my virginity."

~

ime seemed to stop as Anthony stared at Miss Pemberton. Had she just asked him to relieve her of her *virginity*? Who did she think he was, the Marquess of Ripley? Rather, Ripley before he'd fallen in love with Phoebe?

Hell, maybe she did. Anthony had done his best to replace Marcus as London's Most Notorious Rake. He hadn't set out to do so, but that had been the result, apparently.

"I am, ah, flattered, Miss Pemberton, but I'm afraid I'm not the sort of gentleman who—"

She held up her hand and narrowed her eyes at him briefly. "You are *precisely* that sort of gentleman. Or at least you have been the past year or so. Ever since your—"

"There's no need to delve into particulars." He couldn't let her say it out loud. Even so, the end of her sentence crashed around in his brain. *Ever since your parents died.*

Her gaze fixed on him for an uncomfortable moment. He sought to redirect the topic. Quickly.

"Why on earth do you want to divest yourself of your virginity?"

Her brow creased. "Divest myself? It's not a cloak."

He wanted to laugh at her quip, but did not. This was serious. "No, it's not. You can put a cloak back on, and once gone, your virginity will be lost forever."

"I doubt I shall miss it," she said. "It's come to my attention that sexual activity is rather, er, pleasant, and I should like to experience it for myself."

"Pleasant." Anthony's gaze lingered on the swell of her breasts and the lush contours of her heart-shaped mouth. "That's not the word I would use to describe sex or any of the things leading up to the act itself."

She looked skeptical and maybe a bit horrified. "It's not pleasant?"

"It is, but I'd perhaps describe it as thrilling. Rapturous. Perhaps even *heavenly*."

Jane laughed, and he couldn't help but smile in return.

"You have the most infectious laugh," he murmured.

"Thank you. I think. I'd hate to be infectious like a disease."

"Never that," he said. Though if she were, he'd gladly become ill. Did that mean he would accept her proposal? No, he couldn't. And yet, he understood her dilemma. She was young, with little chance for marriage. Could he blame her for wanting to experience physical gratification?

Anthony tipped his head to the side. "Do you pleasure yourself?"

Her eyes widened just before she averted her

gaze. Then she stood and put several feet between herself and the bed—and him. "Yes."

That single word aroused every part of him. His blood surged in his head, his cock.

"But I don't think I'm very good at it."

Holy hell. What was he supposed to do with *that* information?

You could help her.

"How would you know?" The question fell from his mouth before he could think it through, but he realized it was a logical query. If she'd never had an orgasm, how would she know if she'd had one?

His head was starting to hurt again. Just as his cock was starting to throb. He adjusted the bed-clothes to hide his erection. This was unacceptable. He couldn't lust after one of his sister's friends. Even if she was caring, beautiful, and asking him to pleasure her.

"You're considering it," she said, sounding surprised. She hadn't expected him to agree. And he wasn't going to!

"You're a lady. And Sarah's friend. I couldn't do what you're asking."

"Then why ask about me pleasuring myself?"

"Because it seems the least I could do is show you how to do that."

She arched a brow and contemplated him a moment. "And why should that be you? You can't have experience in showing a woman how to find pleasure."

He pinned her with a smoldering stare as heat built inside him. "I can tell you precisely where to put your fingers and how to move them to provoke a release that will make you scream in ecstasy."

"How?" The single word came out high and breathy. Utterly arousing. This conversation was driving him to the very brink.

God, he wanted to invite her back to the bed, toss her skirts up, and show her. "You are testing my restraint." While she sounded breathless, he sounded tortured. Because he was.

"Good. Does that mean you agree?"

"No." But she was right—he *was* considering it. "Dammit, you've cast a spell on me. Perhaps you put something in the headache tonic."

She sauntered toward the bed, her hips swaying in a devastatingly provocative fashion. "Could I?"

Not that he knew of. Anyway, it wasn't necessary. She was quite capable of captivating him all on her own. He scowled at her. "You're making this difficult."

A bright smile lit her face. "Good. I promise this will remain a secret—just between us. And you'll take precautions to prevent a child."

Bloody, bloody hell. Of course he would. He couldn't have a child. He didn't deserve one. Pain—not the physical kind—seared through him. "I haven't agreed to anything."

She sat back down on the edge of the bed. "Not yet, but I've several days to convince you before you return home."

He needed to go home *now*. Before she seduced him. In all honesty, it wouldn't be that hard. Just thinking of what he wanted to do to her was sending him into a fit of desire.

"I should go home tomorrow."

She frowned. "No. We have an agreement. You're staying at least a week." When he didn't argue, she stood up again, her gaze sweeping over him and lingering ever so briefly on his pelvic region.

"I'll move back to the other chamber tomorrow."

As she leaned toward him, her eyes sparked with heat. "If you decide to accept my proposition, you don't have to."

"Jane." He swallowed. "Miss Pemberton. If I decide to accept your proposition, I will still refuse to share your bed. As you said, this would be a secret, between us alone, and I will not be so blatant in our...activity." Damn, he certainly sounded as if he was about to agree.

"However you wish. I'll let you set the rules," she said.

The word "rules" only heightened the lust spiraling through him. Or maybe it was that she would relinquish control to him entirely. He felt light-headed with want.

He managed to form a few words. "We'll see what happens. Now, will you go?" If he didn't frig himself, he was going to be miserable come morning.

"I will. And thank you for considering my request. I must admit, after hearing you talk tonight, I find I'm more curious than ever. I do hope you'll agree. If not, perhaps you can recommend someone else."

He bloody well would not! "No. That I will never do."

"Then I suppose it will have to be you." She gave him a final saucy smile, then departed.

Anthony leaned his head back and groaned. This could be very bad. She wanted him. He wanted her. No one knew he was here, and no one need ever know what went on between them. The temptation was overwhelming and impossibly real.

What the hell had he gotten himself into?

CHAPTER 4

*C*ulpepper walked into the garden room, carrying a small basket. "Miss Pemberton, may I present your kitten."

Jane jumped up from the table where she'd been sipping tea and met him in the middle of the room. "You found one!"

"I did, and if I may say so, she's quite frisky. I might believe she would cause the ruckus you blamed on her the other day during your meeting."

Laughing, Jane peeked into the basket where the bundle of fur was curled into a tiny ball. "Maybe we should have gotten two," she said. "She looks lonely."

"In fact, there was a sister. Would you like me to fetch her too?"

Jane looked up at him. "Could you?" These kittens might be the only companionship she'd ever have.

She flinched inwardly. She was just feeling sorry for herself after her conversation with Lord Colton the night before. Thinking back, she felt a mix of embarrassment for making the proposition, as well as irritation because he'd clearly wanted to accept but was keeping himself from doing so. Was she that re-sistible?

Apparently so. The rumor he'd revealed also rose in her mind and made her upset all over again. She'd been denied the opportunity to make a match, so yes, it might very well be that this kitten—and her sister—would be her only companions.

Taking the basket from Culpepper, she reiterated her wish for the second kitten. "Please fetch her sister at once. I would feel terrible for splitting them up."

He inclined his head. "As you wish, Miss Pemberton." He turned and left, and Jane went to sit on the settee. She set the basket next to her, and the kitten poked her head up. Yellow eyes stared up at Jane from an adorable tawny striped face.

"Well, aren't you the sweetest thing?" Jane murmured.

The kitten mewed softly as Jane set her in her lap. "What shall I call you?"

In answer, the kitten stretched her front paws out and sank her claws into Jane's gown. "Careful, don't ruin it," Jane said without much heat. What did she care if one of her day gowns was ruined? She was probably on her way to becoming a lady hermit. Perhaps she should move out to a folly on some eccentric duke's property. Then she could have a dozen cats. Or more.

Jane giggled, and the cat turned in her lap, gazing up at her with those beautiful golden eyes. "You are so pretty. Perhaps I will call you Jolie. That's French for pretty. Or maybe you need a yellow name to match your gorgeous eyes. Sunny? Daffodil? Oh, I like that."

The kitten jumped from Jane's lap onto the settee and began to explore the cushions. Jane picked up the basket to set it on the floor and noticed a ball of yarn inside. "Is this for you?" she asked, taking it out and placing it on the settee.

Daffodil's eyes widened briefly as she saw the yarn. She squatted down, her backside wiggling, then she leapt forward and attacked the ball. It tumbled to the floor, and Daffodil followed, batting it around and chasing where it rolled.

Grinning at the kitten's antics, Jane felt better than she had all day. Perhaps last night hadn't been as bad as she'd thought. Colton had flirted a little bit, at least. And when he'd asked her if she'd pleasured herself... Well, that had kindled something deep inside Jane, something she'd tried to satisfy when she returned to the guest chamber. She couldn't help but think that he could at least help her in that regard—even if she had told him he couldn't know how to. Clearly, she'd been wrong.

A wave of heat rushed over her, driving her to jump up and pace. Just as had happened half the night, her mind turned to the rumor that had ruined her. How had she never known it existed? It certainly explained why her first Season had been such a disappointment. She'd had interest—several men had paid calls. Had they suddenly stopped? She couldn't recall. She did, however, remember that her mother and father had wondered why none of them had progressed to making an offer. They'd blamed Jane for not being charming or interesting enough, something Jane knew wasn't true.

And yet, doubt had niggled at the back of her mind ever since. Doubt she didn't share with anyone, least of all herself. Except when she was being most honest or feeling most vulnerable. As she was now.

Oh, blast it all. She'd left home and declared her spinsterhood precisely so she could stop worrying about such things. Who cared if she'd been ruined?

You do.

Yes, she did. Her future had been stolen, and she wanted to find out who had done it. And why.

Her pacing became more vigorous, her skirts swirling about her feet as she crisscrossed the room. Then she felt a tug and looked down to see Daffodil attacking the hem, her paws swatting at the moving fabric.

Jane couldn't help but smile, then bent to scoop the kitten into her hands. "We are going to have such fun. Especially when your sister arrives."

Loud voices carried down the stairs and into the garden room where Jane stood just near the door. Carrying Daffodil, Jane hurried upstairs toward the sound—her bedchamber. Not quite her bedchamber, but her sitting room. Inside, Lord Colton stood arguing with Meg.

"My lord, you aren't supposed to leave your bed."

"Then why make my laundered clothing accessible?" he asked, rather astutely. He wore his breeches and shirt, but nothing else.

Jane couldn't help but take in his bare feet and calves and the triangle of his chest and neck that were revealed by the opening of his shirt. She looked to Meg, who stood with a hand on her hip as she regarded Lord Colton with likely well-earned irritation. "I'll handle this, Meg," Jane said as Daffodil squirmed out of her arms and jumped to the floor.

Meg startled. "Oh!"

"This is Daffodil," Jane said as the kitten began exploring the room.

"She's so cute!" Meg squealed. "I'll have Cook make her something to eat. She'd like that, wouldn't she?" The maid turned to Jane.

"I'm sure. And yes, we need to establish a place for her to eat. The kitchen, I suppose?"

Meg nodded. "You may also want to feed her

somewhere else too, at least while she's small. She needs to eat enough so she can grow into a big, strong cat." Meg squatted down, and Daffodil came to sniff her. She then allowed the maid to stroke her head.

"Meg, will you also see that the bedding is changed in the guest chamber, as Lord Colton will be moving there."

"Such a good girl," Meg murmured before standing up. "I'll take care of it, miss." Then she pivoted and left without giving Lord Colton so much as a parting glance.

Jane turned her attention to him. "Please don't annoy the servants."

He blinked in innocence, and she was drawn to just how awful he looked today. His face was a more brilliant array of color, and his right eye was still swollen. "Did I annoy her?"

"It seemed you might have. She was only enforcing what I said—that you need to remain in bed. The physician said bed rest for a week."

"I hardly think he meant staying in an actual bed. In any case, I *have* to get up today so I can move to the guest chamber, don't I?"

He had a point there. "Do you feel better?" It seemed he must since he was upright. And he'd dressed himself. She would have wagered he couldn't do that without help. He certainly couldn't have the day before.

"I do, actually. Head's still a bit achy, and of course my face is a disaster, and my ribs pull here and there, but overall, I feel more human."

That was good to hear. "You certainly don't look better."

He cracked a smile, which did not improve his appearance. "I did peek in the glass, and I'm afraid I must agree. Why you made me, of all people, that proposition last night is a mystery. I'm absolutely ghastly."

Except he wasn't. She recalled exactly how attractive he was underneath the damage, and she'd seen him nearly naked the other day. Ghastly was not a word she'd use to describe him, even in his current state.

"I'm glad you're feeling better, but you still can't go downstairs. I'll help you to the guest chamber after the bedclothes are changed."

"I suggest a compromise. I'll go downstairs just until the bed is refreshed, and then I promise I'll come back up." He started toward her, and Daffodil took that moment to attack his foot.

The viscount wobbled and began to pitch forward. Jane rushed toward him, wrapping her arms around his midsection and keeping him from falling. He was bloody heavy. She had to dig her feet into the floor and presumed he was also preventing himself from toppling over. She doubted she could have stopped him on her own.

He looked into her eyes as they straightened. "There you go saving me again," he murmured.

"Someone has to."

"Apparently." He looked away, and she removed her hands from his waist. The feel of him against her —his warm, strong chest pressed into hers—was emblazoned on her body and mind.

"Here, sit." She looked to the settee and put her arm toward him but stopped short of touching him.

He went and sat, stretching his legs out before him. Daffodil promptly attacked his foot again. "If it weren't for the cat, I would have been fine."

"Maybe, but doesn't it feel better to sit?"

"Actually, it does. I suppose I should rest a bit more." He didn't sound entirely thrilled.

"If you're feeling up to it, perhaps we can play a

game later—cards or backgammon. Or I can bring you some books."

"Either would be lovely, thank you. For now, maybe you could just keep me company until my new jail, I mean new room, is ready."

Jane considered sitting beside him, but ended up taking a chair across from him instead. She was still feeling a bit flustered after last night. "I'd like to hope this doesn't feel like jail."

"It doesn't. I was teasing." He sat up a little straighter, retracting his feet a bit. Daffodil nipped his ankle, but he didn't even flinch. "I am incredibly grateful for your assistance and your concern."

"Daffodil!" Jane admonished, not that the kitten paid her any attention. It would take her some time to learn her name.

"She's not bothering me," Lord Colton said, reaching down to scratch her behind the ear. Daffodil flopped onto her side and then promptly curled herself around his hand and ran her back feet against his wrist. Colton laughed. "She's rather frisky."

"That's what Culpepper said. I've sent him to fetch Daffodil's sister so they will have each other to play with."

"Very thoughtful of you, although I daresay Daffodil can probably turn just about anything into a plaything." He scooped her up in his hand and brought her to his lap, where he alternated between pressing her nose and tickling her belly. She attacked his hand with fervor, flopping this way and that. Their play was most entertaining.

Watching him, she realized he held many attractive qualities, and she was again reminded of the proposition she'd made him last night. She'd wondered if he would pretend it hadn't happened—she considered doing that herself—but he'd already men-

tioned it. Even if it was in the form of a self-depre-
cating comment.

She decided not to raise the issue. She wouldn't
pretend it hadn't happened, but neither would she
press him. He wasn't in any condition to help her
anyway. Oh, why had she been so bold?

Instead, she once again reverted to the subject of
the rumor. "I'm hoping you recalled something else
about that rumor you mentioned last night. I'm
quite keen to find out who started it and why."

He continued to play with Daffodil as he cocked
his head to the side. "I didn't. That was five years ago.
Truly, it's been a very long time since I heard mention of it."

"But have you heard something since then? Does
the rumor continue to follow me?"

"I couldn't say. I'm not exactly on the Marriage
Mart myself."

No, of course he wasn't. But he had been once.
Presumably. "Were you looking for a wife at one
time?"

"Not really. Perhaps you should ask someone else
about the rumor. Or, better yet, forget about it
entirely."

"I'm afraid I can't do that. Whoever started it was
lying and must have had a reason to do so. They ruined my life. Surely I deserve to know why, if not an
apology."

"And what will that accomplish?" he asked flatly.
"What's done is done. You can't change the past,
Miss Pemberton."

She recalled that last night, he'd called her Jane. That
had been after she'd said they could share a bed. Heat
started to rise in her neck. Had she actually said that?

Clutching to the topic at hand, she said, "I plan
to talk to Phoebe."

"Does she know that I'm here?"

"Not yet, but I will tell her at some point—we don't keep secrets from each other." Besides, Phoebe was the closest thing Jane had to family. Her parents certainly weren't going to visit any time soon. Or ever. And her sister Anne would be wed in a fortnight or so. Jane's chest tightened when she thought of how she would miss her sister's celebration. Because her parents wouldn't allow her to attend. They'd said she'd made the decision not to come the moment she'd moved to Cavendish Square. To which Jane had retorted that she'd at least waited until Anne was betrothed.

In hindsight, however, perhaps she should have delayed her departure until after the wedding. Except her parents' pressure regarding Mr. Brinkley had grown untenable. They hadn't been listening to her, and she'd feared they would announce a betrothal any day. She'd felt utterly trapped. This, where she was now—lonely as it might seem at the moment— was far preferable.

"If you tell Phoebe, she'll tell Marcus," Colton said. "I'd prefer he didn't know about my altercation."

Of course Phoebe would tell him. They shouldn't have secrets either. Damn. "Why don't you want him to know? Isn't he your friend?"

"Yes." His tone was measured. "However, I am not in the mood for his…concern."

"Yet, you're satisfied with mine."

"You are far more delightful. And prettier."

Jane laughed even as she realized he hadn't really answered her question. He could be very enigmatic, particularly when it came to his behavior. She was a bit surprised he hadn't asked for spirits yet. Although, maybe that was why he'd been going downstairs. She nearly asked, but decided he probably wouldn't answer that either.

So she couldn't tell Phoebe that Lord Colton was here. That was unfortunate, because not only did she dislike lying to her best friend, she was also now unable to ask for advice as to whether she ought to seduce him.

"What?" he asked. "You're looking at me rather intently."

"Am I? I was thinking about lying to my dearest friend and how uncomfortable that makes me. Alas, I will honor your request, and when I visit her to discuss this disturbing rumor, I will withhold the fact that you are here—and why."

"You don't even need to visit her about that rumor. Not really. As I told you, the past belongs where it resides—behind us. There's no point dredging it up again, especially the unpleasant bits." He spoke with a dark, provoking ferocity.

She leaned forward, earnest in trying to make him understand her perspective. "This isn't just a past mistake or regret. This is a mystery that deeply affected my life. I should like to know why it happened. As *I* said, I think I deserve that."

"Knowing what happened won't change it," he said grimly, his gaze clouding. "So long as you know that." He looked away, and she felt a sudden chill. He had to be speaking about his parents. They'd been murdered by a highwayman, and their death had devastated him and Sarah. Nothing could ever change that past.

Jane stood. "I'll see if your bed is ready."

He glanced down at Daffodil, who was now curled into a ball asleep in his lap. "No rush, as I seem to be trapped."

His tone held a bit of mirth, but she still heard

the darkness beneath it. Perhaps he *was* trapped. And maybe she could help set him free.

~

A nthony had awakened the next morning with not one, but two kittens curled up in a pile between his calves on top of the coverlet. He'd later learned that Daffodil's sister, named Fern, presumably because of her pretty green eyes, had come to the household the previous evening.

He'd heard that from Meg, whom he'd apologized to for being difficult yesterday afternoon. He hadn't seen Miss Pemberton since then.

Standing from the writing desk in his chamber, Anthony went into the narrow dressing room to tie his cravat. He wound the silk around his neck and looked into the glass. At last, the swelling around his right eye had diminished enough so that he could actually see from it. However, the rest of his face still looked fairly awful. Some of the purples had lightened to blue and some of the blues had paled to green, but overall, it remained a colorful chaos.

After tying the cravat into a semblance of style, he picked up his coat and tugged it on, wincing slightly as his ribs pulled. They felt a trifle better, but he understood why the physician had recommended he rest. Even so, he hadn't been able to resist bathing and dressing today. He needed to feel like a human again. He brushed his fingertips over the short beard covering his jaw. Albeit a hairy human.

Going back into the bedchamber, Anthony picked up the letter he'd just written and walked to the door. Before he could open it, someone rapped on the outside.

"Come in," Anthony said as he reached for the

latch. He opened the door to see Miss Pemberton standing in the corridor.

Her gaze swept over him in surprise. "You're dressed."

"Yes."

"You're supposed to be resting. For at least three more days. Four, really. Maybe longer." She pursed her lips, and he couldn't help thinking they looked incredibly kissable.

"I wanted to feel normal for a change," he said. "And I wanted to see if Culpepper could have this delivered." He held up the letter he'd written to his butler and valet.

"Oh. What's that?"

"I've asked my butler and valet to send some clothing. I'm a bit weary of this costume."

"You shouldn't be dressed at all. You have a nightshirt that I purchased for you. If you stay abed, that would be enough." She glanced past him toward the bed. "But you don't want to stay in bed."

"You mentioned cards or backgammon. I was hoping we might play. Lying in bed makes that difficult."

She narrowed her tawny eyes at him. "I still think you were just trying to sneak downstairs."

"If my intent was to play a game with you, how would I have maintained any amount of secrecy?" he asked wryly.

"You determined that once you were downstairs, I wouldn't force you to come back up."

"You have this all sorted out," he said with a hint of admiration. Because she was right.

"I'll allow you to go downstairs—just for a game —if you can make it to the stairs without weaving on your feet."

"Does that mean you aren't going to offer me escort?" He pouted.

A smile teased her heart-shaped mouth. "I will stay close enough to catch you. Again."

"Then allow *me* to escort *you*," he said, presenting his arm.

She hesitated, but then placed her hand on his arm, and they started toward the stairs. Anthony felt much steadier on his feet than since he'd arrived, and he made his way to the stairs—and down them—without so much as a totter.

"Did I pass the test?" he asked when they reached the bottom.

She inclined her head. "Well done, my lord."

He guided her to the garden room. "My lord sounds so formal. You must call me Anthony."

She took her hand from his arm after they moved inside. "I couldn't. That's far too familiar."

"You've tended my wounds, allowed me to sleep in your bed, and seen me naked. What is more familiar than that?"

"I can think of at least one thing," she said, averting her gaze. "Also, I did not see you naked. Just nearly so."

Anthony tried not to think about that one thing. Or any of the other things that went along with that. "Oh, well, if that's all…"

She flashed him a wide, brief smile. "Let me give your letter to Culpepper."

"Thank you." He handed it to her. "Could you send a coach to deliver it and have a footman wait to collect my belongings and then bring them back? That's the only way I can think to keep my location secret."

"Of course." She took the missive. "I'll instruct Culpepper to arrange it."

"And perhaps have him bring some madeira or port?"

She pressed her lips together. "I thought you were avoiding anything stronger than ale."

"Only because you said I had to." He went to the table situated in front of the doors that led to the garden and sat.

She tapped the letter against her hand. "If you can articulate a good reason for needing something stronger than ale, I'll allow you to have it."

"Ha. You're a malicious caregiver."

"If you think so, I suppose you can leave at any time."

"You've adamantly insisted I stay for at least a week." He regarded her with interest. "Why the sudden change?"

She lifted a shoulder. "I can't force you to do anything. If spirits are that important to you, I suppose you must do as you will."

She was right—she couldn't force him to do anything, including accept her proposal. But he was considering that, just as he was abstaining from everything except ale. "As I am healing rather well under your care—malicious or not—I am inclined to stay. And abide by your rules."

"I'll take this to Culpepper," she said, waving the missive. "And ask him to bring some ale." She departed, and the two kittens dashed into the garden room.

"If it isn't Daffodil and Fern," he said, smiling. They came to him and sniffed his boot-clad foot. He reached down and gave each of them a pat. "Are you terrorizing the house yet?" He glanced about the room for something for them to play with. His eyes landed on a ball of yarn, rather a ball with a long tail of yarn that had come unraveled.

Anthony stood and fetched the ball from the corner. Fern's head snapped toward him as he rewound the yarn around the ball. "Looking for this?" he asked.

He squatted down and held the ball out on his palm. Fern scampered to him and swatted the ball, gingerly at first, then more forcefully so it went flying off his hand. Daffodil raced toward it, tackling her sister in the process. They tussled for a moment, seeming to forget about the yarn. Then they both froze and looked for the ball in unison, both launching toward it at once.

Anthony laughed at their antics, feeling better than he had in ages.

"What's so funny?" Miss Pemberton asked. She sauntered toward the table, carrying a backgammon set.

"The kittens. They are incredibly entertaining."

She set the game down on the table. "I adore them so much, and they've only been here a day. Fern hasn't even been here that long, actually."

"What prompted you to get them?" Anthony asked, retaking his seat at the table and helping her to set up the backgammon board.

"You, actually."

Anthony arched a brow at her and couldn't help but chuckle. "Why?"

"Because you were making a racket while I was trying to have a Spitfire Society meeting, and I had to come up with a reason for the noise. I blamed it on a kitten."

"And they believed you?" He didn't remember what had happened, but imagined he'd made more noise than a kitten could.

"They seemed to." She looked at the kittens playing with the yarn. "And watching them some-times, I think it's maybe possible. Daffodil knocked several things off my dressing table this morning. I wonder if they even slept."

"They did. Meg let them into my room last night and kept the door cracked open."

Miss Pemberton looked at him in surprise. "They slept with you?"

"When they weren't attacking my feet."

"I see. How adorable." She snapped her gaze to his. "Except it was probably annoying, and you need your rest. I'll make sure they don't bother you tonight."

"It was fine." He narrowed an eye at her. "Or are you just trying to steal them for yourself?"

She laughed. "Not at all. After you go, perhaps they'll sleep with me."

After he went. He suddenly didn't want to contemplate that. "Shall we play backgammon?"

"Unless we set up the board just to look at it."

"Or for the kittens to jump up and bat the pieces around."

"Shhh." She glanced over at them where Daffodil was launching a sneak attack on her sister. "Don't give them any ideas."

"Shall we roll to see who goes first?"

Miss Pemberton nodded and picked up one of the dice. Anthony plucked the other from the board, and they both rolled. "It's you," he said after rolling a two to her four.

Culpepper appeared with two cups of ale, which he deposited on the table. "Can I bring anything else?"

Miss Pemberton arched a brow at Anthony in question. He looked up at Culpepper to answer his question. "No, thank you."

After Culpepper left, Anthony raised his cup. "To the loveliest caregiver I could have hoped for."

She gave him an arch look. "I thought I was malicious."

He shrugged. "You're still the loveliest." He grinned at her before sipping his ale.

She rolled the dice, and they each took a few turns before he spoke again. He couldn't seem to stop thinking about her proposal. Which wasn't all that shocking. It wasn't every day a beautiful young woman asked him to seduce her. It wasn't ever, actually.

But was it really seduction? "So about this proposition of yours," he said slowly.

She perked up, her gaze meeting his. "Yes?"

"What exactly are you looking for? Something transactional—I give you pleasure in exchange for your hospitality and care, and that's that?"

"Well, I suppose I'd like to give you pleasure in return. That seems only polite."

Polite? "This isn't an exchange of favors, Miss Pemberton. What you're asking will expose you—and me, and not just physically. There is an intimacy when one does these things." He took another drink of ale. How could he have ever thought this—with her—would be transactional? "Well, there can be, and it's better if there is."

"Better how?"

"The pleasure is greater. In my experience anyway. If I merely tupped you with expedience, it would be less satisfying. Would you expect kissing or touching?"

She answered quickly. "Kissing, yes. And I'm not sure how you can do what I asked without touching."

He smiled. "I meant more specific touching. Would you want me to touch your body, specifically your breasts and your... sex?" He'd been about to say pussy, but decided that was perhaps too base.

Her cheeks flushed a delicate shade of pink, and

he felt the heat too. Not in his face, but lower, much lower.

She didn't look away from him, and her gaze seemed to strip him naked. Or maybe that was only his wishful thinking. "It seems like you should? I mean, I don't know. Does that make it better? As you said, more intimate?"

"Yes." He sounded like he'd been wandering a desert for a month. He drank more ale.

"How?"

Hell, she wanted specifics. He leaned slightly forward. "Your breasts are sensitive. I can arouse you by touching them—with my hands and with my mouth."

Her nostrils flared. "You'd put your mouth on them?" She glanced down at herself, and he would've sworn her nipples had hardened, but of course he couldn't tell through the layers of her clothing. More wishful thinking, perhaps. "What else?" she asked, sounding a tad breathless.

Emboldened by her interest, he picked up one of the dice and rolled it between his fingers. "See what I'm doing to this die?" he asked softly. "I'd do this to your nipples. You'd arch up into me, and I'd gently tug. Maybe you'd gasp. Maybe you'd groan. Maybe you'd beg for me to suckle you. And I would. Then perhaps you'd feel the sensation—the desire—deep in your sex."

She didn't blink. Her lips parted. Anthony nearly groaned with need.

"Then you'd touch me there?"

He nodded, unable to speak at that moment.

"And would you put your mouth there too?" The question weighed heavy with skepticism. She expected him to say no—he was sure of it.

"Shouldn't I?" he asked, wondering if she would want him to.

Her eyes widened. "I don't know. That sounds...scandalous."

He laughed, a low sound deep in his throat that reverberated through his chest. He set the die down on the board. "All of this is scandalous, Miss Pemberton."

She looked down at her lap. "Yes, of course it is. I shouldn't have asked."

"I'm not sorry you did. And yes, I would put my mouth on you—if you allowed me to."

When her eyes met his once more, he saw heat and desire. His cock rose, straining against his breeches, and he was glad for the cover of the table.

"I would," she said, her voice cracking slightly. "I trust you to do what you think is best. What would feel best."

She trusted him. Nothing else she could have said would have undone him more.

"Jane," he growled. "*Miss Pemberton*." He shook his head. "No, if I'm going to shag you, I'm going to bloody well call you Jane."

She leaned forward, her gaze expectant. "Does that mean—"

He didn't let her finish. "That means nothing. Yet." Oh hell, he was considering it. More than that. He was *planning* it. He envisioned her lying in her bed upstairs, sprawled nude before him, a veritable feast for his taking. And he would do everything he'd just told her and more, starting with kissing her. "Have you ever been kissed?"

She shook her head.

How in the hell had she gotten a reputation for trying to seduce men when she hadn't even been kissed? It was plainly obvious to anyone who took the time to speak with her that she was as innocent as could be.

Which meant he should keep his bloody hands

—and mouth—to himself. And yet, if she was asking him and she was already off the Marriage Mart...

He finished his ale and was sorry there wasn't more. His mouth felt eternally dry as he sat here across from the most alluring woman he'd ever encountered. Was that true? He'd encountered quite a great many women. Yes, but Jane was different. Jane had seen sides of him now that no one had.

He owed her. Still, that wasn't a reason to take her virginity. He could kiss her, though, couldn't he?

"You should be kissed."

"Is that an offer?" A slight smile lifted her lips.

"Maybe. I'm still deciding. You are making it incredibly difficult to refuse you."

"Oh, good." She grinned then, and something in his chest loosened for the first time in a very, very long while.

"In the meantime, I believe there's a backgammon game going on."

"Is there? I nearly forgot. You were quite distracting." She gave him a saucy stare.

"You think *I'm* distracting?" He shook his head with a short laugh. "You need to stop looking at me like that."

"I'm not sure what you mean," she said coyly.

"I think you do. And it's your turn."

She picked up the dice and held one in her palm while rolling the other between her fingertips. Her message was clear.

This was going to be a very long game.

CHAPTER 5

*J*ane looked around the drawing room of the Marquess of Ripley's house in Hanover Square. It was every bit as elegant as she'd expected, and not a bit improper like the marquess. Or like he *had* been. Although, was he really "proper" all of a sudden because he'd married Phoebe? After all, her reputation had been ruined when she'd called off her wedding last year just before it began.

Oh, what did any of that matter! Reputations and standards were set by the elite and often had nothing to do with a person's true worth. Jane now knew that from personal experience. Every time she thought of the rumor about her, she grew even more livid.

Phoebe swept into the drawing room, beaming as she'd done on her wedding day. "I'm delighted you came to visit!" They embraced, then sat together on the settee, turning toward each other.

"This house is magnificent," Jane said. "I can see why you would prefer it to your house in Cavendish Square."

Phoebe gave her a sheepish look. "Don't tell Marcus, but I miss my garden room."

Jane gently touched her friend's hand. "Oh no!"

"It's all right. He's given me free rein to create one here too. There's a sitting room that will work marvelously—after we have doors put in and several other refurbishments. And his garden *is* larger than mine."

"Well, that will be lovely. I assume you'll want your Gainsborough, as well as a number of other things from the house."

Phoebe's gaze took on a contemplative sheen. "Yes, I suppose I will. I didn't have much time to think before the wedding." She blushed faintly. "Everything happened so quickly."

"Why delay? When you find the person you want to spend the rest of your life with, I imagine you want to begin immediately."

"Exactly so," Phoebe said, beaming once more. "Now, tell me about your cat."

Jane nearly laughed at the absurdity of going from speaking of marriage to getting a cat, but what else could Jane discuss? The thought nearly made her want to weep, but she wasn't the sort who wallowed in despair. Besides, she wasn't despairing, not yet. She was angry about the rumor, but she was also entertaining a handsome, charming gentleman. Entertaining? Was that what she thought was going on?

"She's adorable. So adorable, in fact, that I brought her sister home too. Daffodil and Fern."

Phoebe's brow puckered. "I thought it was a boy. I could have sworn you referred to it as a he."

Jane froze. Had she? Forcing a laugh, she waved her hand. "I thought it was a he at first! Silly of me." Phoebe squinted slightly, as if she wasn't quite sure she believed Jane's story, but that was asinine. Why wouldn't she? Thinking the kitten was a boy was far more believable than thinking the kitten had caused all that noise the other day.

Seeking to divert the conversation, Jane blurted, "I heard the most awful thing, and I need your help."

Phoebe's gaze flickered with alarm. "What?"

"Apparently, someone started an officious rumor during my first Season. They said I was *fast*."

"Who would do such a thing?"

"I've no idea, which is why I need your help. I want to find out who did it and why." She folded her hands in her lap. "They quite ruined my life, Phoebe. That's why I've never wed, why when it seemed I might make a match, the gentleman invariably failed to pursue a courtship."

"And yet the Duke of Seduction still wrote about you," Phoebe noted. "So not everyone was aware of this rumor. I certainly wasn't."

Phoebe referred to the gentleman—the Marquess of Northam, who was now married to their friend Lavinia—who'd taken it upon himself to write poems about unmarried women in an effort to boost their popularity so they could make a match. The marquess was a gifted poet and musician. His ballads had been published and widely read, and they'd led to several matches. Including Phoebe's, which had, unfortunately, ended horribly when her betrothed had showed himself to be a truly awful person.

"It's possible Northam could have been aware of it and decided to write about me anyway," Jane said. "He rather likes flouting convention."

"So he does," Phoebe agreed. Then she laughed. "It seems those men make the best husbands."

Yes, it did seem to be the case, particularly in the instance of Phoebe's husband. "Any ideas on who would have started something so hideous?"

Phoebe's eyes widened briefly as she blew out a breath. "So many people, but *why* would they? I didn't know you very well back then. Was there anyone you spurned or ignored?"

"I've thought and thought and can't come up with a single person. That's what's so damnably frustrating."

Phoebe looked past Jane, her brow furrowed as she was clearly in deep thought. Then she swung her gaze back to Jane's. "You need to ask someone who would have known what was going on during your first Season—someone well connected." She froze for a second then blinked at Jane. "Who told you about this?"

Blast it all, Jane couldn't very well tell her it was Anthony. The omission burned Jane's mind—she longed to tell Phoebe about him and the proposition she'd made. About how she was consumed with thoughts of the things he'd said to her yesterday, with a need she didn't fully understand. "Anne's betrothed's cousin told her, and she told me." That would be all but unverifiable by Phoebe, who would have no cause to speak with Anne since they weren't close.

"I see. Chamberlain's cousin shouldn't have said anything."

"I disagree. I'm glad to finally know that my unmarried state wasn't my fault."

Eyes narrowing briefly, Phoebe leaned toward her. "It was never your fault! Your mother never should have told you that."

"Yes, precisely, and now I'll have proof. When I find out who started the rumor and show that person to be a liar."

"Is that your intent? Finding them will be hard enough. You want revenge?"

"I deserve that, don't I?"

Phoebe exhaled. "Yes, but I'm afraid you won't get it."

Jane had hoped for a bit more support. "I will still try."

"And I will help you." Phoebe tapped her finger against her lip. "Whom can we talk to?"

"It seems to have been a rumor among gentlemen," Jane said. "Could you ask Ripley?"

"Of course. It does seem he may have heard such a thing, given his reputation." She briefly pursed her lips.

"Former reputation," Jane corrected, prompting Phoebe to laugh.

"I daresay that's still his reputation, but I don't care. Most people will never believe he's head over heels in love with someone, let alone with me, but they don't have to."

"No, they don't," Jane said quietly. All that mattered was that Phoebe believed it. And why wouldn't she? One had only to look at Ripley to see he was utterly besotted.

"If Marcus doesn't know, he could probably ask a few gentlemen."

"Can you think of any women who might have heard of it?" Jane asked. "Someone well connected across Society and who wouldn't have spread the rumor, since it wasn't known by everyone."

"What about Lady Satterfield? She knows absolutely everyone, and she's as kind and generous as anyone I've ever met. She would never spread such gossip."

"And neither would she tell me or my mother about it. She wouldn't want to cause upset."

"Exactly so. Yes, I think we should ask her. If Marcus can't just put an end to the query posthaste."

Jane was eager to learn the truth as soon as possible. "Is he here?"

Phoebe shook her head. "I'm afraid not, but I'll speak with him as soon as he arrives and send word."

Feeling a bit of relief, Jane gave her friend a grateful smile. "Thank you." The relief was short-lived, however, as she realized she would likely have no occasion to speak with Lady Satterfield. It wasn't as if Jane would socialize in those circles any longer. "I've just thought of something, unfortunately. How will I ever speak with Lady Satterfield? I haven't received one invitation since I moved to Cavendish Square, and I don't expect that to change."

Phoebe scowled. "There are separate rules for men and women, and it's bloody unfair. You know that I shall always invite you to everything we host—as will all our friends." She gave Jane a pointed look. "And never forget that our friends include dukes."

Jane appreciated Phoebe's support. "I still don't know how I'll be able to see Lady Satterfield any time soon."

"You will when I host a dinner party next week. We'll have it at Brixton Park, and people can spend the night if they like. Maybe we should play hide-and-seek in the maze again." Her eyes sparkled with something Jane was beginning to recognize—a special anticipation. And since she knew that last time they played hide-and-seek in the maze, Phoebe had met Marcus and kissed him for the first time, she could imagine what Phoebe was thinking.

And now Jane was thinking the same thing. She nearly asked if Phoebe would invite Anthony, but that would mean he'd have to be at home to receive the invitation. Which he wasn't. In the end, she said nothing. Thinking of kissing Anthony in the maze at Brixton Park was ludicrous. He hadn't agreed to anything. Still, she could hope.

They spoke for another hour or so before Jane took her leave. As she walked briskly back to Cavendish Square, she prayed Ripley would be able to solve the mystery. Then she just had to determine how to exact revenge on the scoundrel who'd ruined her.

Once home, Jane went upstairs to the guest room to see Anthony. She paused just outside, realizing she'd been first-naming him in her head since the day before when they'd played backgammon. When he'd told her she should call him Anthony because she'd been familiar enough with his person to do so.

And then he'd made them even more familiar by detailing the things he could do to her. Her body tingled. Driven to see him, she went to the door, which was half-open.

"Lord Colton?" She might first-name him in her head, but she wasn't ready to call him Anthony. Yet.

"Come in."

She did so, pushing the door a bit wider as she stepped over the threshold.

"Pardon me for not getting up," he said wryly from a chair near the hearth, where he held a book.

She saw that both kittens were curled in his lap asleep. "You're recovering. You needn't stand even if you weren't covered in cats."

"I'm still a gentleman," he said, closing the book on his finger to hold his place. Then he cracked a smile that made her pulse quicken. "Mostly."

"The kittens really love you," she said, moving to take a seat on the padded bench at the end of the bed.

"So it would seem. I'm not sure I love them, however. They kept me up half the night attacking my feet again. I should wake them up and deprive them of sleep." He glowered down at them in a look of mock disgust.

"Oh, you love them anyway. How can you not?"

He sighed. "I suppose."

"What will they do when you leave?" she wondered aloud, and then wished she hadn't said it. She didn't want to think about him not being here.

She'd become quite used to his presence. No, she *liked* it.

"Well, I still have another few days under your mandate."

"And you'll stay longer if necessary," she said firmly, hoping he would heed her advice. And not just because she wanted him to stay. "How are you feeling today? That's what I came to find out." Also just to see him. But she wouldn't say so.

"Better. My chest doesn't ache quite as much. I can nearly take a deep breath."

"Wonderful!" She was glad to hear it, even if it meant he would leave. "You look better." The swelling around his right eye was much diminished today, and some of the more brilliant bruises had faded somewhat.

"You're very kind. I still look like hell," he said. "There's a looking glass in the dressing chamber, you know."

She laughed. "I know, but I stand by what I said. You didn't see yourself the morning I found you on the step. The bruises may not have been as colorful, but you looked quite horrid."

He grimaced. "I think it will be some time before I look normal."

That was probably true. He certainly didn't look like the gentleman she knew, even without his injuries. Brown whiskers covered his jaw and the space above his lip, and she found it oddly attractive. "The beard isn't bad, to be honest," she said.

He brushed his hand along his jaw. "I was thinking I need to shave. But you like it?"

The question made her belly flutter. "I don't *dislike* it. I admit it's a bit hard to tell because of the bruising."

He smiled faintly, lowering his hand to the arm of the chair. "I'll need to come up with a reason for my injuries when I return home. I don't think I can keep from going out until they're completely healed. I may go mad."

"Is that happening now?" Jane asked. "Madness, I mean."

"No. But then I have quite a bit to divert me here." He gestured toward the kittens with the book.

"Just them?" Jane asked, wondering if she was the only one affected by their flirtation.

"Not just them." There was a dark, provocative edge to his tone that sent a soft shiver up her spine.

Jane fought to find the thread of their conversation before she started asking him to consider her proposal again. She wanted him to come to his own decision and wouldn't mention it further. "Instead of coming up with a reason for your injuries, why not just stay at home until you're fully recovered? Surely that would do you good."

"And what will I tell my retainers happened?"

"The truth? Or at least, part of the truth? Where will you tell them you've been?"

"What they already believe—staying at the home of a friend. I didn't elaborate in the letter you gave to Culpepper."

She took in his blue breeches, ivory shirt, and dark-yellow waistcoat. His open neck and bare feet were scandalous, but they were well past that, of course. "They gathered your clothing rather quickly. Jones said he didn't have to wait very long." A distressing thought occurred to her. "You don't think anyone from your household followed Jones back here, do you?"

"I doubt it." He chuckled softly. "You are a mischievous thing, aren't you?"

"How does that make me mischievous?"

"Because not everyone would have imagined such a scenario."

She shrugged. "My mind tends to do that. I contemplate things rather thoroughly." Now she was thinking of the rumor and her need to find the instigator.

"I suppose I could tell them—my retainers—that I fell from a moving coach."

Jane leaned back against the base of the bed. "Is that believable? I suppose it is if you'd been drinking."

"And we know that's believable," he quipped with a smile.

"What if you fell while trying to climb into a lady's room?"

He laughed. "I'm not *that* much of a reprobate."

"Probably shouldn't admit it, even to your retainers, if you were." She winked at him. "You tumbled down a flight of stairs?"

"I was attacked by swans. They're nasty things."

Jane giggled. "They are indeed. I'm not sure your injuries match that, however. How on earth would they bruise your ribs?"

He waggled his brows. "Perhaps their wings are more dangerous than we realize."

"Maybe a stampede of goats would be more believable."

He shouted with laughter. "Goats?"

She nodded, lifting her shoulder. "Why not?"

"Why not a horse or cow?" he asked between laughs.

"I would think they would do worse damage," she said with great thought. "A goat seems just right."

He was still laughing. "Goats it is. I'll have to determine how I came into contact with attack goats, but I'm sure that will just come to me." His cobalt eyes sparked with mirth.

Jane didn't remember when she'd had such a delightful time with someone. "You'll think of something, just as I did with Phoebe earlier."

He set the book down on the small table beside the chair and looked at her in question. "Oh?"

"I asked her about the rumor, and she plans to speak with Ripley about it to see if he recalls anything."

"You didn't tell her about me?"

"No, that's why I had to come up with something to tell her about the rumor—I couldn't say I'd heard it from you. I said my future brother-in-law's cousin told my sister, who in turn told me."

"Thank you." He sent her a sheepish glance. "I feel bad asking you to lie."

"I understand why it's important to you, but thank you for saying that." She noticed a loose thread on her skirt and tried to gently tug it free. It didn't budge. "Will others have missed you in your absence?"

"Doubtful. As you know, Sarah is in the country awaiting the birth of her child, and she's the only close family I have." He looked down at the kittens and stroked their fur. Fern stretched onto her back, and he rubbed her belly.

"You've friends, though," Jane said, hoping to distract him from his melancholy—if that was what he was experiencing. He seemed to darken and... shrink whenever his family was mentioned.

"Felix is with Sarah, of course." Because they were married. "And Marcus is busy being a newlywed."

Jane wondered if that was all. She recalled they seemed to have a disagreement at the wedding breakfast. Ripley had gone to speak with Anthony, and Anthony had appeared to grow irritated. Then he'd left. She decided not to ask about it. Their diverting conversation had already taken a dim turn. "Anyone else?"

"It's possible a few gentlemen may wonder." He frowned and looked over at her. "I can't say if anyone witnessed the fight. Perhaps it's pointless of me to tell my story of attack goats if the gossip is already speeding through town."

"I don't think it is. I read the gossip pages—a bad habit that I shall blame my mother for, and I've seen nothing about you at all."

"Not everything shows up there," he said with disgust.

"That's true. Otherwise, I would have known about that rumor when it happened." She briefly clenched her hand into a fist, then laid it flat on her lap. "Every time I think of it, I'm so angry. But I have a plan, thanks to Phoebe. As I said, she will talk to Ripley to see if he remembers anything, and I will ask Lady Satterfield. She knows everyone, and if any lady were aware of it, I would wager it's her."

"I still think you should let this go," Anthony said softly. "What good can come of pursuing it?"

Jane straightened as she blistered with ire. "The dastardly knave who ruined me will be knocked down a notch, at least!"

"And how will you accomplish that? You're just going to reveal this years-old scandal—which won't help you at all reputationwise—and the perpetrator will be shunned by all and sundry?"

"I'll find a way. Ripley did it for Phoebe when he successfully maligned her former betrothed's reputation." Phoebe had told her how Ripley had gone to White's and simply talked loudly about Sainsbury. It had been enough to negatively affect his standing.

Anthony rubbed Daffodil's ear. "There's no saying what damage that actually inflicted since he ended up committing murder shortly thereafter and will likely soon be transported, if not hanged."

He had a point, blast it all. Still, she believed she could exact retribution, and she was at least going to try. Had she hoped he would help her? Perhaps. She thought they'd become friends. Were they really, though? Once he left, they'd go back to being acquaintances. In fact, she'd likely see him less since she wouldn't be attending any Society events, not that he went to many anymore. Well, except those hosted by her friends, which were, it seemed, also his friends. So she'd likely see him.

"I can see you're thinking," he said. "And that you're angry. You are angry, aren't you?"

He could read her emotions? Of course he could. She could well imagine her ire was on display for anyone to see. She exhaled and stood. "Yes. I feel betrayed. And I've no idea who did it or why."

"Why betrayed? You think someone you care about would do this?"

"I don't know, and regardless of what happens now, I'm afraid I can't rest until I find out who it was." What the hell else did she have to do anyway?

She suddenly felt a tightness in her chest. What did she have? More importantly, *whom* did she have? Her gaze fell on the two kittens in Anthony's lap and realized even *they* weren't really hers. They'd gravitated to him since coming to live here.

"I don't expect you to understand," she said tightly, then turned on her heel and stalked toward the door.

"I'm sorry," he called after her.

As she left the room, she could have sworn he said something about understanding.

∾

*A*nthony reviewed his appearance in the glass, tilting his head this way and that. It felt strange to be freshly shaven for the first time in nearly a week. He hoped Jane would approve. That was assuming he even encountered her. He hadn't seen her since yesterday afternoon. When she'd left angry.

He'd botched that. Her situation was not the same as his. She wanted to learn more about what had happened in the past, while he wanted to bury it. Who was he to tell her how to behave in her situation?

"My lord?" Culpepper called from just outside the dressing chamber. "Do you require assistance?"

Anthony opened the door with a bit of flourish. "I do not." He'd managed the bath they'd prepared, as well as shaving and dressing himself. He really could go home. But he didn't want to. Not yet. Not until he made things right with Jane.

"You are missing a coat," Culpepper advised.

He was. "Ah, yes." He turned and fetched the coat, then handed it to the butler. "If you wouldn't mind?"

"Not at all."

Anthony put his hand into one sleeve, then turned his back to Culpepper, who helped him don the garment. The butler swiped his hands over each shoulder as Anthony straightened the coat on his frame.

Turning, Anthony asked, "Better?"

"Perfect, my lord."

Laughing, Anthony adjusted the cuffs of his shirt at the end of his sleeves. "Far from it."

"You look much improved. A few of your bruises are only a faint yellow now."

That was true, but his right eye was still a ghastly

bluish purple. "I do feel better, so that's something, I suppose."

"And the ribs?" Culpepper asked.

"Still a bit tight, but I had no difficulty with the bath."

"Excellent. I hope you know you can call on us for anything."

Anthony smiled. "I do, thank you. Miss Pemberton is quite lucky to have you and the rest of the household."

"We're lucky to have her."

"I notice she hasn't had any visitors. Well, except that first day." He wanted to ask why her parents didn't call. "Does her family come to see her very often?"

Culpepper's shoulders stiffened. "They do not. In fact, they have yet to pay a call."

Wresting his expression away from a scowl, Anthony nodded. "I see. That is their loss." Did their inattention make Jane sad? Did she regret declaring herself a spinster? She clearly did—insomuch as she regretted the rumor and what it had done to her marriage prospects. She'd chosen to become a spinster because it had seemed the best option in her current state. A state someone else had manipulated.

Anthony suddenly wanted to get in another fight, and for a far better reason than he'd ever quarreled over before—Jane's honor.

"I agree," Culpepper said, referring to Anthony's comment that her parents were lacking. "We are very happy to have Miss Pemberton here, especially now that Miss Lennox is wed. We have a warm, pleasant household."

"I can see that," Anthony said. "You are particularly skilled, if I may say so, as is the cook. I don't, ah, suppose, you could bring me a glass of madeira? Or port? Any wine will do."

Unease flickered briefly in the butler's gaze, and Anthony regretted asking. "My apologies, my lord, but I have strict instructions to provide you nothing stronger than ale. Would you like me to bring you some?"

"I apologize for putting you in an awkward position, Culpepper. I am fine just now, thank you." In fact, Anthony didn't remember the last time he'd gone so long without drinking stronger spirits. He felt refreshingly clearheaded. He'd been afraid to go out into the light, he realized, but maybe it wasn't as bad as he'd anticipated. Because he had Jane to distract him. And she'd done a marvelous job of it.

"If you don't require anything else, then," Culpepper said, pivoting.

"Is Miss Pemberton at home?"

"She's in the garden room."

"Thank you, Culpepper." Anthony lifted his arm. "After you."

Culpepper inclined his head and preceded Anthony from the chamber.

Anthony went downstairs and paused in the doorway of the garden room. Jane sat at the table in front of the garden doors, one of which stood ajar. Her hand steered a quill across the paper in front of her, and a single golden curl brushed her ear. He longed to be that curl—close to her scent and the soft silk of her skin.

He walked into the room. "Good afternoon, Miss Pemberton."

The quill stopped scratching, and she set it down on the blotter. Reaching for a small cloth, she wiped her fingertips as she turned. Then her eyes widened in surprise. "Lord Colton, you shaved."

He brought his hand up and lightly massaged his chin. "I did. Bad decision?"

"I don't think so. You look quite handsome, in fact. I can actually see that it's you for the first time."

He laughed softly. "You mean I could have been an imposter this whole time?"

Her eyes danced with mirth. "I never considered that, but I suppose it's possible. What would have been the motivation for such a ruse, however?"

"Why, to spend time with you, of course. How else can a gentleman find himself in your bed and at your mercy?" He was flirting with her, which he probably shouldn't do. Not when her proposition still stood between them. Not when he was incredibly close to agreeing to fulfill it.

She set the cloth down on the table and stood. "I wanted to apologize—"

He couldn't let her do that. "No, the fault was mine. I shouldn't advise you on what to do, particularly when you didn't even ask for my input. Please accept my apology. I never meant to anger you or cause you upset in any way."

She hesitated, seeming surprised by his apology. "Thank you. I appreciate that, although I do realized I've been a bit…relentless about the rumor since you told me."

"I wish I never had," he said softly. At the flash of indignation in her eyes, he clarified, "Only because it causes you pain, and I would never wish to do that."

Her shoulders relaxed. "It's good to know the truth—or at least part of it. Knowing that it wasn't my fault… Well, it helps." She gave him a weak smile, and he realized she'd carried a burden for years of perceived failure. He thought of her parents not visiting and now wanted to start a new fight. Though, a physical altercation with her family was not something to *actually* consider. Still, he could imagine it.

He stepped toward her, closing the gap between

them to maybe half a yard. "It would never have been your fault. You're lovely. Any gentleman would be lucky to have you as his wife. I can't believe no one ignored that ridiculous rumor and snapped you up in spite of it."

"You didn't." She said this with a smile. "I'm teasing. I appreciate your kind words. I know it's hard for you—a man—to understand, but this literally changed the course of my life. It's hard not to feel powerless and a bit...empty."

He knew precisely how that felt. He'd made a decision not to go home to his family's estate to oversee something his father had asked him to do. He'd been too busy with his life in London. So his parents had gone instead. And in an instant, their family had changed forever at the hands of a highwayman. It didn't matter that he'd been caught and hanged. Anthony felt no relief, no sense of justice. All he felt was an overriding guilt and soul-deep emptiness.

Now he wanted a bloody drink.

"Anthony?"

Her use of his name drew him from the abyss. He blinked and looked at her, focusing on the concern in her tawny gaze.

She narrowed the distance between them by two small steps. "You keep doing that."

"What?" He twitched, knowing precisely what she meant, but hoping she really hadn't seen through him.

"I lose you for a moment." She touched his sleeve. "Where do you go?"

"Nowhere." Nowhere he wanted to share with her. She was grace and light—the epitome of everything he was not. Everything he could never be.

"I don't think that's true," she murmured. "But I won't pester you." She pulled her hand back. "Just know that I'm here if you ever want to talk about anything."

He captured the hand she'd just removed from his sleeve, twining her fingers with his. "Maybe I can help you with regard to the rumor."

She blinked twice. "Thank you. I appreciate the assistance. Phoebe sent a note earlier—Ripley didn't recall the rumor at all."

"That's unfortunate. Tell me about your first Season. Who courted you?"

"No one officially."

"You can't think of anyone who paid you attention? Maybe took you for a promenade in a dark garden during a ball? I'm trying to determine why such a rumor was even believable."

She glanced at their joined hands. "This is about as close as I've ever been to a gentleman. There weren't any clandestine meetings or walks. I don't even remember being invited to do anything like that. And you know I haven't been kissed."

Yes, he knew that. "Which is a bloody crime."

Her gaze met his, and heat leapt between them. "Is it?"

"Of the most grievous kind," he whispered, leaning toward her. He lifted his other hand and gently cupped her cheek just before he lowered his lips to hers. Closing his eyes, he brushed his mouth over hers. The kiss was soft, chaste, and the effect of it jolted through him like lightning.

He opened his eyes in wonder as he stood back. She stared up at him. "Is that all?"

Time stopped for a second, and then he laughed. "For someone with no experience, you know too much."

"Only because you told me," she said without guile.

"So this is *my* fault."

She arched her brow in a thoroughly saucy, provocative fashion. Maybe she had plenty of guile. "I'd like it to be."

And just like that, his cock went completely hard. "Careful what you ask for, Jane." He let go of her hand and wrapped his arm around her waist, drawing her against him. She felt so good, and he knew she would taste even better.

Closing his eyes, he swept his mouth over hers. He moved his hand back, his fingers driving into her hair behind her ear while he stroked her cheek with his thumb. He dragged it down, pulling on her jaw and then slipping his tongue past her lips.

She put one hand on his shoulder and the other on his waist, her fingertips digging into him as he kissed her, exploring her mouth with his tongue. Silently, he coaxed her to kiss him back.

Then she did, her tongue gliding against his, tentative at first, then with more purpose. He drew back and whispered, "Yes, just like that." Angling his head, he kissed her again, moving his hand to cup her nape and pulling her more tightly against him.

Her hand curled against his neck as she gave herself to him in complete abandon, her head tipping back and her mouth opening to accommodate him. Then she grew bolder, pushing her tongue into his mouth and demonstrating how quickly she learned.

Anthony's hips twitched as he tried not to move against her. He wanted her with a stark desperation that shocked the hell out of him.

And she was his for the taking. She'd made that very clear. He could turn around and close the door and lay her down on the settee...

He pulled away, his breath coming in fast pants as he released her.

"What's wrong?" She looked up at him with desire-hazed eyes and kiss-reddened lips, her breath as rapid as his.

"Nothing." He forced himself to take deep breaths and urged his lust to diminish. He couldn't take her on the settee. He wouldn't. She deserved far better than that.

She deserved far better than *him*.

"I have to go." He turned and fled the room before she could question him further. Before he exposed anything else about the void in his soul. Before he ruined her just as he ruined everything else.

CHAPTER 6

*T*oday was day seven. Anthony could very well leave her tomorrow. In fact, she expected him to. He'd been distant since they'd kissed the day before. Oh, he'd still played backgammon and cards after dinner. And he'd flirted with her—benignly. But he hadn't mentioned the kiss, and neither had she.

She'd thought he'd changed his mind about her proposition, especially when he'd kissed her. Clearly, that wasn't the case. The kiss, she assumed, had unnerved him.

Furthermore, he was doing exceptionally well. They'd spent time in the garden that afternoon, and while his eye still looked terrible, most of his other injuries were nearly healed.

Tonight, they were going to have dinner in the dining room, and she wondered if it would be their final evening together. She expected it even as she dreaded it.

She was suddenly irritated with herself and her defeatist attitude. If this was to be their last night together, she wanted to enjoy it. And she wanted to know if it was truly to be their last.

Dressed for dinner, Jane went to his room and knocked on the door.

"Come in," he called.

Jane opened the door and closed it behind her. The bedchamber was empty, but the narrow door to the dressing room stood open. She crossed the room and went to the threshold. He stood with his back to her, his hands tying his cravat.

The lawn of his white shirt stretched across his broad shoulders as he worked. Her gaze dipped down the muscles of his back, barely visible beneath the cotton, and settled on the curve of his backside. She'd never paid attention to how attractive that body part was on a man. Or maybe it was just his. Her fingers itched to touch it. Yesterday she'd gotten a frustratingly small taste of him. She wanted more.

His eyes met hers in the mirror, and his fingers stopped moving. "Jane. Miss Pemberton."

He'd reverted to calling her Miss Pemberton after the kiss. She'd followed his lead and gone back to calling him Lord Colton. But in her head, he would forever be Anthony.

Turning, he gave up on the cravat, letting the silk fall into a half-tied knot. "Please pardon my dishabille."

"No need to excuse yourself. I'm intruding. Please pardon *me*."

He grinned. "We are nothing if not unfailingly polite."

She nodded. "I wondered if you planned to leave tomorrow. I realize I could have asked at dinner, but I find I…" She fought to find the right words. "I wanted to know. Now."

He looked bemused. "Why?"

She stepped farther into the small room. "If it's to be our last night together, I want to know."

He swallowed, his Adam's apple moving while

the rest of him remained stock-still. "It should be. I'm nearly healed, and I should go home."

She moved closer, emboldened by the electricity she felt in the air. "But you aren't *fully* healed. You *could* stay."

"We both know I should not."

"Why? Because I might beat you at backgammon again?"

He smiled, his eyes crinkling in the way that made her insides flutter and her lungs feel like they couldn't draw a deep breath. "Clearly. My manhood can't support another loss."

She refused to sidestep the attraction between them like they had since the kiss. She'd regret it forever. Moving to stand directly in front of him so he had nowhere to hide, she placed her hand on his chest. With only his shirt between them, she felt the strong beat of his heart, the tantalizing heat of his flesh. "Or is it because you might kiss me again?"

"I won't do that. I overstepped yesterday."

She narrowed her eyes up at him, frustrated by his unnecessary chivalry. "How can you overstep when I invited you to take my virginity? A kiss is well within the bounds of what I've already asked you to do. And what will you do if I kiss you?"

A low growl sounded from somewhere deep in his throat. "Jane, you are the embodiment of temptation."

She twitched her hips and pushed her hand up to his cravat. Bringing up her other hand, she plucked up the silk between her fingers. "Should I tie this for you or take it off?"

"Fuck."

Surprise leapt through her, and for a moment, she froze.

"God, I'm sorry." He closed his eyes briefly and groaned. When he looked into her eyes again, there was naked desire. "You completely rob me of my senses. I want you to take it off, but you should tie it."

She gave him an apologetic grimace. "Sadly, I don't actually know how to knot a cravat." She pulled the silk loose and gripped the ends in each hand. Then she used it to tug his head down. "I have, however, recently learned how to kiss."

Standing on her toes, she pressed her mouth to his. She'd expected to have to coax him, but his arms came around her, and he lifted her against him.

She swallowed a gasp as he plundered her mouth. So much for kissing *him*. Not that she didn't. Because she *had* learned to kiss and had thought of little else since yesterday.

Releasing the cravat, she curled her arms around his neck and held on tight. Oh, this was everything she'd hoped it would be. He felt so good against her —strong, warm, secure. And he made her feel desired, special. He wanted to resist, but wasn't able to. Her insides cartwheeled.

He slowly lowered her back down to the floor. Her body slid down his, and she was all too aware of his hard length—his *cock*—against her. A pulse that had started between her legs when he'd kissed her the day before returned and grew to an insistent throb. She knew she could try to quiet the ache, but suspected he would do it better. Maybe he would at least show her how—hadn't he offered to do that?

He ended the kiss, but didn't move away. He spoke against her mouth. "You are a temptress. I know I'm repeating myself. I can't help it. Jane, you should go."

"Probably, but I'm not going to. I've been clear with you about what I want. Nothing has changed. Unless…you've changed your mind?" It seemed he had, or was at least on the verge of doing so.

"I can't do everything you want." He pulled back slightly then so he could look at her. "It's not that I don't want to. God, I want to. But I can't. Not everything."

Disappointment curled in her gut, but he hadn't outright denied her. "What can you do? Can you at least show me how to properly pleasure myself?"

The heat between them grew to an almost unbearable level before he answered. "Yes." The word was barely audible, but she saw his lips move. His lovely, kissable, enchanting lips.

She stood on her toes to kiss him again. "Oh, good."

"Jane," he growled before claiming her mouth and kissing her with wild abandon. They clung to each other as if they were the only solid objects in a storm raging about them. When at last they parted, they were both panting.

"Later, after dinner?" he asked.

Jane shook her head. She didn't want to wait. Hell, why not now *and* later? "Now, please. And after dinner, if you're so inclined."

He took her hand and led her back to the bedroom. "I make no promises about later, but now… Get on the bed."

Jane kicked off her slippers and started to climb on the bed.

"On second thought, that's going to rumple your dress, and we still have to dine."

She put both feet back on the floor. "We could dine here, and it doesn't matter what we wear." She curled her lips into a sultry smile. "We could wear nothing, in fact."

"Temptress is perhaps not a strong enough word. Siren is better." He stared at her with a fiery intensity. "Jane, you're a siren. And you're going to be the death of me. But I daresay it will be the best death anyone could hope for."

"I don't want to kill you," she said softly, then turned to present her back. "Why don't you unlace my dress, and I'll just remove it for now. Then I can put it back on...after."

In answer, he began to pluck at her laces. She'd been undressed by her maid more times than she could count, but it had *never* felt like this. Each pull reverberated through her body, echoing in her core, pushing her desire even higher. By the time he finished, she was breathing heavily, her chest rising and falling rapidly.

She took her arms from the sleeves, and he whisked the garment over her head. Pivoting, she watched him carefully lay it over the back of the chair near the hearth.

Then he came toward her again and twirled his finger. "Turn back around."

Puzzled by the request but eager to do anything he asked, she faced the bed. His fingers touched her nape, gently stroking her and sending ripples of sensation down her spine and out to her extremities. She shivered. He moved down until he reached the top of her corset.

"I want to take this off too. But we don't really have to."

She heard the battle in his voice. He was holding himself back. She didn't want him to. "I think I'd prefer if you took it off." He'd mentioned touching her breasts, which wouldn't be possible with the corset on.

Again, he unfastened her garment, the sound of the laces pulling through the fabric whispering in the air around them. As the corset loosened, she tried to calm her racing pulse, taking a deep breath and closing her eyes.

He tugged the corset from her, sliding it over her hips and down her legs until she stepped out of it. She kept her eyes closed, allowing him to guide her.

"I suppose I shouldn't take your hair down." He spoke near her ear, his breath tickling her neck.

"You could."

"I won't."

But she heard the desire in his voice. Then his lips were against her skin. She gasped softly as he kissed her neck and shoulder. He lightly clasped her waist, then splayed his hand over her hip so that his fingers nearly touched her sex. Well, her sex covered by the petticoat and chemise she still wore. It was too much.

Jane reached behind her waist and untied the petticoat. It fell to the floor, and she kicked it aside. "That's better," she murmured.

His hand pressed on her, bringing her backside against him. "Lift your chemise."

It reached her midthigh. Using her left hand, she pulled the hem up to her hips.

"Higher," he whispered against her ear. He kissed her there, his lips and tongue tracing a seductive trail along the outer edge.

She did as he said and lifted the chemise to her waist, exposing herself.

"Show me what you do when you pleasure yourself," he said, keeping his voice low. It was dark and seductive, enveloping her in a world of sensation where touch and sound were paramount.

Heat flooded her, and she wondered if she had the courage to do as he asked. Only, he wasn't asking. And that made it all the more enticing. She lowered her right hand to her sex and pressed gently. "I just rub here," she barely whispered.

"You don't put your finger inside?"

She shook her head, her cheeks flaming even as her thighs trembled.

He put his hand over hers. "Widen your legs farther apart."

When she did so, he began to move her hand against herself, rotating her fingertips against that spot that felt good.

"Your clitoris is very sensitive. I could probably make you come just by doing this—going faster and faster. But if I add my finger—or my tongue—inside you, you might come harder. Do you know what that means, Jane? To come?"

She shook her head, unable to speak as desire unfurled inside her. He hadn't stopped moving their fingers, and the sparks he'd ignited were now burning into flame, licking at her from all sides.

"It means orgasm—that release that sweeps over you, overwhelming your senses and stealing your reason. Some compare it to a loss of consciousness or even death—tumbling into a darkness that is at once terrifying and welcome."

He made it sound so wondrous. She was certain she'd never experienced anything like *that*. "You've set my expectations quite high," she said on a gasp as he widened his pattern of movement, their fingers moving lower over her sex and dipping into her heat before circling back up.

"Then I'd better meet them," he said with a masculine confidence that made her shudder.

He continued their play in silence. No, not silence, because she was nearly panting and her blood was pounding in her ears.

He lifted his other hand to the top of her chemise and tugged it down, exposing her breasts. "You never touch yourself here?" He gently cupped one globe.

Jane was glad for the security of his body behind

her, because she felt as if she might collapse. "No," she managed to answer.

"Remember the die?"

"Yes." She nearly whimpered when his fingers closed over her nipple, and he repeated what he'd done the day before to the die. He rolled her flesh, then softly squeezed, pulling on her. She felt the pleasure deep in her core, her pelvis twitching in response as she moaned.

"See what you've been missing?" he teased as he moved between stroking her flesh, rolling her nipple, and then lightly pinching before repeating the sequence. All the while, he used her fingers to delve deeper into her sex. "Are you usually this wet?"

She'd noticed wetness before, but not like this. But then she hadn't put her finger inside herself before. "No. I don't know. Is that normal?"

"Yes, when you're aroused. It makes it easier for entry." He pushed her finger inside her and kissed her neck, his mouth latching on her as he pumped her finger in and out. The tip of his finger went in too, and she wanted more. More than that, she wanted his finger—or fingers—not hers.

Slipping her hand from beneath his, she reversed their positions so she could slide his finger inside herself. "Please."

"Kiss me, Jane."

"I—" She gasped as he drove deep into her. Yes, she could see how she might come harder…

"Turn your head and kiss me." His command, dark and demanding, made her body thrum.

She turned her head, and he claimed her mouth, spearing his tongue into her as he did the same with his finger. But he broke this kiss briefly. "Don't stop touching yourself, Jane. Let's do this together. Keep stroking your clitoris."

She did as he said, and the pleasure of it along

with his finger and his hand on her breast built the pleasure inside her to a harrowing degree. Then he kissed her again, and the storm increased, buoying her to unimaginable heights.

"Faster, Jane," he rasped against her mouth. Then there was more inside her—he was using two fingers, stretching her.

Her legs buckled, and he kept her from falling, moving his hand to her other breast and holding her more tightly against him. "Come for me, Jane. *Come*."

Mindless, she couldn't keep up the pace even as her impending release demanded it. "Anthony, *please*."

He withdrew his fingers and took over her clitoris, moving rapidly over her flesh, showing her how she was deficient. The spiraling pleasure burst inside her. She cried out as spasms rocked her body. He kept moving, alternating his fingers between her sheath and her clitoris. She was absolutely lost in a torrent of ecstasy.

When she began to calm, he turned her and perched her on the edge of the bed. She opened her eyes and looked up at him in wonder. "I never imagined…"

He kissed her, his hand cupping the back of her head. She wrapped her hand around his wrist and kissed him back, so grateful for his gift.

When they pulled apart, she blinked up at him. "Thank you."

"You're welcome."

She couldn't help but notice that he looked pained, his face drawn into tight lines. "Are you all right?" She touched his cheek.

"Fine. Wonderful, actually."

"Except you didn't come. Right?"

"I, ah, will take care of that after you leave. Before I come down for dinner."

He meant to pleasure himself, of course. Presumably he was much better at it than she was—although, now she felt much better prepared. "I noticed it felt better when you did the pleasuring." Which was why she'd unabashedly begged him to put *his* fingers inside her. "Would it feel better for you if I did the same?"

"My God, Jane, are you even real?" He laughed briefly. "Yes, it would, but I'm not letting you do that."

She slitted her eyes as she looked up at him. "Not even if I really, really want to?"

He closed his eyes and tipped his head back for a second before looking back at her, his gaze bright with heat. "Are you sure?"

She nodded. "Yes, please. Tell me what to do."

∼

This was madness.

Anthony should walk away. No, he should run. He did neither.

"You don't have to do this," he croaked.

"I know. But I want to." She stood from the bed, her chemise still pulled down to reveal her breasts, their nipples hard and the color of dark, dusky pink roses. He ached to take one in his mouth. He was a beast, as depraved and selfish as he knew himself to be.

Still he didn't move, not even when she put her hand on his chest.

Her lips curled into a seductive smile. "If someone had told me a week ago that I'd be here with you doing…this, I would have laughed. Just before I told them they were insane. And yet, now there is nowhere else I'd rather be, and I honestly can't understand why I never considered you in this way." She trailed her finger up until she met his bare flesh above the open neck of his shirt.

Her touch singed him, burning desire into every part of him. He struggled to speak, but he feared if he didn't, he would entirely lose his grasp on reality. "In what way is that?"

"To be honest, I don't think I've considered any man in this way. It's hard to do that when you don't know what goes on once you're wed."

"Your mother told you nothing?" He found that almost criminal. Cruel, to be sure, since some young women seemed terrified. He'd frightened more than one by merely asking them to dance.

She shook her head. "She said my husband would explain everything, and that it was better that way." She traced her fingertip up to the hollow of his throat, her gaze following her movement. "I have to admit, I appreciated your explanation. And your demonstration." She lifted her eyes to his, and her lids lowered slightly, making her look seductive and…confident. Wasn't she supposed to be a virginal miss?

He'd clearly underestimated her. Perhaps allowing her to help him wouldn't send him straight to hell. Oh, what did it matter when he was headed there anyway?

Anthony lifted his hand and captured hers, stilling her finger against his flesh. "You're sure you want another demonstration?"

"Yes, please." She looked at him with such eagerness, such…hunger that it took his breath away.

"You have more courage than any woman I've met."

"Are you sure it isn't brazenness?" She laughed softly, her eyes twinkling in the early evening light filtering between the curtains. He realized it had grown darker in the room since they'd come from the dressing chamber. He was tempted to light a candle, but decided it might be better to leave them in twilight.

"You are a minx." He kissed her, using his teeth to gently tug on her lower lip.

She gasped softly, and he reached down to cup her backside, pulling her flush against him. After a thorough kiss that made his already aching cock throb with want, he raised his head. "Feel that?" He pressed her more tightly against his erection.

"How could I not?"

He let out a laugh. She was delightful, and he didn't deserve any of this. He looked into her tawny eyes and tried to be serious. "Do you want to touch it?"

"I think I must."

He couldn't help but smile. "That's not the same as wanting to."

"Of course I want to." She backed away slightly and brought her hands to his waistband, then immediately began unbuttoning his fall.

If he had any doubts as to her intent—or desire—she disabused him of every single one. He still doubted the intelligence and decency of allowing her to do this, but then she touched him, and he had no thoughts of any kind. Just blissful sensation and desperate longing.

He closed his eyes and cast his head back, whispering, "Jesus."

"This is good?" she asked.

"If you didn't do anything else, this would be lovely."

"Well, you're easy."

He opened his eyes as she drew another laugh

from him. "And you're unlike any woman I've ever met. This isn't supposed to be amusing."

"Isn't it? I suppose not. I didn't feel at all like laughing when you were touching me, but why not. Laughter feels good, and every single thing you did to me felt better than good." She sighed. "It was wonderful."

It took every ounce of self-control Anthony possessed not to toss her on the bed, lift her chemise, and sink himself deep into her wet heat. He closed his eyes again, thinking that might help preserve what was left of his sanity. "Jane. I think it's time you took it out."

"Oh, this?" She guided his cock from his breeches. "Should I take off your clothing?"

"Not necessary." He sounded like he was being strangled, but that made sense because he could barely draw breath through his lust.

"Actually, I disagree. Your shirt is quite in the way." She hadn't finished speaking before he'd pulled the garment over his head and tossed it away.

"Better?"

"*Oh yes.*" She touched his chest with her other hand, splaying her palm over the center as her fingers pressed into his flesh. "Anthony, you're magnificent. So hard and contoured... I had no idea how beautiful a man could be."

Christ, he was going to spill himself. He opened his eyes and saw the admiration in her gaze and nearly did just that. "Jane, I need you to move your hand." Hell, he was supposed to be showing her. It was far easier to instruct her with regard to herself, he realized.

She caressed his chest, her fingertip grazing his nipple. He sucked in a sharp breath and felt his cock jump against her palm. "Not that hand," he groaned. "*The other one.*"

"Oh! Of course," she murmured.

He put his hand over hers and demonstrated. "Like this," he hissed, sliding her palm over his shaft from tip to root and back again. "And just like we did with you, you'll move faster and faster."

"I see speed is important. That felt incredible when you did it to me. I'll endeavor to do my best."

"Jane, it's taking effort not to spill my seed at this very moment, so I don't think you'll have to try too hard."

"Is that right? You *are* easy." She looked up at him with a saucy smirk. "But I think you're lying. I think you'd much prefer if I took as long as possible, to draw out your pleasure. Isn't that what you did with me?"

The entire time she spoke, she worked his cock with a novice expertise that likely would have scandalized anyone else. But he was a scoundrel and the worst sort of man, so he only wanted more. "Faster," he breathed. "And tighter." He clasped her hand more securely around him.

She followed his lead, and he let his hand fall away. Closing his eyes again, he let his head fall back as he surrendered to her. He clasped her waist and moved with her, his hips thrusting. She brought her other hand down his chest and to the side, to caress his hip. Her palm brushed his backside and then came forward over his hip, gliding atop his thigh. Then she cupped his balls.

How in the fuck did she—

Anthony groaned. "Jane. Don't."

She pulled her hand away but kept up the pressure on his cock.

"No, I didn't mean." He couldn't speak coherently. "Don't *stop*. Do that. Again."

Her hand came back to his balls.

"Just squeeze. Lightly."

She did as he asked, and it was the end of him. He cried out as a vicious orgasm ripped through him. Mindless, he held her tight as he spent himself into her incredible hand.

"*Jane.*" He said her name over and over again, diminishing in volume as his body quieted.

"Well, that was messy."

He opened his eyes, his heart racing at an impossible speed. He sucked in air. "I'm sorry. I should have told you that was coming." He really was the worst.

"It's not a problem," she said calmly. "I was merely making an observation."

He looked down and saw that the front of her chemise was quite wet. "Hell. I *am* sorry."

She brought her hand up—not the one covered in his seed—and curled it around his neck. "Anthony, don't be. I asked for this, and I don't regret a single thing, least of all a soiled chemise. Though perhaps I'll launder this myself." She winked at him, and he could only stare at her.

What had he done to deserve this charming, intelligent, caring young woman? How he'd ever managed to find his way to her doorstep at his darkest hour would remain a mystery—and one he wasn't sure he would ever solve. It didn't matter. He would be forever grateful, for this had been the best week of his life, battered and beaten though he'd been.

Something soft nudged his calf. He looked down to see Daffodil. She mewed up at him.

Jane smiled. "I think she's trying to say she's hungry. I am too, actually. Which means I need to get ready for dinner. I'll meet you downstairs shortly?"

She turned from him and went to fetch her corset, petticoat, and dress before sliding her feet into her slippers.

He tucked himself back into his breeches and

buttoned the fall. "You're just going to go to your room like that?"

"I don't particularly want to wear the chemise in its current state," she said.

"What if someone sees you?"

"Everyone's busy preparing for dinner. Meg might be in my chamber." She shrugged. "I'll tell her I had a problem with my corset and then covertly change my chemise. She cocked her head. "Are you worried about my reputation with my servants?"

"Maybe. I don't want to contribute to your ruin."

She reached up and caressed his cheek, giving him a soft smile. "You haven't. You've given me something I will remember—and treasure—forever. I'll see you at dinner, and we can discuss whether you'll accept my original proposal."

Then she was gone.

And he was well and truly fucked.

He couldn't take her virginity. He was already the most vile person for doing what he'd done with her. Yes, she'd been a willing participant, but she wasn't a courtesan or a prostitute. She was a lady, and he'd taken advantage of her curiosity. But then he was as selfish and callous as a person could be.

Except she'd told him that she had no plans to wed and didn't expect to experience sex at all. While she might believe that right now, he wasn't sure it was true. Marriage clearly meant something to her, or that bloody rumor wouldn't have bothered her so much.

She likely wanted to fall in love and have a family, even if she didn't want to admit it. And why would she if she was convinced it would never come to pass? Was there anything more painful than loss— whether it was a dream or…something else?

Anthony wasn't going to be the one to ruin her chance for a future, because despite that rumor and her recent spinsterhood, he believed she could still find happiness. There was a gentleman out there who would see past Society's rules and appreciate her for the wonderful woman she was—a gentleman who would honor and love her, and, most importantly, deserve her.

That man wasn't him.

But maybe he could help her. He nearly laughed. How could he expect to do that when he couldn't even help himself?

One thing was certain—he had to go home to-morrow. Early. Before she could try to persuade him to stay. Which meant he just had to get through din-ner. And then plead a headache lest she try to seduce him with talk of her proposition again.

He wouldn't surrender a second time. Once had been enough. No, once had been too much, because now her touch, her laugh, her sweet passion would haunt him until his dying day.

$\mathcal{A}$nthony alighted from the hack and carried his portmanteau up the steps to his house on Grosvenor Street. His butler, Purcell, opened the door, his stoic expression betraying only the slightest surprise. "Good morning, my lord." His tone was even and pleasant, as if Anthony hadn't disappeared for a week.

"Good morning, Purcell." He walked into the hall and briefly felt a rush of familiarity, of home. Until the arrival of the also familiar sense of guilt and despair that always chased those sensations away.

"I'll take that," the butler offered, reaching for the portmanteau. If he noticed the bruising that was still visible around Anthony's eye, he didn't say so. But then he was as stoic and adept as a butler could be, which was why Anthony found him comforting. From his dark hair speckled with gray to his calming dark eyes to his rigid frame, he presented a portrait of equanimity. He'd never bowed to grief after Anthony's parents had died. He'd carried on—almost—as if nothing had happened.

"Did I hear his lordship?" The sound of Anthony's valet's deep voice slid into the hall just before he appeared. Tabor was tall and thin, with a mop of

blond hair that he could barely tame and round blue
eyes that nearly always saw right through Anthony.
His personality was completely at odds with that of
the butler, and yet Anthony found him comforting
too.

"Good morning, Tabor," Anthony said.

Tabor's eyes widened as soon as he fixed his gaze
on Anthony. "Good heavens, what happened to your
eye? Another fight?"

"With a goat, if you must know."

"A goat?" Tabor squinted at him briefly, clearly
skeptical of Anthony's story. "How does one fight
with a goat?"

"I was staying with a friend outside town. He
has goats. Aggressive goats." Anthony smiled inwardly as he recalled the delightful conversation he'd
had with Jane about those nonexistent goats. But the
warm sensation didn't last. He'd left her that
morning with only a note of gratitude. He'd had to
go, but doing so hadn't been easy. Especially after
last night.

Their dinner together had been lovely, as full of
laughter and flirtation as he'd come to expect when
he was in her company. He'd nearly thrown caution
out the window—again—and taken her to bed. He
knew she wanted him to.

Instead, he'd pleaded a headache, kissed her forehead, and bade her good night. And she'd given him
a warm smile and told him to sleep well, that she'd
see him today.

Only she wouldn't. He was an ass, but necessarily
so. Someday, she'd thank him for leaving before she
could become too entangled in the tragedy of his pathetic existence.

Tabor snorted. "I don't buy that at all. Aggressive
goats, you say?" He shook his head with a laugh.
"You got into another fight." He took the portman-

teau from Purcell, who looked a bit uncomfortable to be witnessing the exchange.

"Purcell," Anthony said. "Would you mind bringing coffee to my study? I presume I have correspondence to review."

"Quite a bit, my lord." Purcell inclined his head and left the hall.

"Coffee?" Tabor narrowed his eyes. "I haven't heard you ask for that in—" He seemed to think better of saying when because that would clearly indicate it had been since his parents' death.

"I have coffee on occasion." Rarely.

"More often than not, it's port or gin or something along those lines." Tabor stepped close to him and sniffed. "Are you sober?"

Anthony rolled his eyes. "Yes. Don't act as if it's an anomaly."

"Isn't it, though?"

Anthony exhaled, knowing it was pointless to argue with the one person who perhaps knew him better than himself. "Yes. Fine. I find I like being… clearheaded." He did, in fact. He didn't wish to dull any of the time he spent with Jane.

Except there would be no more time with Jane.

A ripple of unease tripped through him.

"I must congratulate you, my lord. Despite the ruin to your eye, you look quite fit, if I may say so. It's good to see." He gazed at Anthony with such approval and warmth that Anthony felt slightly uncomfortable. Had he really been that much of a disaster?

Of course you were. That was the point—destroying yourself. And the sooner you get back to it, the easier things will be.

Easier? Were they hard just now? No, and he would work to keep them that way. If he couldn't see Jane anymore, at least her influence would persist.

"Your parents would be pleased," Tabor said softly.

Anthony snapped his gaze to Tabor and clenched his jaw. The valet, who was just a few years older than Anthony, ducked his head. "My apologies, my lord." Then he took himself off with alacrity.

Taking a deep breath, Anthony headed to his study. The stack of correspondence on his desk was rather large. He rubbed his hands together in anticipation of the distraction from his parents, from Jane, from all of it. He sat down to read just as Purcell brought his coffee and set it on the desk.

"Will there be anything else, my lord?" the butler asked.

"No, thank you," Anthony said before sipping the steaming-hot beverage and turning his attention to the correspondence.

The first few missives were about various committee meetings at Westminster he should attend. Anthony set them aside to review again later. For the first time in ages, he looked forward to returning to the House of Lords.

The next handful were invitations. Though he wasn't invited to as many events as in the past due to the decline of his reputation, he still received more than he cared to accept. But there was one from Marcus and Phoebe. They were hosting a dinner party later in the week at Brixton Park. Guests were welcome to stay the night after if they didn't want to return to town.

Was he ready to see Marcus again? They'd argued at Marcus's wedding breakfast, when he'd tried to convince Anthony to stop drinking so much. It seemed that was becoming a theme. Or a problem.

Hell, he knew it was a problem. He knew he drank too much and had since his parents had been murdered. Anguish swept through him, and he nearly went straight to the sideboard where he kept his spirits. Perhaps he should have Purcell remove it from the study entirely. Yes, he should do that.

Because he *did* like being clearheaded. Where Marcus had failed, Jane had succeeded in persuading Anthony to stop. But then Jane hadn't so much persuaded him as insisted he follow her rules if he wanted to stay and recuperate at her house. He told himself it had been easier to stay with her than suffer the pain of coming home, but was that the truth?

He shook his head. None of it really mattered. Except she had made a difference with him. Perhaps she'd been precisely what he needed at that moment.

Anthony took another sip of coffee and redirected his focus to the correspondence. The next letter, drafted in familiar handwriting, made his breath catch. He tore it open and read the words quickly, then went back and reread them. His sister had given birth. He was now an uncle to a baby girl. Named Marianne for their mother.

A riot of emotions tumbled through him, none of them worth exploring—or feeling. Clearheadedness suddenly seemed an awful idea.

Lifting his gaze from the letter, Anthony stared at the portrait of his grandfather that hung on the wall opposite his desk. Now that Anthony was viscount, he should replace it with a portrait of his father, but he hadn't been able to do it. Almost a year had gone by since his father had been murdered, and Anthony still couldn't bring himself to look at his face.

The letter from Sarah dropped from Anthony's fingertips. He blinked and looked down at it. She'd given birth five days ago. The letter had likely been sitting here for at least a couple of days. She would have had it delivered as soon as possible to share the news. And she would be expecting his response, which was now delayed because he hadn't been here.

Self-loathing tore through him. He glanced toward the sideboard where bottles of port, rum, and gin beckoned. His foot twitched, and he nearly stood. It took every ounce of self-control he possessed not to pour a drink. More specifically, not to succumb to the desire to be numb. It was so much easier than this. Than feeling.

With Herculean effort, Anthony pushed Sarah's letter aside. He'd somehow find the courage to write her back later. He would. His gaze drifted to the sideboard once more.

Cursing, he ripped open the next letter. The words chilled him to his very soul, or rather, what was left of it.

Colton,

I know what you did, how you killed your parents. Unless you want everyone to know your sins, I require two hundred pounds, delivered to the barkeep at The Stinking Sheep in Blackfriars. You must deliver the funds personally on the seventeenth of May, or everyone in London will know the embarrassing and tawdry details of your transgressions—gambling, debt, drinking, womanizing, but most of all, murder.

Air fought its way into his lungs. He wasn't a murderer.

Yes, you are. They wouldn't have died if you hadn't gotten into trouble and if you hadn't refused your father's request.

Fuck, what day was it? He scrambled to think. He'd lost track of time while he was at Jane's. At last, he realized *today* was the seventeenth. If he hadn't come home today, he would have missed this entirely.

Clutching the letter in his hand, he stood and

walked around the desk. Did that mean he was going to pay it? Two hundred pounds wasn't a paltry sum. And yet, if he didn't, everyone would know the specifics of his crimes, just how far he had fallen. His friends, his sister, Jane...

Anthony crumpled the parchment and threw it across the room. He stalked to the sideboard and poured gin into a glass, then tossed the entire contents down his throat. Welcome heat snaked through him. He closed his eyes to savor the taste and the sensation that all would soon be right.

No, not right. Never right. Only better. More tolerable.

Numb.

He poured another drink and swallowed it down too. Filling the glass a third time, he went to the settee against the wall and lay down upon it, waiting for the apathy to take over. To immerse himself in comfortable darkness.

He couldn't bear anything else.

~

"*H*e's the worst, isn't he?" Jane asked the kittens who'd awakened her rather early that morning with their antics. They hadn't done that before. Presumably because they were typically in Anthony's chamber. That should have been her first inkling that something was amiss. Then, later that morning, when she'd gone downstairs to breakfast, Culpepper had handed her the note from Anthony informing her that he'd left.

My dear Jane,
Words cannot adequately convey my gratitude for your care this past week. I hope that I have repaid

*your kindness in satisfactory measure, but I daresay
that will never truly be possible. You were a light in
the darkness when I needed guidance most.*

> *Thank you.*
> *Colton*

He hadn't even had the grace to sign his given name. After everything they'd shared! Last night, he'd indicated she would see him today, and the whole time, he'd known he wouldn't be here.

Unless he'd awakened this morning and decided to go. He *had* suffered a headache last night. Perhaps he was regressing in his recovery.

Or *perhaps* she was making excuses for him.

Jane paced the garden room, and the kittens batted at her skirts until Fern jumped on Daffodil, and they somersaulted across the carpet. "Well, at least you don't seem too upset," she murmured. "But then you did wake me at an ungodly hour this morning. Was that because you were missing Anthony? Did you wake him up at that time every day?" Savagely, she hoped they did. He deserved that much.

The kittens ceased their wrestling and looked up at her. Daffodil mewed, then walked over to nuzzle her face against Jane's slipper. Jane bent and scooped her up. The kitten began to purr as Jane cuddled her and scratched her head. "How could he just leave like that? The least he could have done was to say goodbye in person."

Daffodil nudged her head into Jane's hand as if she agreed.

"Thank you, Daffodil." Jane looked down at Fern, who was now pulling on a thread from the carpet. "What do you think?"

Fern sat back from the thread, then wiggled her behind before launching forward once more.

"I should go after him?" Jane asked. Of course she should. She would go to his house right now and demand to know why he'd left so covertly. "Thank you, girls." Jane dropped a kiss on Daffodil's head before depositing her on the carpet next to her sister.

A short time later, Jane was in Phoebe's coach on her way to Anthony's house on Grosvenor Street. A dozen things went through her head as to what she could say, none of them very polite.

As the coach stopped in front of the house, her ire wilted. She'd never been here before, but she knew it had been his parents' house. Was it hard for him to live there? She knew from their conversations —or rather his reactions to some of their conversations—that the loss of his parents still weighed heavily on him. As it should. They were his parents, after all, and it hadn't even been a year since they'd died.

It's been nearly a month since you've seen your parents.

Yes, it had been, and they hadn't written or paid a call. She, on the other hand, had written to them. She'd asked how the wedding plans were coming and whether they would soon forgive her. Jane had hoped it would be in time for the wedding, but they hadn't responded. Her sister Anne had, however, saying that they needed time and for now, Jane just needed to be patient.

The coachman opened the door and helped Jane out. She went up the steps and was greeted immediately by the butler.

"Good afternoon." Anthony's butler carried an air of austere dignity. He was not at all what she might have expected. But then, he'd likely been Anthony's parents' butler. She wondered if that was painful for him too.

The anger she'd felt upon learning he'd left sputtered and died.

"Good afternoon," Jane said warmly. "Miss Pemberton to see Lord Colton."

A single crease marred the butler's forehead, and only for a moment. "I'm sorry...*miss*, but his lordship is not at home. I will tell him you called."

Jane noted the way he hesitated before stressing that she was a miss. Who should never call on a gentleman, let alone without a chaperone. Being a spinster was bloody difficult. And not nearly as wonderful as she'd hoped.

Except she had been able to take care of Anthony, something that never would have happened if not for her situation. Or the ruin she'd never been aware of. Had that rumor never started five years ago, Jane would undoubtedly be married to some other gentleman, with children to boot.

The thought of never having come to know Anthony as she had, without sharing that wonderful evening of bliss...

"Good afternoon," the butler said, closing the door.

Jane frowned. The butler's attitude chafed, but what did she expect?

Frustrated, she turned and went back to the coach but didn't direct the driver to go home. Perhaps a stroll along Bond Street would drive her doldrums away.

A scant five minutes later, Jane walked into one of her favorite shops. She adored their embroidery on things as varied as pillow slips and stockings.

"Miss Pemberton?"

Jane turned to see Lady Gresham. "Good afternoon, Lady Gresham. How lovely to see you. Allow me to apologize for the brevity of our meeting last week. I need to convene another very soon." Perhaps she'd do that later in the week. It wasn't as if she was occupied with anything—or anyone—else.

"That would be delightful," Lady Gresham said with a smile. "I'm quite keen to continue our discussion regarding a charitable endeavor we might support—something to aid women in need. That is a cause for which my sister and I are strongly in favor."

"I've been thinking about it, and I wonder if we should find a hospital or a workhouse we can help, somewhere that is specific to women?"

"There is a hospital in Whitechapel that provides reformation for former prostitutes. Perhaps we can help there somehow?"

Prostitutes? Jane wasn't sure what she thought of that, but if a woman wanted to change her fortunes, she could certainly support that endeavor. "I'll consider that, thank you." Jane's attention was drawn to the window through which she saw a woman walking outside the store. Not just any woman—Lady Satterfield.

Jane resisted the urge to rush outside and speak with her about the rumor. What if she didn't get another chance? Phoebe was hosting a dinner, but what if Lady Satterfield didn't attend? Jane would have no occasion to see her at another event because Jane wasn't invited to any.

Ice crept through her like a glacier moving over the earth, chilling everything in its path. Had she made a terrible mistake moving to Cavendish Square? She'd ruined any chance she had at making a match in Society.

You didn't have much of a chance anyway after that rumor started.

Yes, but if she was able to somehow undo the damage now, to convince people that she'd never behaved improperly, perhaps she could have salvaged her reputation enough to secure a match. But that wasn't possible now.

Did she even want it to be? She'd found most men on the Marriage Mart tiresome or disgusting. Not one had sparked her interest, her affection, her desire.

Well, there had been one...

"Miss Pemberton?"

Jane pulled herself from her reverie. "My apologies, Lady Gresham, I'm afraid I was distracted."

"I could tell." Lady Gresham's brow creased with concern. "Can I help somehow?"

"No, this is an old problem, something not worth worrying about." Jane was parroting what Anthony had said. Was he right? Should she let the rumor go? It was, as she'd just deduced, too late to change anything.

"I find old problems sometimes have a way of resurfacing when we least want them to," Lady Gresham said softly. "Best to eliminate them completely. If you can."

"Excellent advice." Jane didn't know if she could eliminate the problem, but she could certainly seek justice and right the wrong that was done to her—to the extent that she could find the person who'd started the rumor and exact an apology, preferably a public one. "Thank you, Lady Gresham."

"My pleasure, Miss Pemberton. My offer for assistance still stands."

"I appreciate that. Now, let us discuss when to hold our next meeting." Jane's day might have started poorly, but renewed purpose gave her hope.

CHAPTER 8

*T*he subscription room at Brooks's was lively two nights later as Anthony sat in the corner nursing a brandy. The last two days had passed in a comfortable blur as he'd returned to the embrace of his best friend: alcohol.

Perhaps not comfortable. Tolerable was more accurate. And it would do.

It had to, because the alternative was sobriety, which he'd accidentally awakened to that morning. For an hour, he'd been tortured by thoughts of the extortion note he'd received, the fact that he was two hundred pounds lighter, and, of course, images and memories of Jane. Those were by far the worst.

And it wasn't as if he didn't think of those things in his inebriated state, it was that he was less tormented by them. He could think of Jane and her sweet scent, her inquisitive touch, her delicious mouth and not fall into a pit of despair.

"Anthony!"

He hadn't heard that voice in weeks. Anthony sat up straighter as Marcus approached the table. Tall and muscular, with dark hair and dark blue eyes, the marquess was an attractive fiend. He was also a good friend, despite his scandalous reputation. Most of the time.

"Ripley." Anthony raised his glass. "Join me."

Marcus did just that, taking the chair to Anthony's left so they both faced the room with their backs to the wall. "Brandy?" he asked, glancing at the drink as Anthony set it back on the table.

Anthony nodded.

"For the eye? No, it looks like an old injury. When did you get into another fight?"

"Last week. An aggressive goat." Anthony smiled. The lie never got old. Because it always reminded him of Jane. Of their time together.

Marcus snorted. "Horseshit. What really happened?" He inclined his head at a passing footman.

"Don't press me," Anthony warned, thinking of their last meeting at Marcus's wedding breakfast.

Marcus arched a dark brow at him. "And here I thought you might apologize for stalking out of my wedding celebration."

"I will when you apologize for—and stop—meddling."

"I'm not meddling," he said quietly. "You're my friend, and I care that you don't overly abuse yourself or find yourself in a situation from which you can't recover."

It was far too late for that.

"Anyway," Marcus's tone turned bright. "Let us speak of pleasant things."

"Marriage has ruined you."

Marcus let out a laugh as the footman delivered his brandy. "Not at all, but I can see why you'd think so. I'm disgustingly happy, if you can imagine. Marriage is not at all what I expected."

"You were fortunate to meet Phoebe."

"Indeed I was, and I will be grateful for her every

moment of every day of my life." He tapped his glass to Anthony's and drank.

Anthony, of course, didn't need the excuse to drink too.

"Has your sister delivered yet?" Marcus asked.

"Yes, last week. A girl." Anthony had written back to her with congratulations but hadn't asked to visit. He wasn't sure he was ready to meet his niece who was named for his mother. Anthony's gut clenched. His dead mother.

"Wonderful news. I'll tell Phoebe. She'll be thrilled." Marcus sipped his brandy. "Can we expect you for dinner tomorrow night? You didn't send a response. If I didn't see you here tonight, I was going to hunt you down."

Anthony hadn't responded because he hadn't decided. He wondered if Jane had been invited, but couldn't ask. Marcus would want to know why, and there was no explanation that wasn't soaked in scandal. Besides, he'd asked Jane to keep his visit a secret with her friend, so he couldn't very well share it with his. Furthermore, Marcus, in his offensive happiness, would certainly tell his wife, and that could cause strife between her and Jane. Anthony had committed enough transgressions without adding friendship killer to his list.

Killer.

The word pounded in his brain. He finished his brandy and stood abruptly. Suddenly, his friend's company was more than he could endure. Not his company, his contentment.

"Where are you going?" Marcus asked. "I just got here."

"Sorry, I've somewhere to be."

"Mrs. Alban's?" Marcus gave him a knowing look. That had been Marcus's favorite brothel, and Mrs. Alban was his close friend—or had been before he wed Phoebe. They hadn't been lovers, but she made sure Marcus was always well cared for by her employees. As his friend, Anthony had received the same attention.

But Anthony hadn't been there since before his fight. Perhaps he should go there. He'd likely feel a hell of a lot better if he did. "Yes. I'd ask you to join me, but I daresay your days there are over."

"Quite." Marcus shook his head. "It's a bloody reversal, isn't it? If someone had wagered on this happening, I would have told them that they'd lose their fortune."

Anthony clasped his friend's shoulder. "You deserve every bit of it." More than Anthony ever would.

"You're coming tomorrow night, then?" Marcus asked, narrowing his eyes up at Anthony. "I won't take no for an answer. You owe it to Phoebe to come and apologize for leaving her wedding breakfast early."

Damn, had he hurt her feelings? "I hope I didn't upset her. I never meant to."

"Of course you didn't. She cares about you too. Just come. I promise it will be diverting, and I won't harass you about what you drink, all right?"

"But will there be anyone for me to fight with?" Anthony asked, grinning.

Marcus cocked his head to the side. "I'm afraid not, but I've time to fetch an aggressive goat or two. Will that suffice?"

"Brilliant. I'll be there."

Anthony left the club and caught a hack. Only he didn't go to Mrs. Alban's. He ended up in Cavendish Square, staring at Jane's house.

The mystery of how he'd ended up at Jane's still bothered him, but only because he wanted to be grateful for whatever—or whoever—had driven him there. What if it had just been him? He'd found himself nearby, and, for some reason, he'd gone there, maybe recalling that it was Miss Lennox's house. He wasn't sure he believed he could have purposely done something that had turned out to be so helpful. He had a history of incredibly bad decisions with even worse results.

If he hadn't allowed his gambling losses to get the better of him. If he hadn't borrowed money from the Vicar. If he'd gone to Oaklands instead of his parents.

Then he'd be dead instead of them.

He deserved nothing less. And as he looked across the square toward where Jane was likely tucked into her bed, he knew she deserved far better.

Anthony turned and walked into the night.

~

*a*nxiety tripped through Jane as she strolled into the drawing room at Brixton Park. She smoothed her right hand over her left forearm, adjusting her glove while surveying the room. Phoebe had told her there would be sixteen attendees at the dinner, and most planned to spend the night. Jane had wanted to ask for the guest list outright, but had stopped short of that.

Anthony wasn't there.

She exhaled in disappointment but had to admit she wasn't terribly surprised. Perhaps he knew she would be here and wanted to continue avoiding her. She'd sent him a note that morning asking how he was faring. It seemed the kind thing to do since she'd overseen at least the start of his recovery. She was also just plain curious. Because she cared about him.

It seemed, however, he did not return the sentiment.

Jane pushed him from her mind. He wasn't the reason this dinner was important anyway. It was Lady Satterfield, and she *was* here. That made Jane smile with anticipation.

Phoebe came toward her. "You look lovely, Jane. Is that a new gown?"

"It is," Jane said, glancing down at the pink confection with its sheer overlay that shimmered in the candlelight. "Thank you for leaving me a small allowance," she added quietly.

"Thank *you* for letting me. I know your parents won't give you a farthing."

That was true. Jane touched Phoebe's hand briefly. "I am so grateful for your generosity. And your friendship."

"As I am for yours." Phoebe's eyes sparkled with warmth. "Now, to the matter at hand. Shall we go speak with Lady Satterfield?"

"Yes, please."

As they made their way across the drawing room, Jane noted some of the other people in attendance, including Phoebe's parents, the Duke and Duchess of Clare, and the Earl and Countess of Sutton. The Duchess of Clare's sister, the Countess of St. Ives, or Fanny, as she was known to Jane, was a good friend.

Jane noted that the Duke of Clare had once gone by the moniker the Duke of Desire while the Earl of Sutton had been known as the Duke of Deception. It occurred to Jane that she, as an outcast, ought to feel right at home with this group, and the realization made her smile.

"What?" Phoebe asked as they neared Lady Satterfield.

"I was just noticing that this party is rife with people like us, those that don't necessarily fit into Society's expectations."

"You're right. Well, we must band together." Phoebe looped her arm through Jane's with a grin.

They arrived at Lady Satterfield, whose husband had just departed to go speak with some other guests.

"Lady Satterfield, you know Miss Jane Pemberton?" Phoebe said, taking her arm from Jane.

The Countess of Satterfield was a tall woman in her late fifties. Her dark hair was liberally streaked with gray and dressed in a regal style that perfectly matched her bearing. She looked at Jane with warm welcome in her gray eyes. "Of course. How lovely to see you, Miss Pemberton."

Jane dipped a curtsey. "Good evening, my lady."

Lady Satterfield looked between Jane and Phoebe. "How is your Spitfire Society? You're down a member with Her Grace, the Duchess of Halstead, gone from town." She referred to Arabella, who was at her husband's country seat and would be for the duration of the Season. They had much to do there.

"We are currently adding members," Jane said. "And we are focusing our efforts on supporting a charitable organization, such as a hospital or workhouse." She glanced toward Phoebe. "I saw Lady Gresham yesterday on Bond Street, and she mentioned a hospital that, er, helps women in Whitechapel."

Lady Satterfield clasped her hands together and smiled. "Well, that sounds wonderful. It's too bad I can't be a spitfire too, for I would love to participate in supporting such a cause."

Was there any reason she couldn't? Jane looked at Phoebe in question, and she seemed to have the same thought, because she lifted her shoulder and nodded.

Jane turned her attention back to the countess. "Then you must join us. There's nothing to say the

Spitfire Society can't include spitfires of all marital states, ages, or anything else."

"Wonderful!" Lady Satterfield declared with a laugh. "Lord Satterfield has long said I was a spitfire, and now it's official." She sent a glance toward the Countess of Sutton. "You must invite Lady Sutton too. She's been a force of wonder at Bethlehem Hospital. And Ivy—Lady Clare—too. She's been a champion of supporting women, particularly those in workhouses, for some time. In fact, her sister, Lady St. Ives, had been looking for a place to start a workhouse entirely for women before she married. I wonder where she left that project?" Lady Satterfield cocked her head to the side in thought.

Jane vaguely remembered that now. "I'd forgotten about that. I'll write to Lady St. Ives tomorrow and inquire. It would be splendid if we could all join forces and work together. I think that's an excellent purpose for the Spitfire Society, don't you, Phoebe?"

Phoebe nodded. "I do indeed."

It was time for Jane to turn the conversation where she needed. She pivoted toward the countess. "Speaking of recalling things…" It wasn't the best transition, but it was all Jane could come up with. "I wonder if you might remember something of a rather, ah, delicate nature."

Lady Satterfield's brows dipped into a V as she stepped a bit closer to Jane.

Phoebe also moved in, and Jane lowered her voice a tad. "It's come to my attention recently that a rumor circulated about me during my first Season. It seemed to have just been among the young bucks, so you may not have heard about it, but given your stature in Society and the esteem in which everyone holds you, I thought it possible you may have heard mention of it."

"Oh dear, may I assume this rumor was not flattering?"

Jane's jaw clenched briefly. "That's correct. Someone spread the notion that I was loose. It explains why none of my casual suitors offered for me and why, by the end of that Season, I felt as if I was moving quickly toward the shelf." She vividly remembered her mother's anger and disappointment and the regimen she'd put Jane on before the next Season: painting, dancing, practicing the pianoforte, riding until she probably could have bested any gentleman in a race along Rotten Row in the early morning. In the end, none if it had made a difference. Her second Season was as much a failure as her first.

"We'd like to find out who started this rumor and, if possible, why," Phoebe said.

Jane's heart swelled at her use of the word "we." She cast a grateful glance toward her friend.

"I don't recall this rumor," Lady Satterfield said. "But, if it was truly just among the bucks, that isn't unusual." She tapped her finger against her chin. "That was 1814. Let me recall what was happening. My second grandchild, Christopher, was born that year." She smiled. "He was such a delightful baby." Her brow creased as she lapsed into thought once more. Then she looked around the drawing room. "Clare and Sutton were unmarried men at that time. Perhaps they heard something."

Jane wasn't sure she could ask them. Not only did she not know them well enough, how did one broach such a topic with a duke and an earl? It had been difficult enough with Lady Satterfield.

Lady Satterfield seemed to understand her concern. She reached over and patted Jane's arm. "I'll speak with them and see what I can learn. Would that help?"

Exhaling, Jane smiled in relief. "Thank you, yes."

"I'd be happy to," Lady Satterfield said. Her brow furrowed once more. "What do you plan to do with this information, dear? It can't be helpful to you now. The damage was, unfortunately, done quite some time ago. Perhaps we should focus our energies on rehabilitating your reputation, as I was able to do for my stepdaughter-in-law when I took her on as my companion."

She referred to Eleanor St. John, who'd been ruined as a young lady during her first Season. Afterward, she'd fled to the country for a very long time—almost ten years, if Jane recalled the story correctly—and returned to London only when she found herself in need of employment. She'd accepted a position as Lady Satterfield's companion, who'd taken a particular liking to her. Now she was the Duchess of Kendal, and, of course, Lady Satterfield's stepdaughter-in-law.

Not that Jane expected to make such a match or to be Lady Satterfield's companion. She didn't need either of those things, just an improved reputation with which to go forward. That was all she wanted, and it was what she deserved.

"How would you do that?" Jane asked. "Rehabilitate my reputation?"

"Well, this rumor happened quite some time ago, and it was just a rumor, unlike what happened with my stepdaughter-in-law. Lord Haywood had coerced her into an embrace, and it was seen."

Jane flicked a glance toward Phoebe. She'd been betrothed to Haywood's cousin and refused to marry him after he'd behaved even worse with her. "Why is it men never have to pay for their mistakes—at least not has handsomely—as women?"

"And some of our 'mistakes' aren't even that,"

Phoebe said with considerable disgust. "They are beyond our control, as is your case."

"It is certainly unfair," Lady Satterfield agreed, pressing her lips together. "However, and I do hate to say this, Miss Pemberton, but leaving your parents' house and taking up residence alone has nothing to do with the past and will not help you in the present."

"It has everything to do with the past," Jane said, trying to keep her outrage in check. Her anger wasn't directed at Lady Satterfield. What she said was true. But it also wasn't fair. "If not for the rumor that set me on the trajectory of failure, I might be married now. Happily ensconced in a life that Society approves. That was stolen from me, and I have done the best I could."

The countess grimaced. "I do understand. You had no marriage prospects whatsoever?"

Jane thought of her parents' neighbor, Mr. Brinkley. "I did, but no one I wanted to wed. Shouldn't we be able to marry someone we choose?"

"Of course. But surely you must realize that even without the rumor, you may still be unwed. What if the man you were meant to marry simply hasn't come along yet?"

Anthony came to her mind, and she nearly laughed. He *wasn't* marriage material.

Jane straightened toward Lady Satterfield. "He definitely hasn't."

"Well then, let us work on reestablishing you in a position to find him, shall we?" She inhaled and adopted a practical tone. "Can you return to your parents' house?"

That was not what Jane had expected her to say. She blinked, searching for an appropriate response since "hell no" was not acceptable. "I don't think they'd allow that."

Lady Satterfield frowned. "What if I spoke with your mother?"

Again, Jane had to bite back her response. "I don't think that would be wise. My sister is marrying soon, and their focus is on that happy occasion, as it should be. Perhaps afterward, I will call on them." She smiled at Lady Satterfield even as emotions swirled inside her. She suddenly wasn't sure she was on the right path at all.

Perhaps Anthony was right—the past didn't matter. As the countess had pointed out, it wasn't as if Jane had met a man and hadn't been able to marry him as a result of the rumor. While it was possible that not meeting a man was due to that rumor, she could never know for sure. And why torture herself with that possibility? Wasn't it better to look to the future, to what happiness she may find?

Furthermore, Jane didn't want to go back to her parents. They hadn't supported her in her time of "failure," and they would push her into a marriage she didn't want. She was far happier in Cavendish Square with her cats.

Especially when you have a handsome and seductive male houseguest.

As if drawn by the thought in her mind, Jane looked toward the main entrance to the drawing room just as Anthony walked in. Her breath snagged in her lungs as she took in his near-perfect appearance. His wavy brown hair was brushed back from his high forehead into an immaculate style. His features had entirely returned to normal with the exception of a faint bruise around his right eye. He wore a stark black suit of clothing with a cobalt-blue waistcoat that made his eyes gleam like jewels. Jane felt an almost visceral pull to go to him, to touch him, to claim him.

And, most of all, to re-blacken his eye.

CHAPTER 9

Q quick scan of the room told Anthony what he most wanted to know: Jane was present, and she looked magnificent. Her lush frame was draped in a gauzy pink dress that made her look like something he wanted to eat. Her blonde curls were swept into a fetching style with jewels that glistened as she moved her head. She wore a simple ribbon around her neck with a bauble that grazed the hollow of her throat. He wanted to put his lips there and then strip every other thing away from her body so she wore that and nothing else.

Hell, he couldn't walk around the bloody drawing room with a raging erection. He turned from her and went to a footman to pick up a glass of whatever was on his tray.

"You came," Marcus said, coming up behind him. "And you went straight for the brandy."

Anthony smiled and tried not to look at Jane. "Of course I did."

"Well, I'm glad you're here. Try not to drink too much, if you don't mind."

"I've gotten better at doing that." He hadn't really, at least not since he'd left Jane's. But while he'd been there, she'd kept him sober. Because she'd insisted. In hindsight, however, he was glad he'd done it. He might not have appreciated their time together if not for his clear head.

The butler came in to announce dinner, and everyone paired up to walk into the dining room. Hell and the devil, Jane was not partnered. Anthony looked around. They seemed to be the only unmarried people here. Bloody, bloody hell. He briefly wondered if Marcus had arranged this. Had Jane told Phoebe what had happened after all?

Not even Anthony would ignore propriety in this instance. He crossed the room to Jane's side and bowed. "May I escort you to dinner, Miss Pemberton?"

She curtsied in response. "Thank you, my lord."

He offered his arm and braced himself for the electric charge that would surely come when she touched him. She placed her hand on his sleeve, and though he'd prepared, he was still shaken by how deeply he felt the connection.

As they walked in the procession to the dining room, he sensed her tension. Or maybe that was his.

"You look well," she whispered. "Did you get my note today? Perhaps you sent a response after I left to come here." Her tone was just slightly accusatory, which he deserved.

"I did get your note." And he hadn't written a response because he was a massive cad. He'd also wondered if he'd see her tonight. "I expected to see you here." It was a bit of a fib, but not entirely.

"Did you? I had no idea if you were even invited."

"So you didn't arrange it?"

Her fingers dug into his sleeve. "You think I told Phoebe about us even after you asked me not to? You're a cad."

He nearly laughed since she used the same word

he'd just thought about himself. "I know. A massive one, really, but then I've never tried to disguise my true nature."

"No, I suppose you haven't, particularly with the manner in which you departed my care."

There was no mistaking the accusation there, or the hurt.

"It was for the best," he said even more quietly than they were already speaking.

They walked into the dining room and, as Anthony's luck would have it, they were seated next to each other near the end of the table. Anthony was between Phoebe on his right, at the end, and Jane on his left. Wonderful.

He shouldn't have come. He almost hadn't, but the lure of seeing her had been too great. Even he could admit to himself that was why he was here. Massive cad didn't begin to describe him. He had no business wanting to see her. Hadn't he already decided that?

Anthony helped her into her chair, then sat down beside her.

"And no, I didn't have anything to do with this seating arrangement either," she said softly. "Or the fact that we are the only unmarried people here. If I'd known, I would have demanded Phoebe invite others. Or maybe I wouldn't have come at all."

The anger in her voice pierced his chest. He leaned slightly toward her. "I'm sorry, Jane. Truly. But I had to leave. You must see that."

She turned her head toward him, and he saw the heat blazing in her tawny eyes, like brandy in front of a fire. "Yes, it would have been just horrible if you'd stayed. It was the absolute worst week ever."

Anthony smiled in spite of himself. "Your sarcasm undoes me, Miss Pemberton."

"Good. I will do my best to eviscerate you with it over dinner."

"Please do," he murmured as the wine was poured and the first course was served.

A few minutes later, after they'd sampled the soup, Jane asked, "Do you like turtle soup? I did at first, but sometimes it's not quite what I expect. I find it…disappointing."

"I know what you mean," Anthony agreed. "But I like this one. Do you?"

She looked him squarely in the eye. "I thought I did, but I can't decide. Ask me later." She reached for her wine and took a sip.

The soup was removed shortly thereafter and replaced with the next course. Anthony sampled the turbot and the trout, as well as tongue and oyster patties. "I just realized most of my plate starts with the letter T."

"Hmm." Jane swallowed a bite of trout. "T is for terrible. And thoughtless. It's also for trust, a word I like very much."

He lowered his voice to a bare whisper and leaned toward her. "It also begins temptation, a word *I* like very much."

She narrowed her eyes at him, her jaw clenching. "Are you flirting with me?"

Hell yes, he was flirting with her. And he shouldn't. "My apologies. It's my natural manner with you, I'm afraid, and here we are, stuck next to each other for a long period of time."

"Unfortunately," she muttered. "T is also for thickheaded."

Oh. *Oh.* Realization smacked him in the face. Yes, it was.

She was doing as he'd invited—treating him to a course of sarcasm. Or several courses, as it were.

"T is for talented and thrilling." He gave her a half smile.

She ignored him as she focused on her plate and also spoke to the man on her other side—Mr. Lennox.

"I'm glad you came tonight, Anthony," Phoebe said from his right.

He turned toward her. "Thank you for inviting me. I owe you an apology for leaving your wedding breakfast."

She arched a dark brow at him. "Did Marcus ask you to say that?"

"Should I lie?"

Phoebe laughed. "It didn't bother me that you left, so long as you're all right and all is well between you and Marcus. It seems to be?"

He nodded before taking a sip of wine. "Quite." A thought occurred to him. Had he and Jane been invited simply because they were Marcus and Phoebe's close friends, or was there more to it? "Ja— Miss Pemberton and I couldn't help but notice she and I are the only non-married guests. Are you and Marcus trying to play matchmaker?"

Phoebe leaned toward him, her eyes sparkling and her lips curving into an anticipatory smile. "Should we?"

Hell, he'd set his own bloody trap. "Not at all." He went back to his plate.

Soon the course was replaced with the next. This one included turkey, asparagus, mutton, and several other meats and vegetables.

Anthony looked over at Jane, but she spoke first. "Are you going to comment on my turkey?" She emphasized the T.

He chuckled. "No. Would you like to find a way to compare me to the mutton?"

"What can I say except that you are old enough

to behave better than you have." Because mutton was an older sheep.

He touched his breast. "A direct hit."

She looked at her plate, but not before he caught the faintest hint of a smile.

"Will you be participating in the hide-and-seek after dinner?" Mr. Lennox asked Jane.

"I think so," Jane said. "The maze is wonderful. Have you seen it?"

"I have not," Mr. Lennox said. "I am looking forward to it."

Anthony imagined finding Jane in a darkened nook of the maze. Then he imagined taking her in his arms and kissing her. Maybe tossing up her skirts and sinking his fingers into her sweet heat, driving her to the brink of release and then swallowing her cries with his mouth. He finished his wine and willed his erection to diminish.

The footman refilled his glass, and he saw Jane take note. He also saw the slight crease of her forehead and downturn of her mouth. He swept the glass up and took a long drink.

He spent the rest of dinner eating and drinking and trying very hard not to even look at Jane. When he'd said she was a temptation, that had been a gross understatement. He wanted her more than anything. More than the bloody wine he was drinking too much of.

Too much? Did he really think so? Yes, probably.

And then he stopped drinking, and that really pricked his temper.

At the conclusion of dessert, he stood with the rest of the gentlemen as the women left the room. Jane looked up at him before departing. He swallowed, hating that he'd disappointed her but knowing no matter what he did, he would always do so. Better to do it on purpose now.

The footman brought port, and several of the men smoked. Anthony sipped his wine, but mostly left it untouched.

Marcus moved to Phoebe's vacant chair after a while. He scooted the chair close to Anthony and spoke in a low tone. "Am I mistaken, or is there something going on between you and Jane Pemberton?"

"Why would you think that?" Anthony decided he should have one more drink of port.

"You kept speaking to each other in what looked like a somewhat intense exchange. Am I wrong?"

"We disagreed about the turtle soup."

Marcus narrowed his eyes at Anthony, but said nothing.

"Shall we join the ladies?" Clare asked, standing.

Anthony looked toward the duke, who he knew was an old friend of Marcus's. They'd been brothers in debauchery at one point. "Yes." Anthony joined him in standing.

"Looking forward to seeing Miss Pemberton?" Marcus murmured.

"I'm going to the billiard room." Anthony departed the dining room and did exactly as he'd said, making his way to the other side of the house to the billiard room.

Only a few lamps burned in the room, and the table was not illuminated. Still, Anthony set the three balls on the table and practiced making shots. It was some time before he realized he hadn't poured a drink. He scanned the room for a sideboard. Surely there were spirits in here, of all places. There it was, over near the window.

A flash of pink drew his eye to the doorway. Jane came into the room, and the space seemed to contract.

What the hell was she doing here? Now he really

needed a drink. He stalked to the sideboard and poured a brandy. When he turned, she stood only a few feet away, her gaze focused on the drink in his hand.

"What poison do you choose?" he drawled, citing a question often used by an American he drank with on occasion.

"Poison?" She sauntered closer. "If you think it's injurious, why drink it?"

He snorted in answer, then sipped his brandy before walking back to the billiard table. He set his glass down on the edge and picked up the mace. "Shouldn't you be out in the maze?"

She moved to stand at the end of the table. "Why aren't you there?"

"I'd rather play billiards."

"Me too," she said, going to take a mace from the case hanging on the wall.

"Have you any idea how to play?" he asked.

"Not really."

He leaned over and hit the white ball into a red one. When he stood, he fixed her with a dark stare. "Why come to play billiards by yourself if you don't know how?"

"Fine. I learned you were here." She came around the table and stopped a foot from him, leaning her hip against the table. "You owe me an explanation."

"About what?" He moved around her, careful not to inhale her too-familiar and too-intoxicating scent. Bending, he made another shot, sending a red ball into a pocket on the other side of the table.

She touched his arm. "Don't be like this. I thought we were…friends. Did I drive you away?"

He heard the pain in her question, and his irritation completely evaporated. Setting the mace on the table, he turned to her. "No. Don't ever think that."

"How could I not? I asked you to take my virginity and then we... Well, we got closer, and then you left."

"I told you before, Jane, I can't be that man. I won't be."

She edged closer to him. "What man?"

He clenched his jaw. "The man who ruins you."

"How can you ruin me when I ask for you to take me, to show me? Please don't tell me you regret what we did."

"I should."

"Please don't. I don't think I could bear it."

He couldn't bear the near break in her voice. Moving past her, he picked up his glass and took another drink, keeping his back to her.

"And there you go, straight to the spirits."

He spun around. "Yes. That's where I go. Where I am welcome."

"You were welcome with me. Why do you do this to yourself? You deny closeness—what we shared was lovely, wasn't it? And you drown yourself in wine or brandy or whatever you can find." She crossed her arms and glared at him with a mix of anger and concern. "Why?"

"Because I prefer to be numb." He hadn't meant to answer. To reveal.

She dropped her arms to her side and came to him, her hips swaying. Taking the glass from his fingertips, she set it back on the edge of the table. Then she cupped his face, her touch gentle against his jaw. "Why do you want to be numb?"

He didn't want to answer this question either, but it was like she was pulling something out of him. He tried to hold on, but she was stronger than he was. "I don't like to...feel."

"Tell me why. Let me feel for you."

He stared at her, knowing she wasn't going to let him go. And he didn't want to. "I can't."

"Yes, you can. I know you have guilt. I can see it in you. It's about your parents. Tell me."

His parents. He let out a sound that was part sob and part gasp. "They died because of me."

"They were killed by a highwayman. How could they have?"

"I was supposed to go to Oaklands." His voice was small and hollow. "But I didn't want to. I should have been the one to die, not them." He was surprised at the lack of emotion in his words, because the anguish nearly ripped him in two.

Her hands clasped him more tightly, her thumbs pressing into his face. "The dastardly act of a highwayman isn't your fault. How could you have known that would happen?"

"Because it was *supposed* to be me. The Vicar sent the highwayman to kill me, not them."

Her eyes clouded, and her hands slipped from his face. "The Vicar?"

He stepped away from her, swearing violently. "The man I borrowed money from to pay my gambling debts after my father refused to give me any more funds." He turned away from her and put his hands on the edge of the billiard table, hanging his head in torment. "I lost everything and couldn't pay him back. He said I had to find a way, and if I couldn't, that he would take it anyhow. I didn't realize what that meant."

Clutching the edge of the table until his hands hurt, he finally pushed away and turned back to face her. "Don't you understand, Jane? *I'm* the poison. I ruin everything and everyone. How can I defile you with my body, my very presence?"

"Anthony." Her voice cracked as she came toward him, her arms outstretched.

He backed away. "You have to go. Please."

She shook her head, lowering her arms to her

sides but continuing toward him until he was against the wall and had nowhere else to go. "I won't leave you." She touched his face again, her fingertips soft and cool against the heat of his flesh. She dragged her fingers down his jaw just before she kissed him.

The contact was fleeting, a tease that sent his body into a frenzy of desire. She didn't back away as she looked up at him, her lips inches from his. "If you want to forget, to lose yourself, do it with me."

"You know what you're asking me, Jane?"

"I'm not asking you." She curled one hand around his neck and dropped the other to his waist, then lower, until she cupped his cock over his breeches.

"Jane." He'd never felt so torn, so absolutely broken. Yet here she was, offering to put him back together, at least for a little while.

In the end, he was powerless to resist. Letting out a low groan, he picked her up and kissed her with all the pain and longing pent up inside him. Yes, he wanted to lose himself, but he feared he was already lost.

～

*J*ane curled her arms around Anthony's neck, desperate for the feel of him against her. He moved a hand down to her backside, cupping her as their tongues met in a ravenous kiss. She'd come here seeking answers and reconciliation, but honestly hadn't expected this.

She'd hoped, however. With him, she would always hope.

He pushed away from the wall and walked forward, holding her against him. He tilted his head and lashed his tongue against hers. She felt something against the backs of her thighs, and then he lowered her. She realized it was the billiard table.

She heard him shove the mace and one of the balls away before he laid her down on the baize. His mouth moved from hers, kissing along her jaw to her ear, where he gently bit her earlobe. Jane gasped as she clutched his neck and shoulders.

His lips and tongue traced down her neck, licking and sucking. Jane closed her eyes and surrendered to sensation and need. He cupped her breast, pushing it up as his mouth latched on to the flesh above her bodice. She wished she wasn't wearing any clothes so she could feel him as well as she had the other night.

He pulled his mouth from her, and she felt her gown slide up her legs. "Lift your backside."

She arched up and opened her eyes as he shoved her gown up around her waist. She wanted to ask what he was doing, but words seemed unnecessary or even jarring.

He clasped her knees and pushed her legs farther apart, opening her to a startling degree. She gasped, watching as he stared at her a long moment, his hands slowly sliding up her thighs. With each inch of flesh he touched, desire coiled inside her, creating an insistent throb between her legs, in that very place he'd so completely exposed.

Then his gaze moved up, connecting with hers, holding her captive. He continued his path along her thighs until he dragged his thumbs along either side of her sex, gently parting her. She quivered in response, desperate for him to touch her there, to coax the shattering release he'd given her the other night.

"What do you want, Jane?" His voice, husky and raw, intensified her need.

"You. I want you."

He slid his finger along her crease. "Do you want this?"

She couldn't look away from the erotic magnetism in his gaze. "Yes."

He rubbed her clitoris, making her body contract. She flattened her hands against the baize and rose up against his hand. "That's right," he said softly. "You want more?"

She nodded.

"Tell me, Jane."

"I want more. Inside me. Please." Her thighs shook.

He slid one finger into her sheath, and she cried out, closing her eyes. "Jane, look at me," he instructed. She opened her eyes once more as he slowly pumped his finger in and out. "I'm putting my mouth on you now. Try not to scream." He gave her a wicked smile before finally breaking eye contact and lowering his head between her legs.

Then his tongue was on her clitoris, licking her gently. She opened her mouth, but no sound escaped. She rose up on her elbows, desperate to see what she was feeling, but all she saw was the top of his head moving as his lips and tongue wreaked havoc on her sex.

Not havoc, but an intense pleasure. His finger continued to move inside her as he suckled her. Her muscles contracted as her passion mounted. She began to move beneath him, seeking more of everything. He replaced his finger with his tongue, his hands splayed on her inner thighs as he stroked inside her.

She cried out, arching up into his mouth, her release building inside her. He put her legs over his shoulders and cupped her backside, holding her captive to his mouth. She couldn't have imagined the ferocity of her first orgasm with him, but this was already more devastating. Her body trembled as her muscles tensed, the pleasure pulsing inside her. She was unable to stop the cascade, not that she wanted to. His fingers dug into her backside as his tongue plunged deep, and she was lost in a torrent of ecstasy.

When his hand pressed over her mouth, she realized she *had* screamed. She let out a sob against his hand as her legs quivered around him. He didn't stop with his mouth, and as her orgasm subsided, she could sense another beginning. She wanted more. She needed more.

She needed *him.*

Jane plunged her hands into his hair, tugging him away from her. He straightened, his breath coming hard and fast, his eyes dark and intense. She pushed up from the table and scooted to the edge. Grabbing his lapels, she shoved his coat from his shoulders.

He didn't help her, and she had to drag the garment from his arms. It fell to the floor, and she unbuttoned his waistcoat.

His hands came over hers. "Stop. Please."

"Why?" Her body pulsed with need for him, her mind screamed to have him against her, *inside* her.

"Because we must."

"No, we mustn't. I want you, Anthony, and you want me." She lowered her hand and stroked his rigid cock through his clothes. "Don't turn away from this. From me."

"*Jane.*" His voice was harsh and broken, his gaze tormented.

She unbuttoned his fall and slipped her hand inside his breeches to stroke his cock. "I want you, Anthony. This may be the only chance I ever have. *We* ever have." She wasn't sure she believed that, but the moment was desperate.

He caressed her face softly, his expression turning sad. "Jane. You make it impossible to deny you, even as I know I must."

"But you won't." She sat up on the edge of the table and put the tip of him against her sex. "I don't know what to do. Show me, please."

He positioned her legs around his waist, then placed his hand over hers. He guided his shaft into her, stretching her, filling her. There was discomfort but also an urgency to bring him deeper, to move, to create the delicious friction that would see them both home.

She released him, then moved her hand to his backside, pressing him toward her. He drove forward, and she sucked in a breath at the new sensation.

"Jane, breathe," he whispered against her ear, his hand cupping her nape. "Are you all right?"

She heard the agony in his voice and wanted to reassure him. "I'm fine." The discomfort was already beginning to recede. But the need was not. "Please don't stop."

He clasped her neck and withdrew before sliding into her again. Then he kissed her, his tongue delving into her mouth as his cock did the same to her body, thrusting into her with glorious precision. Joy spread through her as she reveled in this intimacy, in this shared experience. She kissed him back with passionate fervor, tangling her fingers in his hair.

He began to move more quickly, his hips snapping into hers. The second orgasm she'd tasted began to build again. The climb was faster, less steep this time, and when he held her tight against him and ground against her, she exploded, her sex contracting around him as she shuddered through her release.

Then he was suddenly gone. He let out an almost

inhuman sound, hushed though it was, and she felt his seed on her thigh.

The only sound in the room was their panting breaths, the only scent the musk between them. They stayed like that, his forehead against hers as their minds and bodies returned to the present.

Jane drew a deep breath. "Why did you leave?"

"To prevent a child." He swore under his breath and took a step back from her, rapidly buttoning his fall.

Her gown fell over her thighs. "Oh. Thank you."

His gaze met hers, and she was shocked at the fiery anger she saw there. "Why did you do that?"

"Do what?" She slid from the edge of the table, smoothing her skirts down. She felt his seed dampen her chemise and was for once glad for an excess of undergarments.

"I told you I didn't want to take your virginity." He rebuttoned his waistcoat.

She sucked in a breath at the raw revulsion in his voice. He despised her. "I'm sorry. I wanted you. I was sure you wanted me."

"I do. I did. But that doesn't matter. When I do what I want, when I take what I want, bad things happen." He turned from her and swept his coat from the floor. "You need to stay away from me. Dammit, Jane, I tried to keep us apart."

"I know you did, and I don't want that." She moved toward him, her own ire rising. "Look at me, Anthony. You need to stop this...this self-loathing. We both wanted this tonight, and there's nothing bad about it. I don't feel bad. Why should you? In fact, I feel better than I ever have." Except for his anguish. The despair inside him was palpable, and she would do anything to banish it. She took his hand, gripping it between both of hers. "Whatever happened in the past, whatever wrongs you think you committed, they are in the past. A wise person told me we should leave that where it belongs —behind us."

Some of the storm in his eyes dissipated. "A wise person?" He snorted. "I doubt that."

"Well, I'm beginning to think he is. Tonight, I spoke with Lady Satterfield about the rumor that was started about me, and she urged me to focus on fixing what I could now. And she's right. If my reputation is that important to me, I should do something to repair it. I realize it's only important to me insofar as I am able to do the things I want."

"And what's that?"

"Participate in the Spitfire Society and, right now, be with you. Neither of those things requires the approval of anyone but me." She smiled softly. "And you."

"You want us to have an affair?"

"Why not? Phoebe and Ripley did."

His gaze darkened once more. "They ended up married." He took his hand from between hers and stepped closer so that she had to tip her head back to look up at him. "That will not happen, Jane. Ever. Do you understand?"

She nodded, swallowing at the savagery of his vow.

"Tell me you understand. I am not the man you think I am."

Notching her chin up, she challenged him. "And who is that?"

"The kind who will fall in love with you, marry you, and give you a lifetime of happiness. I will disappoint you. I've already done so." He turned away from her.

She put her hands on her hips, growing irritated with his intent to self-destruct. "Do you want to be that man, the one who disappoints me?"

"No!" He swung back around, his eyes wild. He ran his hand through his hair, making it stand up in places.

"Then let me help you not to be. Let me help you bury the past so that you can be a different man, the man you want to be." She watched his chest rise and fall as he struggled for breath. Her heart ached for him.

"I don't know who that is."

She gave him a warm, encouraging smile. "Then let's find out together."

CHAPTER 10

*A*nthony willed his hands to stop shaking. He wanted to believe what she was saying—that he could be someone else. That he could change.

He doubted that was possible, but what if there was a chance she was right? "You're going to give up on the rumor?" he asked.

"I am. You were right—nothing I do will change anything, so it's better to focus on here and now, as well as tomorrow."

If she could bury the past, maybe he could too. His past was far worse since it was entirely his fault, whereas hers was not. She'd been the victim of someone else's bad behavior. Anthony had been the perpetrator, and his victims…

He swallowed. How was he supposed to move forward when he was mired in guilt?

Jane came toward him and took his hand again. "I'm going to help you. You are not alone—you *must* remember that. Promise me?"

No, he wasn't alone. She'd said they would do this together.

Hell, they were *together*. While everyone else was out in the maze.

"Jane, aren't you supposed to be playing hide-and-seek?"

"I suppose." She didn't look the least bit concerned.

"You'll be missed. There aren't that many people here."

"I'll just say I changed my mind."

That would work, but it would be better if she were seen just so there was no suspicion. "I think since we are both missing from the event, our joint absence might be noted."

Her eyes widened briefly. "Oh! You don't think people will assume we were together?"

Anthony wasn't sure, but he thought of Marcus and how he'd noticed their behavior at dinner. "It's possible they will. I think you should go out to the maze." Hopefully, they weren't finished. "You can just pretend you were very well hidden. I'll walk you to the door." He offered her his arm.

She curled her hand around his sleeve and gave him a sultry smile. "Will you meet me in the maze?"

"I don't think that's wise." Still, his body reacted, thrumming with desire.

"Then you can come to my room later. I'm in the north wing, in the corner overlooking the maze."

He chuckled as he escorted her from the billiard room. "You're incorrigible."

"Isn't insatiable a better word?"

He lifted her hand and kissed her palm, looking into her eyes. "Incomparable."

They made their way to the drawing room, which opened to the gardens. Thankfully, there was no one there, including servants. He walked her to the door, and she took her hand from his arm.

"I'll see you later?" she asked.

A bright lamp burned to the left of the door. Anthony pulled her to the right, into the shadows, then dipped his head and kissed her. He kept the connection disappointingly brief. "Let's not risk it, and anyway, you need a recovery period."

She clutched the front of his coat for a moment. "Remember, we're doing this together." Her eyes narrowed. "I won't let you ignore me again."

He laughed. "I wouldn't dream of it." He exhaled. "One more kiss."

She stood on her toes and put her hand on his jaw, her lips sliding over his. Then they broke apart, and she danced away, grinning, as she hurried toward the maze.

Anthony watched her, surprised to find he was filled with something he hadn't felt in a very, very long time: hope.

"What the hell are you doing?"

Marcus's angry voice cut through the night air. Anthony turned to see Marcus striding toward him.

Stopping before Anthony, Marcus glowered at him in the lamplight. "Explain," Marcus ground out.

"It's none of your business."

"You kissed my wife's best friend."

Anthony let out a sharp laugh. "For you, of all people, to be outraged by such a thing is rather hypocritical, don't you think?"

Marcus grimaced. "Maybe. However, Jane Pemberton is not a courtesan or a prostitute."

"And neither was Phoebe when you were shagging her."

Marcus swore. "Is that what's going on?"

"Marcus, this is none of your affair. Jane—Miss Pemberton—is a grown woman. It was just a bloody kiss."

Silence reigned for a moment as Marcus continued to glare at him. Then he exhaled, and his expression relaxed. "Don't hurt her. That would hurt Phoebe, and I can't have that."

"For Christ's sake, this has nothing to do with Phoebe. Stop looking for excuses to play the champion." Anthony rolled his eyes.

Marcus speared him with a threatening stare. "Don't hurt her."

"I won't." Except he very well might. He'd clearly told her what to expect from him—rather, what not to expect. He'd be sure to remind her at every opportunity. "You won't tell Phoebe, will you?" He wanted Jane to be able to make that decision, not Marcus.

"We don't keep secrets."

"I would prefer you allow Jane to confide in her friend—if she wants to. As I said, it was just a kiss."

Marcus grunted in response. "She'd be good for you. I like her."

"I like her too."

"I mean, she'd make a good viscountess."

"*Don't*." Anthony clipped the word out with speed and bite.

"Someday, you're going to have to climb out of the abyss. She could be the one to help you. If you'd let her."

"As it happens, that's precisely what I'm trying to do." She'd given him a glimmer at the end of a very dark tunnel.

Marcus blinked in surprise. He clasped Anthony's shoulder. "I'm glad. Love could change your life —it did mine. Speaking of which, I need to get to the maze and find my wife." He grinned. "And, I suppose, the rest of our guests." He clapped Anthony before removing his hand and taking off into the night.

Love was not what Anthony was after. If he could move on from the past and try to live in the light, that would be enough. That was all he could expect, and far more than he deserved.

∽

*B*rixton Park disappeared from view as the coach rounded a bend. Jane sat back against the squab, sorry the short party was over. No, she was sorry to leave Anthony after not having a chance to speak with him that morning. Nor had he come to see her last night.

But then, he'd said he wouldn't. Still, she'd hoped he might.

Hadn't he said he would disappoint her?

That wasn't what he'd meant. And anyway, it was hard to be too disappointed after the way he'd kissed her when he'd escorted her outside—with warmth and promise. She hadn't expected it, not after the emotional upheaval in the billiard room.

She'd lain awake for quite some time last night, and not just because she'd been waiting for him. She'd relived his pain and anguish and hoped she'd given him some amount of succor. He had to find a way to forgive himself for his mistakes.

Learning he'd accumulated gambling debts that his father had refused to pay had been a surprise. She'd never heard of him being a wastrel, but then that wouldn't have been the first bit of gossip—true or not—that she hadn't heard. She couldn't help but think of the rumor about herself and then feel the subsequent outrage. It was a bit less, however, perhaps because she'd decided to let it go.

Or maybe because she was still reveling in the satisfaction of being with Anthony last night. She had no regrets about what they'd done in the billiard room. Well, maybe one. That it hadn't lasted longer. With each moment she spent with him, each taste he gave her, she wanted more. She rather thought insatiable was the perfect word.

Now that she was going to help him find peace

with his past, there would be more time. More...opportunity. Were they actually going to have an affair? He'd asked if that was what she wanted, but hadn't confirmed that was what they'd be doing. She wanted confirmation. She wanted to know what to expect. And she really didn't want to be disappointed.

The coach began to slow and move to the side of the lane. Suddenly tense, Jane brushed the curtain aside and looked out the window. Highwaymen wouldn't strike in daylight, would they? Except, she was fairly certain that was what had happened to Anthony's parents. Her blood chilled.

A man walked toward the coach, and Jane's breath caught. Anthony pulled open the door and climbed inside. "Mind if I join you?"

She laughed as relief poured through her. "What are you doing?"

He removed his hat and tossed it on the rear-facing seat. "My coach is too slow."

"I doubt that, since you managed to catch up to me."

Shrugging, he sat down beside her. "Then it's too lonely."

Jane sat back and crossed her arms. "I was lonely last night."

The coach started moving.

"Were you?" Anthony murmured, scooting closer so his right side touched her left. "My apologies, but then I did tell you I wouldn't come to your room."

"You did."

He angled himself toward her and put his finger beneath her chin, turning her head. "Jane, I will always be honest with you about expectations. If I say I'm not going to do something, I mean it. If I say I will, I mean that too. Do you understand?"

"Yes. However, you didn't do that when you

abruptly left my house. That was *completely* unexpected."

He grimaced. "It was, and is, why I shall endeavor to do better."

She gave him a single nod. "And I will always ask for what I want. You shall always know where I stand. Do *you* understand?"

He dropped his hand to his lap. "I do." He settled back against the squab beside her. "Now, tell me your plan for putting the past behind us."

She smoothed her hand over her skirt, brushing away an invisible speck. "As I said last night, I'm going to forget about that stupid, horrid rumor. I'm going to embrace the life I've chosen as a spinster. To that end, I'm going to have an affair." She turned her head to look at him.

"With me." He slid her a glance that sparked heat in her core.

"If you agree. I couldn't tell after last night."

"I agree. So long as you remember what I said—I won't marry, and I won't fall in love with you."

How he could be so sure about not falling in love didn't make sense to Jane, but she wasn't going to debate him. She wanted an affair. Anything else could come later. Or not, probably.

She refused to think about that. She wanted to focus on the present while they moved on from the past. The future could be damned for all she cared at the moment.

"So you will have an affair to get over your past, which includes a rumor in which you were maybe trying to have an affair?"

She heard the sardonic edge to his tone and stifled a smile. Swatting his arm lightly, she sent him a mock glower. "Was that what I was trying to do, start an affair with someone?"

"Not quite." He smiled. "Anyway, it doesn't matter. That's the past, remember? We're not paying attention to it anymore."

She turned toward him, glad to hear him say so. "Yes! That's it exactly. What are you going to do to ignore your past?"

"I suppose drinking myself numb is out of the question?"

"It doesn't seem to have worked for you so far," she answered wryly.

He faced her. "What do you suggest, then?"

She was surprised at his openness. "I think you need to forgive yourself for what you did. For the gambling debts and for not going to Oaklands." She watched him tense, his jaw clenching and his shoulders stiffening. "I know it's hard to talk about," she said softly. "Perhaps that's the first step—learning to talk about it without feeling overwhelmed."

"I can't imagine that ever happening."

"I couldn't ever imagine feeling the sensations you aroused in me last night, and yet I did."

His mouth curled into a wicked smile. "I don't think those are comparable things."

"Why not? I'm merely trying to illustrate how we never know what we're capable of, what might happen if we try."

"I can think of other things I'd like to try...to arouse you."

Her body heated in response. "You're trying to distract me, to deflect from the conversation."

"Yes."

She let out a surprised laugh. "You *are* being honest."

"I said I would be."

Shaking her shoulders, she picked up where he'd interrupted. "Let's talk about your parents. What do you miss about them?"

He leaned back against the squab, looking forward. "God, everything. They were annoying as hell sometimes—my mother was desperate for me to wed —but I would give anything to have her harass me one more time. And my father." He fell silent for a moment. When he finally spoke, his voice was deep and soft. "He was disappointed with my gambling, but he never told my mother. And he never stopped believing that I could put it behind me."

Jane put her hand over his. "See? Even he wanted you to bury the past."

"I suppose he did."

She hesitated, wanting to say something, but unsure if she should. Gathering her courage, she said, "Wouldn't you like to go forward in a manner that would make him—them—proud?"

He drew in a ragged breath. "I don't know if that's possible."

She wanted to argue, but thought of her own parents. She didn't think it was possible to make them proud. Not unless she could rewind time and make a successful marriage.

In Anthony's case, it was even worse. His parents weren't here to be proud. She suddenly felt like she was fighting a losing battle.

She refused to give up. "I think it is. You don't gamble anymore. That's something. Wouldn't that have pleased your father?"

"Yes." He sounded a bit uncertain, and she squeezed his hand. "Yes, it would." That sounded more confident.

He looked over at her. "What about your parents?"

She brought her hand to her lap, wondering if he genuinely wanted to know or just wanted to stop talking about *his* parents. "What about them?"

"Is there any hope for repairing your relationship with them?" He sounded quite caring, and she believed he genuinely wanted to know. "I'm aware they haven't visited you since you moved to Cavendish Square."

She snapped her gaze to his. "How do you know that?"

"Culpepper told me."

She snorted. "What else has my butler divulged?"

"That he loves your household."

Warmth expanded Jane's heart. "I love it too." Which was why she wouldn't go back home. She'd never felt as comfortable there, as though she belonged. How strange was it to finally experience that sentiment with a household full of servants she'd only recently come to know?

"You aren't going to tell me about your parents, are you?" he asked. "And after I endured you asking about mine."

Jane exhaled. She couldn't expect him to do all the hard work. "You make a good point. I don't think I could ever do anything to make my parents proud of me. My failure on the Marriage Mart disappointed them, and my moving to Cavendish Square ensured they would never approve of me."

"Does that mean you'll have no relationship with them whatsoever?"

She hadn't considered that. "I don't know. I haven't really tried." Because it hurt to think about their rejection. "I have no reason to believe they've changed their opinions about me. My sister is getting married on Thursday, and I am not invited."

"That's criminal," he whispered. "Family is family. Nothing should keep you apart—they'll regret their behavior," he said rather viciously.

Jane turned toward him and touched his face. She didn't like having her glove between them, so she took it off and tossed it across the coach. Then she did the same with her other glove. Bare-handed, she caressed his cheek and murmured, "Much better. Thank you for your support. After the wedding, perhaps I'll invite them to visit."

"Why not before? Better yet, why not just show up at the wedding?"

Jane hadn't considered that. "And risk making them even angrier at me?"

His gaze held hers. "If they would be angry with you for wanting to see your sister wed, to share in her joy, then they are perhaps a lost cause." He pressed his lips together in frustration.

She rose up slightly off the seat and kissed him, intending to just briefly sweep her mouth over his. But his arms came around her, and he held her close to deepen the kiss.

Sighing, Jane lifted her hand to his nape, tucking her fingers beneath his collar and cradling his warm flesh. She slid her tongue along his. Anthony tilted her back into the corner and cupped her breast. Then he abruptly sat her up. "Good idea with the gloves." He stripped his away and resumed their embrace, pressing her back with a smile. "This is a lovely way to pass the journey." His mouth descended on hers, and she clutched his neck and shoulder as desire pulsed in her core.

He caressed her breast again, dragging his finger across her nipple, which she could barely feel due to her corset. He kissed along her jaw and neck, his teeth nipping her flesh at intervals, making her shudder with need.

"I suppose it's too much to want to be naked," she muttered.

"It is not," he said against her flesh. "But wanting and doing are not the same thing, and I'm afraid disrobing you in these confines would be quite difficult."

"If memory serves, I don't *have* to be naked…"
She let the suggestion hang between them.

He pulled his head up and gave her a wicked
grin. "Are you trying to seduce me again, Miss
Pemberton?"

"Is it working?"

"Always. We are, after all, having an affair." He
tossed her skirts up and pushed her leg to part her
thighs, then skimmed his hand along her flesh until
he met her sex.

Jane dug her fingers into his shoulder. He teased
her for a bit, kissing her and stroking her folds until
she was begging him to end her misery.

"Is it really miserable?" he asked, smiling.

"No. But it will be if we don't finish before we
arrive in Cavendish Square."

"Actually, we don't have even that long. My
coachman instructed yours to stop outside town so
I'm not seen getting out of your coach."

"Then we'd better hurry." She pulled his head
down and kissed him thoroughly. He thrust his
finger into her, and she bucked up as sensation exploded within her. She tore her lips from his. "I want
you, Anthony."

"I'm right here, my sweet." He stroked her clitoris to make his point.

"No, *all* of you."

"I see." He clasped her waist. "Straddle me." He
held her gown up around her waist while she complied, inelegantly throwing her leg over him as if she
were mounting a horse.

"I've never ridden astride," she said, then gasped
at the feel of him between her legs, his erection
straining against his breeches.

He chuckled. "Aren't you a saucy minx?" He
reached between them and unbuttoned his fall. His

movements brushed against her, sparking pleasure and need.

"Hurry."

"I'll add impatient," he said. "Now, we must be careful so you don't hit your head." He glanced up at the roof of the coach, which was just a few inches above her bonnet.

She untied the ribbon beneath her chin and threw the hat aside. "That's better. My goodness, but clothing, especially accessories, is overrated."

"I couldn't agree more." He pulled his cock from his breeches and slid it across her opening.

Jane dropped her hands to his shoulders and ground down against him, seeking his entry. He guided his flesh into hers, then gripped her hips. He rolled his pelvis against hers, showing her a slow, steady, rapturous rhythm.

He filled her, then rocked back, then filled her again, creating a delicious friction that shot through her with devastating effect. She closed her eyes, giving in to the sensation.

"Jane, I'm not going to last long." He sounded strained, as if he were in pain.

She opened her eyes and moved her hands to cup his neck, her thumbs meeting at the base of his throat. "Me neither."

"Then don't." He slid one hand under her skirt and stroked her clitoris. The slow build of pleasure crashed over her with sudden violence. Jane jerked her hips, moving faster over him.

He came up, driving into her, intensifying her orgasm as he hit that spot inside her that made her see darkness followed by dizzying bright lights. "Jane, I have to—" He wrenched her off him just as she felt the rush of his seed against her.

She swung her leg back and sat on the seat beside him, then used the edge of her petticoat to clean him off. He gave her a lopsided smile. "Thank you."

"Pity you have to finish that way. It seems like it would feel better if you remained inside me." She lowered her skirts and arranged them around her legs.

"Did that ruin the end of your orgasm?" he asked with concern as he tucked himself back into his breeches and buttoned his fall.

"No, but did it ruin yours?"

He shrugged. "It's been a long time since I came inside a woman. When I do now, I always wear a French letter."

She stared at him, aghast. "*Now?*"

"Not, *now* now. I meant before…us."

Us. She liked the sound of that. "I don't know that I want to hear about your French-letter exploits. However, I'd be interested in trying that if it meant you could finish inside me."

He smiled at her and kissed her cheek. "Very thoughtful of you."

"So they prevent a child as well as disease?" she asked.

"They seem to, but maybe I've been lucky."

She thought about the countless women he'd probably used French letters with and decided she didn't like this conversation. Before she could change the subject, he leaned over and kissed her soundly.

"One of these days, I'm going to shag you properly. In a bed." He sat back, winking at her.

"I see you can wink again."

"I can."

"In fact, your face is almost back to its normal handsome state."

"You find me handsome?" He waggled his brows, and she rolled her eyes.

"Stop fishing for compliments. You know I find

you utterly irresistible. Or at least you should. I would think I'd made it obvious. How are your ribs?"

"Much better, thank you." He winced slightly. "Though I wonder if that exercise was perhaps not the best for my recovery. Ah well, I have no regrets." He glanced out the window. "We're nearly to town."

He picked up her bonnet and handed it to her, then set her gloves on the seat next to her. Then he retrieved his gloves and drew them on.

"When will I see you next?" she asked, already eagerly anticipating it.

"Even though you are unconcerned with your reputation, we should be as discreet as possible."

She arched a brow at him. "Why, are you concerned with yours?"

He laughed. "Not particularly, but I will admit the gossips would go mad if they knew we were having an affair." He sobered, taking her hand. "Mostly, I don't want anyone who knew about that old, disgusting rumor to think they were right about you."

Gratitude and something far deeper bloomed in her chest. "Thank you."

The coach slowed, signaling their time was at an end.

"I'm glad you stopped the coach," she said. "I hope I'll see you soon."

He kissed her wrist. "You will."

The coach stopped, he grabbed his hat and gloves, then he was gone.

Jane sat back against the squab and smiled as she relived the time they'd just spent together. Until she thought about the conversation regarding their parents. She said she'd think about inviting hers over, but she was actually warming to his suggestion that she show up at Anne's wedding.

Did she dare?

Anthony's words rose in her mind: *family is family; nothing should keep you apart.* He was right, and she didn't want to live with regret. That was the entire reason she'd chosen this path—to live the life she chose without apology.

And that was what she meant to do.

CHAPTER 11

The late May night was warm and the air softly scented with the trees and flowers of spring as Anthony made his way toward Cavendish Square. He ducked into the mews on his way to Jane's garden. Though he'd just seen her yesterday morning on their return to London, he looked forward to seeing her again.

Even if she did want him to forgive himself and try to let the past go.

It wasn't that he didn't want to. All right, maybe he wasn't ready to forgive himself and feared he might never be. But he saw the benefit in no longer being shackled to the past. Still, could he move forward and stop looking back?

He'd awakened this morning thinking he could, and then he'd received another letter from Sarah detailing the joy and delight of her daughter. When he thought of his sister and his niece and the fact that he'd deprived Marianne of her grandparents, he was once again overwhelmed with grief and regret. He had, however, kept himself from diving into a bottle of gin or brandy.

That was a small victory, and one he wasn't quite

sure he ought to maintain. Numbness could not be overrated.

The clarity in his brain, however, had only led to more thinking. He'd spent the day contemplating whether he should tell his sister the truth behind their parents' death. Just the thought of doing so made him want to toss up his accounts. And it wasn't because she would think less of him. He had to think she already did. He didn't want her to have to share the burden that their deaths weren't random, that they could have been avoided.

But maybe it wasn't fair of him to keep the truth from her. He wanted to know what Jane thought. So here he was stealing into her garden.

He knew her household's schedule, so he'd timed his arrival for after dinner, when she'd be in the garden room. He made his way through the garden to the doors. He tried the latch, but it was locked, so he knocked softly on the glass.

A flash of green silk caught his eye as she came to open the door. Her lips curved into a smile that sent flutters through his midsection. "Anthony." She opened the door wide and gestured for him to come inside.

As soon as he stepped into the garden room, two balls of fur rushed toward him. "Daffodil, Fern." He removed his gloves and tossed them on the table, then squatted down to pet the kittens simultaneously. Daffodil attacked his hand, while Fern flopped onto her back, inviting him to stroke her belly.

"They've missed you," Jane said.

Surprisingly, he'd missed them too. "Of course they have." He stood and looked at her. "Have you?"

"I just saw you yesterday."

He took off his hat and placed it on the table by the doors. "My question still stands."

She tried not to smile. "Yes."

He took her hand and kissed her wrist, his lips lingering against the softness of her skin. "Good." He inhaled her delicious scent—apples and almond—and felt like he was…home. The thought shook him, so he pushed it away.

"Is that why you came?" she asked. "Because you missed me?"

Anthony went to sit on the settee. He draped his arm along the back and crossed his legs. "Did I say I missed you?" He tipped his head to the side in exaggerated contemplation. "I don't recall saying that."

She sat at the opposite end of the settee and rolled her eyes. "Why did you come, then?"

"To ask you something." Now that he was here, he didn't want to talk about her plan for him to let go of the past or ask her about his sister. He wanted to carry her upstairs and shag her senseless.

Her eyes narrowed slightly. "What's that?"

He took a deep breath and forced himself to speak. "I've been thinking about my parents' deaths."

She gave him an encouraging smile. "I think that's good. Even though our goal is to leave the past where it belongs, grieving will help you do that."

Grieving? He wasn't sure that was what he was doing. That would invite more emotion than he wanted to deal with. "I didn't drink while I was doing it—thinking, I mean. That's good too, right?"

She moved closer to him so their thighs almost touched. "That's brilliant. I'm so proud of you." She caressed his cheek and jaw, her touch soft and arousing.

Anthony tried to focus on what he'd come to say. "You're distracting me, Jane."

"Sorry." She dropped her hand.

"I received a letter from my sister today. About Marianne."

"I received a letter from Sarah yesterday. She

sounds so happy."

"Yes, and I want her to remain that way. However, I wonder if I need to tell her what happened to our parents, that it wasn't some random act by a highwayman."

Jane's lashes fluttered, and she glanced toward the hearth for a moment. When she looked back at him, her gaze had darkened to a deep amber. "I think you should not."

"Doesn't she deserve to know the truth?"

"Does she deserve the heartache that will come along with knowing that?" She lowered her voice to a soft, supportive tone. "Because I do think it will cause her heartache, don't you?"

He nodded. Taking his hand from the back of the settee, he ran it through his hair and braced the side of his head, as if he couldn't support the weight of his thoughts without assistance. It wasn't just that she'd likely despise him forever—and he wouldn't blame her for that—it was that he would cause her additional pain. She *didn't* deserve that, especially as she delighted in her newborn daughter. Anthony could well imagine Felix, her husband and his closest friend, hating him and maybe even wanting to beat the hell out of him.

Which Anthony more than deserved.

"Would it absolve your guilt?" she asked softly.

His gaze connected with hers, and he saw how much she cared. It made his lungs contract. He fought to take a breath. "Nothing could do that."

She took his other hand, the one on his leg, and twined their fingers together. "You'll heal. In time."

He couldn't see how. His heart, his very soul, felt permanently broken. The only light he'd seen in the last eleven months had been with her. And even that didn't last. There were still plenty of moments when the darkness claimed him.

Fern jumped onto the settee and crawled onto his lap, where she promptly curled around herself and went to sleep. Maybe Jane wasn't the only source of light. And if there was more than one…

Jane smiled briefly at the kitten before looking back at him. "As you said, you didn't drink today. You wanted to?"

"Yes. It's far better than the alternative."

She stroked her thumb along the back of his hand. "Which is?"

"Remembering. Thinking. Feeling."

"Maybe you need more memories—better ones —to block out the others." Her gaze began to smolder.

"Do I?"

She lifted a shoulder. "It seems a reasonable theory. Take yesterday's coach ride. That's a lovely memory."

His cock surged as his blood heated. "It is indeed." He glanced toward the open door leading to the hall. "Maybe you should close that. I'd get up, but…" He looked down at the sleeping Fern.

Jane chuckled as she let go of his hand and stood. After closing the door, she returned. "What can we possibly do with a kitten nestled on your lap?"

"That's a very good point, particularly when I'd rather it was you there." He snagged her hand and pulled her down beside him. The movement startled Fern, who jumped down. Anthony guided Jane to straddle him as she'd done in the coach the day before. "I didn't come here to shag you."

She traced her fingers along his hairline and down the side of his face to his jaw. "Well, that's disappointing. Are you going to leave?"

"I should. Probably."

"Seems a pity to end your visit so soon." She leaned forward and whispered in his ear, "We won't be disturbed." Then she bit his earlobe, and he groaned with need.

"Hoyden," he murmured before clasping the back of her head and dragging her mouth to his, where he ravaged her with his tongue.

She ground her hips down over him, and he knew he wasn't leaving.

He came up off the settee and flipped her to her back, settling himself between her legs. "Hmm, this is a rather small space for what I have planned."

She inclined her head toward the far wall, opposite the garden. "There's a chaise over here. Would that be better?"

He looked over the edge of the settee and grinned, envisioning her legs spread with her gown tossed up to her waist. "Perfect."

Standing from the settee, he swept her into his arms. She gasped softly, then wound her arms around his neck as he bore her across the room. He laid her gently on the chaise.

"This gown has a drop front," she said helpfully.

"How convenient. It's almost as if you knew I was coming."

Her eyes sparked with desire as she stared up at him. "Hope springs eternal."

That she wanted him as much as he wanted her was devastatingly arousing and astonishingly humbling. Grateful, he kissed her and gave himself over to the light, if only for a short while.

❧

"*M*iss Anne Pemberton," Culpepper announced as Jane's sister came into the garden room on Monday afternoon.

Anne was a couple of inches shorter than Jane, with dimpled cheeks and green-brown eyes that crinkled at the edges at the slightest provocation. Her hair was the same curly blonde, but she could never quite keep all of it in place without a hundred pins and other styling aids. She often wore a bandeau, as it kept the locks from falling in her face.

She was trailed by a woman in her middle fifties whom Jane recognized as their mother's friend Grace Hammond. No doubt she was serving as chaperone since their mother wasn't there. Jane had wondered if she would come when she'd invited Anne.

"Anne," Jane greeted her sister warmly before looking past her to the chaperone. "Mrs. Hammond, how lovely to see you. I hope you won't mind if I ask you to wait in the front sitting room so Anne and I might speak privately?"

Mrs. Hammond briefly pursed her lips, then smiled kindly, her blue eyes fixing on Jane. "Of course not. You look well, Miss Pemberton."

"I am, thank you." Jane was grateful for the woman's understanding.

Once she'd gone, she turned to Anne, who'd gone to look at the Gainsborough landscape, which Phoebe still hadn't taken to Hanover Square.

"Is this a Gainsborough?" Anne asked.

"Yes, it belongs to Phoebe, of course. As does everything here." Jane had not forgotten that if not for her friend's generosity, she would have nothing, not even a roof over her head. When she thought about it too much, however, she felt uncomfortable. And if she dwelled too long, she began to think she shouldn't have left her parents' house, for there was no expectation that Jane would ever live independently of Phoebe's kindness. To that end, she'd begun to think of what she could do to earn money. Anthony's sister, Sarah, owned a millinery shop. It had been a bit of a scandal at first, but she didn't actually work there much, especially since she'd left town to have her baby. Now hats designed by Sarah were all the rage.

"It's lovely," Anne said, turning from the painting. "You appear quite comfortable here."

"I am. And how are you?" She gestured to the settee and went to sit in Phoebe's favorite chair near the hearth.

Anne perched on the settee and clasped her gloved hands in her lap. She was the picture of elegance and respectability.

"Busy preparing to wed."

Jane noted she didn't say anything about how she *felt*. "I can only imagine." Because Jane had never been in Anne's position and likely never would be. "I was, ah, hoping I might be able to attend."

Anne looked down and plucked at her skirt. "Mama and Papa say no." She raised her apologetic gaze to Jane's. "I do ask them."

It sounded as if she hadn't accepted their refusal. Jane felt a surge of love for her sister. "I expected as much. I suppose that's why I didn't include them when I invited you to come."

"Should I have brought them? I assumed you didn't want me to. In truth, I assumed you were as angry with them as they are with you."

"Angry? No." Jane shook her head sadly. She hadn't realized until that moment that she'd hoped they were no longer angry with her. "I'm...hurt. I recently learned that there was a rumor started about me during my first Season—that I was unchaste."

Anne's eyes shot wide, and her jaw dropped. "Is that why you left?"

"Actually, no. I learned about it after I moved here. It certainly explained a great many things, or perhaps just one very big thing that has had repercussions ever since."

"What's that?"

"Why I was a failure my first Season. I had as much interest as you've had this year."

"I remember that. I also remember Mama and Papa's disappointment when you failed to wed. They've contrasted our two debut Seasons *many* times. I'm glad I've been able to please them."

Jane winced inwardly. Anne had done what Jane could not. "You are the antithesis of me, it seems." A wry smile pulled at Jane's lips.

"Why do you do that?" Anne asked, her blonde brows pitching down. "You smile and brush away the bad. Why *aren't* you angry?"

"I was, especially about the rumor. It ruined my life. Or so I thought." Considering how happy she was with Anthony right now, that didn't seem an accurate characterization. "Mostly, I am upset that Mama and Papa blamed me for something that was never my fault—rumor or not."

"Upset isn't the same as angry."

Jane laughed softly. "No, it isn't. But I've recently decided that life is perhaps too short to nurture such feelings anyway. In addition to asking you about attending the wedding, I also invited you here to see if there's any hope that I might repair the relationship between myself and Mama and Papa. Or do you think it's a lost cause?" She hoped it wasn't. When she thought of Anthony's grief over losing his parents, she couldn't bring herself to give up.

Anne blew out a breath. "I don't know. Papa didn't want me to come today. Neither did Mama at first, but I told her I'd come whether they wanted me to or not, so Mama arranged for Mrs. Hammond to accompany me."

"Because she didn't want to come herself."

"No." Anne grimaced faintly. "I'm sorry, Jane."

"It's not for you to be sorry about. Maybe they'll come around." Perhaps she'd start writing to them, wear them down. To what end, though? It wasn't as if things would go back to the way they were. They had to learn to accept her for who and what—a spinster—she was.

"Enough of that," Jane said, brightening. "Tell me about the wedding and your betrothed. Are you happy?"

Anne nodded. "Gil is attentive and charming. And quite wealthy. Mama is positively giddy about that. She's always saying it's better than a title, really."

Jane wasn't sure she believed that, not after all the years Mama had spent drilling into Jane how wonderful it would be if she could at least wed a baronet. Which wasn't even in the peerage. "I'm glad you're happy. That's really all that matters."

"Happy…yes. He kisses well enough."

"Anne!" Jane laughed. "How would you know that?"

Anne blinked at her. "Because I've kissed him."

"Clearly. But how can you judge his skill unless you've kissed someone else?"

Giving Jane an innocent look, Anne lifted her shoulder as she turned her head to look out at the garden. "Isn't it obvious?"

Jane recalled that Anne had said she was in love with someone earlier in the Season. "You kissed that other man?"

Anne nodded.

"What happened with him?" Jane asked. "You said you loved him."

"There was no way we could be together." Anne straightened and turned her head back toward Jane. "Anyway, Gil—and his kisses—will be fine."

Suddenly, Jane felt incredibly naïve. She was three years older than Anne, and yet Anne had kissed someone first. "I didn't kiss anyone until just this year."

Anne stared at her in surprise. "Truly?"

Jane nodded. "A few gentlemen tried, but I never let them. That's what makes the rumor about me so laughable."

"I see. Well, I didn't want to marry someone without at least kissing them first," Anne said. "Not after…" She shook her head. "Never mind."

Not after what? That other man, surely. What had gone on between them? Good heavens, Anne was far more educated about these things than Jane had been at her age! "It sounds as if you've more experience in kissing and whatever else than I could have imagined." Jane thought of her own experience with Anthony, which brought a flush to her skin.

"Am I embarrassing you?" Anne asked.

"Not at all," Jane said, waving her hand.

"Does it bother you that I'm marrying before you? That you might not marry at all?" Anne looked away, and Jane could tell she regretted asking.

"It does not," Jane assured her. "I want you to be happy, and I'm sorry your debut was delayed because I didn't wed."

"Don't apologize. I didn't want to come out until you were married. You know that. But Mama and Papa insisted this had to be the Season." There was a bit of resignation in her voice. She shrugged again. "So here I am."

Something about the way she said that made Jane pause. There was almost a…hollow quality to her tone. And she glanced away again, as if she were uncomfortable.

"You're truly happy?" Jane pressed, worried that wasn't the case. She would hate to think Anne had been forced into both a Season and a marriage.

"This is easier than the path you've chosen, I'm afraid."

Jane's insides turned to ice. Had she driven her

sister toward something she didn't really want but felt she had to accept? "Promise me you won't do anything you'll regret. Your marriage will be long and unbreakable."

"I know that, and anyway, Mama consulted Madame Sybila. The cards indicated this is an excellent match."

"Madam Sybila?" She was a fortune-teller who'd recently gained notoriety for reading cards and palms. Jane was surprised their mother had gone to see her.

"Indeed. It's a bit strange for Mama to do such a thing, isn't it?" Anne's eyes sparkled with mirth. "I was disappointed she didn't take me along." She stood. "I suppose I should be going."

Jane rose and stepped toward her sister. "Maybe I'll steal into the back of the church on Thursday in disguise."

Anne grinned. "I will look for an old woman with a hunched back."

"Yes!" Jane actually considered it and would thank Anthony for the suggestion.

Anne's smile faded. "You mustn't. I wouldn't want Mama or Papa to see you there. The wedding is very important to them."

To *them*. Anne hadn't said it was important to her.

"I understand." Jane went to hug her sister. The embrace was warm but brief. They said goodbye, and after Anne and Mrs. Hammond left, Jane went into the front sitting room to watch the coach pull into the square.

She couldn't shake the feeling that Anne was hiding something, that she was perhaps not happy at all. Jane's failure had put an incredible burden on her sister—to succeed where Jane had not. What if she'd doomed her sister to a marriage she didn't want?

CHAPTER 12

*A*nthony went into his study, where Monday's correspondence sat on his desk. He picked through it, looking for something of interest, when his skin turned to ice. The handwriting on the last one was familiar—thick and stark.

Tearing it open, his heart began to pound.

Colton,

I require a second payment for my silence regarding your gambling debts and the resulting murder of your parents. Same place, Wednesday, the twenty-sixth of May before dinnertime. Three hundred pounds.

"Bloody fucking hell!" Anthony squeezed the parchment in his fist and dropped it to the desk.

That would make a total of five hundred pounds. He had the money—his father had left him a tidy fortune—but he wouldn't keep paying this blackguard.

Anthony stalked to the sideboard. He reached for the brandy, desperate for some calm in his raging mind. He spun on his heel and walked back to the other side of the room.

Who the bloody hell was it? The barkeep had said he only knew that someone would pick up Anthony's package and deliver it somewhere else. And that if Anthony stayed to see who it was, the delivery wouldn't happen.

His hands began to shake, and he went back to the sideboard. This time, he picked up the brandy and poured it into a glass. After setting the decanter back down, he swooped up the drink. Just before he raised it to his mouth, Purcell stepped inside the door, which Anthony had left partially open.

"I beg your pardon, my lord, but Miss Pemberton is here to see you."

Jane? He didn't want to see her right now. Not like this.

"Tell her I'm occupied."

"I can hear that you aren't." She slipped into the study behind Purcell, moving to the butler's side and standing in front of the hearth. Her gaze riveted on the glass in Anthony's hand and then on his face, which surely looked as upset as he felt.

Purcell's eyes narrowed slightly as he looked down at Jane. "Miss Pemberton, I'm afraid I must ask—"

"It's fine, Purcell," Anthony ground out. He nodded toward the butler, whose brows rose briefly before he bowed and left.

"I'm sorry I followed your butler into your study, but I needed to see you. I didn't imagine you'd turn me away." She frowned at him.

"What do you want, Jane?" He raised the glass to his lips.

She stepped farther into the room, moving toward him. "Why are you drinking?"

He lowered his arm partially. "It's late afternoon. Why does it matter? As you know, I often drink."

Irritation blistered through him. He didn't want her here. He wanted to be alone with his anger.

"Yes, but from the look of you, there is some reason." She stopped just in front of him. "Tell me."

"It's nothing." He tried to school his features into a careless expression, but he feared it was impossible. He was too enraged.

She took the glass from him and pivoted, going back to the other side of his desk. "It's clearly not nothing." She sipped the brandy.

"Now you're going to drink it?"

"I'll give it back to you when you tell me why you're upset. Don't lie to me, Anthony. I know you well enough to recognize when you're angry. Or hurt." She lowered her voice, her gaze caressing him. "Which is it?"

He didn't want to tell her about the extortion. What he'd done was bad enough, but now this was bringing everything back up, making it the present instead of the past. And how the hell was he supposed to bury that?

She looked toward his desk, her gaze landing on the rumpled parchment. "What's that?"

Dammit. He strode to the desk and, from the flash in her eyes, realized he'd cursed aloud. He picked up the letter and folded it. "Nothing."

She set the glass down. "I'll leave you to your brandy, then. I'm sorry to have bothered you."

Turning, she took a step toward the door. Anthony reached for her, his hand closing around her forearm. "Don't go. Why did you come? Why do you need to see me?"

She pivoted, her expression a mix of hurt and disappointment. It nearly broke him. He couldn't do that to her, not when he did it to everyone else.

He let go of her arm. "It's an extortion note." He handed it to her so she could read it.

She opened the paper, looking at him in question. He gave her the barest nod, then watched as she scanned the paper, her eyes widening and her lips parting. The precise moment she reached the end was clear: she swore.

"Bloody hell, Anthony. What is this?" She waved the paper. "Never mind, I know what it is. *Who* is this?"

"I don't know." Or maybe he did. He needed to think.

"You already paid them?"

"The day I came back from your house. Two hundred pounds." The words flowed from him. It felt good to release them. "This is the second demand."

"Oh, Anthony." She went to him and put her hands on his chest.

"I was out of time. The letter had been here for who knows how long—while I was at your house. I had to make the payment that very day, or he would reveal my terrible secrets." All of them.

"How would he do that? Or she—since you don't know who's behind this."

He couldn't imagine it being a woman. And the only man he could think of was the Vicar.

How would he reveal Anthony's secrets? Admittedly, Anthony hadn't thought through the specifics. He'd been too worried about not getting to the Stinking Sheep in time. "I don't know. But the first letter said everyone in London would know of it. Maybe he was going to publish it in one of the papers." Anthony felt sick.

She pressed her hands into him, then clutched his lapel in her hands, drawing his attention to her instead of the nausea swirling in his belly. "You can't keep paying this person. Can you go to Bow Street?"

He hadn't thought of that. And he should have.

One of Marcus's good friends was a Runner. He could likely help Anthony.

"You wouldn't have to tell them any of your secrets," Jane said soothingly.

No, he wouldn't. "But the moment I involve Bow Street, the extortionist may expose me."

"How would they know?"

If it was the Vicar, he'd know. And right now, Anthony had to believe it was.

"You *do* know who this is," she said softly, flattening her hands against his chest. "You're hiding their identity."

He put his hands over hers and looked into her eyes. "No. I don't know who it is for certain, but the only person I can think it would be is the man I borrowed from to pay my debts."

"The Vicar?" She remembered his name.

Anthony nodded, anguish sweeping through him when he thought of how much damage this man had caused. And, because of the first note, Anthony had given him more money than was owed and was contemplating paying him even more.

"You must go to Bow Street," she said with certainty. "You can't allow this criminal—this murderer —to extort you. Why didn't you go to Bow Street after he killed your parents?"

Anthony took her hands from his chest and stepped back from her, self-revulsion coursing through him. "I wanted to, but the man who did it threatened my sister. Then he was arrested and hanged. It wasn't the justice I wanted, but at least the man who committed the crime was punished."

"What justice do you want?"

He stared at her, realizing he didn't know. Did he want the Vicar to hang? Yes. But that still wasn't justice. "I should be punished."

Her lips parted, and she lifted her hand to her

mouth. The tears in her eyes gutted him. He turned away, unable to bear her pain in addition to his own. He was such a coward.

And then she was in front of him, her chin jutting and her eyes sparking. "Stop this. You do not need to be punished. I think you've done quite enough of that. Tomorrow, you're going to visit Bow Street and let them handle this."

"What if they can't?" he whispered, his voice ragged. "What if everyone finds out what I've done?"

"They won't," she insisted, cupping his face. "They won't. I told you we'd work through this together, we'd move forward *together*." She stood on her toes and kissed him, her lips soft and urgent against his.

He wrapped his arms around her and swept her against his chest, desperate for the solace of her embrace. She caressed his face and slid her hands back through his hair.

Her gloves were smooth against him, but he wanted her flesh. He wanted all of her.

Lifting his head, he looked down at her with abject need. "I want to take you upstairs. To my bed."

"A proper shagging at last?"

The humor in her tone unfurled the tightness in his chest. He'd never been more grateful for another human being. Clasping her hand, he led her from the study and through a door that led to the narrow servant stairs. He hurried up two flights, and they were both breathless when they reached the landing. He guided her along a corridor to a door at the end.

Opening the door, he swept her into his dressing chamber and then into his bedroom.

"Oh, that was a neat trick," she said, looking around as she removed her gloves.

Eager to have her naked beneath him, he cupped her face and kissed her, then moved his hands down to untie her bonnet, which he then sailed across the room.

He pulled his coat off and tossed it toward a chair, missing it spectacularly, then focused on disrobing her. He turned her around and unlaced her gown, pulling perhaps a bit too savagely at the ties in his impatience.

Once they had the gown off, he took more care with it than he had his coat, laying it gently over the chair. When he turned back, he saw that she'd already stepped out of her petticoat and draped it over another chair. Then she sat down and unlaced her boots, her gaze finding his intermittently as she worked.

Anthony removed his boots and unbuttoned his waistcoat. His body thrummed with desire and anticipation. It was not their first time together, yet something felt different. Perhaps it was the presence of a bed at long last.

She began to remove her stockings, but he rushed to kneel before her, taking over the task. He unfastened her garters, then peeled each stocking from her leg, his fingers caressing each new inch of flesh he exposed. When he was finished, he brought his hands up over her knees, skimming them along her thighs and beneath her shift.

Ducking her head, she kissed him as she untied his cravat. Then her hands were against his neck as she drove her tongue deep into his mouth. He clutched her hips and moved between her legs.

He reached up behind her and unlaced her corset. When it was loose, she pushed it down and rose up off the chair so he could pull the corset from her body. And then there was just the shift. The curves of her breasts were clearly visible beneath the thin white lawn, as was the dusky pink of her nipples. He leaned forward and tongued her through the fabric, drawing a cry from her.

She clutched his head and whispered his name. Overcome, he rested his forehead against her and pulled in a shaky breath.

Pressing on him, she urged him to stand and rose with him. Then she took his hand and led him to the bed, where she pulled her shift over her head and let it drop to the floor. She stood nude before him. He was speechless as he took in her form—from the alabaster slope of her neck and shoulder to the rose-hued peaks of her breasts to the curve of her slender hip to the bevy of golden curls between her thighs.

Anthony would never believe he'd deserve this—her—but he'd always be grateful. "You are beautiful," he breathed.

"You make me feel that way," she said, pulling his shirt from his waistband.

He took off his waistcoat and quickly divested himself of the remainder of his clothes. She traced her fingers over his chest, then flattened her palms against him. "You're beautiful too."

"There is no comparison." He reached behind her and pulled back the coverlet, then swept her up and laid her on the bedclothes.

He climbed in next to her and drew her into his arms, content to just hold her, skin to skin, her heart beating against his. He kissed her temple, her cheek, her jaw.

She nuzzled him, her lips gliding over his neck, her tongue licking along his flesh. He shivered, in awe at the power she had over him. He was utterly at her mercy, and there was nowhere else he'd rather be.

Rolling her to her back, he rose up on his elbow and kissed her. He trailed his hand over her shoulder, down to her breast, cupping her and teasing her nipple until she arched up off the bed and moaned into his mouth. Sliding farther down, he stroked her abdomen and then her hip. She twitched, opening her legs as he skimmed over her thigh and found her sex.

She was already wet for him, her body welcoming him as he pushed one finger into her and used another on her clitoris. His cock, heavy against her leg, throbbed with need.

Her hand encircled him, stroking him from base to tip. He groaned and moved over her, settling between her legs.

She clasped his neck, and he pulled back so he could look down at her. Perhaps sensing him watching her, she opened her eyes. The emotion in her gaze stole his breath.

With her help, he guided his cock to her entrance. He hesitated the barest moment before sliding inside. Her heat enveloped him, making him gasp.

She grasped his hip and widened her legs as he thrust fully inside her. He brushed his hand over her temple, holding her gaze as he withdrew and drove into her again. He went slowly, precisely, cherishing every motion, every breath.

Her body rolled with his, arching and dipping, moving in concert. He barely thought. He just felt. Currents of desire, of pleasure, of the sweetest passion he'd ever known flowed between them. The broken pieces inside him felt as if they might knit together. It seemed repair—redemption—was perhaps in reach.

She brought her legs up and wrapped them around his waist, pulling him more deeply inside her. Her eyes widened as she cried out. "Oh *yes*." Then her eyes closed, breaking the connection they'd shared. But then a new one was forged as she began to move faster beneath him.

His body reacted, thrusting into her with greater speed and depth. She gasped over and over, and her muscles tightened around him.

"Please, Anthony. *Yes.*" She spoke to him, urging him with words, and with her body too, her hands clutching at him as her heels dug into his backside.

Then she began to spasm around him, her body shuddering as she came. He'd never felt anything so potent, so magnificent. His orgasm rushed over him, and he felt wetness on his cheeks as he cried her name over and over.

They rode the storm together, their bodies entwined. He collapsed against her, his breath coming hard and fast. She kissed his jaw, his cheek, murmuring nonsensical words, at least words he couldn't comprehend in his current state.

He realized, far too late, what he'd done. He muttered a curse and rolled to his side, leaving her body.

"That reaction wasn't what I expected," she murmured. "I thought that was rather spectacular."

He wiped his hand over his face, the bliss and contentment he'd known disappearing beneath the weight of his blunder. "I came inside you."

"Oh. I suppose you did." She rolled to her side to face him. "Well, what's done is done."

"Please don't tell me we need to forget this along with everything else we don't like that's happened in our pasts?"

She laughed, surprising him. "Goodness, no. I'll remember this day for the rest of my life. And, no matter what happens, I'll never regret a moment of it." She reached over and put her hand on his cheek, turning his face so that he had to look at her. "Not one moment."

He hoped that would always be true and would pray there wasn't a child. The emotion of the day had drained him. Or maybe it was because he'd just experienced the best sexual encounter of his life. Whatever the reason, he didn't want to dwell on the negative.

He tucked a blonde curl that had come loose behind her ear. "You never told me why you needed to see me."

Skimming his jaw, she brought her hand down to his collarbone. "I didn't, did I? We were distracted. My sister came to visit me today—I invited her."

"Your parents didn't accompany her?"

She shook her head. "My mother enlisted a friend of hers to act as chaperone."

Anthony wanted to yell at her mother. She had a lovely daughter in Jane, and someday, she'd regret the way she was treating her. "I'm sorry."

"It's all right." She traced circles on his shoulder with her fingertips. "I wasn't expecting them to come."

He pulled the bedclothes up over them. "You weren't upset?" She'd seemed that way when she'd arrived—she'd followed Purcell to his study.

"Not about that." Her hand stilled. "After talking to Anne, I think… I think she feels she has to marry. Because of me."

"What do you mean?"

"Her debut was delayed because I hadn't wed. Then this year, they decided it was time—past time, really—for Anne to have her first Season. They've compared it endlessly to my first Season, which was a disaster. I can well imagine the pressure they've put on Anne to be what I could not."

"And what's that?"

"A success."

The hurt in her voice pierced straight to his heart. He put his arms around her and drew her close, kissing her temple. She exhaled against his neck. "It's my fault that she feels she must marry, and I'm not entirely convinced she's happy."

"Jane, you mustn't feel guilty."

She tipped her head back and looked at him. "That's a bit rich coming from you," she said archly.

"You're right. You may feel guilty if you wish, but don't do so for long. It will ravage you inside." His chest tightened again, and the broken pieces faltered. Healing, he realized, was going to take time. He only hoped he could get there—someday.

She laid her palm against his cheek. "Yes, it will. I'll find a way to move forward, and so will you. Starting with going to Bow Street tomorrow. Will you go?"

"I will." But he planned to visit the Vicar first. Jane was right about one thing—it was past time to bury all this, and he couldn't do that if the Vicar kept dredging it up.

Anthony would stop him—once and for all.

CHAPTER 13

"*L*ady Ripley," Culpepper announced as Phoebe walked into the garden room.

It was strange to see her here as a guest, and Jane wondered if she'd ever get over that. "Phoebe, please pardon me if I don't get up. I wasn't expecting you this soon." Jane gestured to the two sleeping kittens in her lap.

Phoebe smiled as she pulled off her gloves and hat and handed them to Culpepper. "Thank you," she said, flicking him a glance before she walked to Jane. She stroked Daffodil's head, waking the kitten, who responded with a massive yawn. "They are *so* cute."

Daffodil started to purr loudly, and Fern stirred. Stretching, she thrust her head against Phoebe's hand, wanting her attention too.

"Aww." Phoebe picked Fern up and kissed her head. "I may need a kitten. I wonder if Marcus will mind."

"As if he would deprive you of anything."

"My apologies for arriving early," Phoebe said, taking the other chair and setting Fern on her lap. She petted the kitten's head and ears. "I hope you don't mind."

"Not at all. I'm glad for the chance to catch up before the others arrive." It would be a larger group since Lady Satterfield was also joining them, and she was bringing her stepdaughter-in-law, the Duchess of Kendal.

Jane was humbled that both of them would visit her. She wondered if it would help her reputation. More accurately, she wondered if her parents would take note and be less disappointed in her. Damn, when would she stop seeking their approval?

"Yes, tell me how you're enjoying being a self-declared spinster. Is it everything you hoped for?"

Jane wasn't sure what she'd hoped for. Freedom, she supposed. And she certainly had that given that she'd secreted her way into Anthony's house yesterday. Not to mention the fact that he'd stayed here for an entire week without anyone knowing. She suddenly felt very bad about keeping all that from Phoebe.

"When you came back to London and moved into this house, how did you see your future?" Jane asked.

Phoebe inhaled as she settled back against the chair. "I was glad to be free of others' expectations and judgment. After Sainsbury," she shuddered at the mention of her former betrothed, "I was glad to be alone."

Jane understood that. Sainsbury had treated her horribly, and she'd narrowly avoided marriage to him. "I thought I would be glad to be alone too—and I definitely don't miss my parents' expectations and judgment."

"I'm sensing there's more. Perhaps a however?" Phoebe knew her so well.

"I'm afraid I'm not that happy being alone. I find myself thinking about marriage—about missing out on a union. Maybe it's from seeing you so happy. And Arabella."

"And soon Anne will be wed too," Phoebe said softly. She gave Jane a sympathetic look.

That was true. Even Jane's sister would be married.

"I can see why you'd feel alone. I'm so sorry, Jane."

"But I'm not actually," Jane whispered.

Phoebe's eyes widened. "You're not?"

Jane shook her head. "I can't tell you everything." She wouldn't disclose Anthony's fight or him staying here since he'd asked her not to. "But Anthony and I… Well, Anthony and I." She left it at that.

Phoebe sat forward, disrupting Fern, who jumped down from her lap. Daffodil did the same, leaping from Jane to chase her sister.

"You can't just say that and nothing else. Anthony and you *what*?" Phoebe demanded.

Jane laughed. It came out with a bit of a giggle quality, and Phoebe narrowed her eyes as she pinned Jane with an insistent stare. "Are you going to tell me or not?"

"Yes." Jane took a deep breath. "We've become close."

"When? How?" Phoebe's eyes danced with delight. "Tell me *everything*. Wait, you said you couldn't." She exhaled with disappointment. "Tell me what you can." She cocked her head to the side. "While you're at it, tell me why you can't tell me everything."

"Because Anthony asked me not to, and I will respect his wishes. We've become good friends." She believed that to be true and hoped he saw them that way too. "I can't say how, exactly, but we've spent a great deal of time together."

"At Brixton Park?" Phoebe asked.

"Yes."

Phoebe's brow puckered. "But you're just friends?"

"Friends with some…extra bits?" Jane's voice rose at the end.

Phoebe blinked, stifling a smile. "Oh. Can I hope you've finally been kissed?"

"Ah, yes. Rest assured, I have become rather, ah, accomplished."

"I see. I will also rest assured that you are being careful. Anthony is quite the rakehell these days." Her features darkened briefly. "Marcus worries about him."

"I can understand that. To be honest, I worry about him too." But then they shared a day like yesterday, and she could see that he was healing. "However, I think our relationship is helping him. Finally."

"Truly?" Phoebe's face brightened. "I'm so happy. For both of you. Do you think this will lead to marriage?"

Anthony's promise to her—that he wouldn't fall in love with her and they wouldn't marry—vaulted to the front of her mind. She swallowed, not ready to think of an end to what they shared. "I don't have any reason to believe it will, no."

Phoebe scooted forward in her chair. "Jane. I don't know what to say. Do you want to marry him?"

"I don't know." She hadn't allowed herself to think about it. "I'm just enjoying each day for now. Maybe when he's fully healed…" If that day ever came. She prayed it would, but there was still so much darkness inside him.

"He'd be foolish to let you slip away," Phoebe said with an edge of disgust.

"You mustn't judge him. I don't know that I want to marry him." What if the darkness never went away? Could she live with that? "Anyway, it doesn't matter now. When you took up with Marcus, you didn't think you'd wed."

Phoebe exhaled. "That's true. I never expected—or imagined—things would turn out as they did. I suppose you'll just have to see what lies in store for you and Anthony. So long as he doesn't hurt you. I won't be able to forgive that."

"He won't," Jane said. So far, he was doing a good job of keeping himself at bay, of ensuring he didn't do damage. But what if she opened her heart too much?

Culpepper appeared in the doorway. "Lady Satterfield, miss."

The countess entered the garden room having already removed her hat and gloves. "Good afternoon, I hope you don't mind that I arrived early." Her gaze settled on Phoebe. "Oh, I see I wasn't the only one. My apologies. I hope I'm not interrupting."

"Not at all," Jane said, rising to welcome the countess. "Please join us." She gestured to the settee, and Lady Satterfield came to sit.

Jane inclined her head toward Culpepper, and he responded with a slight nod. She knew he'd return in a bit with the refreshments since it seemed their meeting was to begin early.

"Good afternoon, Lady Satterfield," Phoebe said cheerfully.

"I'm pleased to see you, Lady Ripley. I know I said this at Brixton Park, but it bears repeating: marriage certainly agrees with you. And with the marquess. He is as smitten as I've ever seen a man." Her eyes gleamed with approval as she added, "Well done."

Phoebe laughed softly. "Thank you."

Lady Satterfield turned her gaze to Jane. "I came early to tell you what I'd learned about that matter

we discussed, but we can talk about it another time."
She flicked a glance toward Phoebe.

"Phoebe knows all about the rumor," Jane said.
"If you don't mind sharing now, I'd be delighted to
hear what you learned."

"Very well," the countess said warmly. "I spoke to
a few people about it, and while it was well known
among the young men of the *ton* five years ago, no
one else was aware. I talked to Nora, and she hadn't
heard a word of it. Oh, by the by, she won't be
joining us today. Her youngest didn't sleep well last
night, and Nora didn't want to leave him."

"I hope all is well," Phoebe said.

"Oh yes. Lucas is not the best sleeper," Lady Satterfield noted. "And the less he sleeps, the more he
wants his mama. As to the matter of the rumor, if it
helps, Clare mentioned a few gentlemen who undoubtedly knew of the rumor: Lord Edgecombe, Mr.
Adair, and Lord Rockbourne."

All the names were familiar to Jane, but one was
particularly so. "Rockbourne was one of my suitors
that first Season—before he inherited and became
Lord Rockbourne. We didn't have an official
courtship, but I had hoped we might. He ended up
marrying Dorothea Chamberlain at the end of the
Season. I remember because she was so very happy."
They'd been friends, but like so many women,
Dorothea had abandoned her unmarried friends the
following Season.

"Is there any reason he would have started the
rumor?" Phoebe asked.

Jane shook her head. "Thomas, I mean Rockbourne, was—is—one of the kindest gentlemen I've
ever met. I can't imagine him starting a rumor of any
kind, let alone one that painted me as a wanton."

"I'm sorry I wasn't able to be of more help," Lady
Satterfield said.

Jane gave her a warm, grateful smile. "Please don't apologize. I've decided you were right anyway —there's no point in looking backward. What's done is done, and I'd rather live in the present." Yes, the present—no past and no future. Just the here and now. With Anthony.

Lady Satterfield smiled approvingly. "Brilliant. I think that's the right attitude, my dear. You have this wonderful new endeavor with the Spitfire Society to focus on. I am absolutely delighted to be able to participate."

"And I'm delighted to have you." Jane looked toward the door as Culpepper brought in a tray of refreshments. A few minutes later, Lady Gresham and Miss Whitford arrived.

Yes, Jane had a wonderful present on which to center her attention. The past wasn't worth worrying about, and the future... Well, she'd just avoid thinking about that entirely.

❧

*T*he double-faced clock hanging over the street greeted Anthony as he arrived at St. Dunstan-in-the-West, sending a bead of dread up his spine along with a rush of apprehension. He hadn't been to the church in some time, but it wasn't long enough. He'd never wanted to see this place again.

Moving into the dim interior, he ducked into an alcove and waited. A few minutes later, a boy came to him. He wasn't familiar, but the Vicar employed many.

"Are ye here to light a candle or make a donation?" the boy, who was maybe ten years old, asked.

"Light a candle." It was code for requesting a meeting with the Vicar. Donations were payments. On his last visit, Anthony had made his final donation. Or so he'd thought. If the Vicar was behind the extortion letters, then that wasn't the case. Anthony was curious, however, why the Vicar hadn't directed the extortion payments to be made here instead of some tavern in Blackfriars. Maybe he wanted to keep these types of "donations" separate. And the Stinking Sheep was very close. Close enough for Anthony to believe the Vicar might use both establishments. He ruled this neighborhood. Or so Anthony had been told.

The boy took himself off, leaving Anthony for quite some time. Leaning against the wall, Anthony took deep breaths and calmed his racing heart by thinking of Jane. The time he'd spent with her in his bed yesterday—and not just the part when they'd shagged—lingered in his mind, giving him the greatest sense of peace he'd known in more than a year. He tried to cling to that feeling.

At last the boy returned and led him to a small room downstairs in the bowels of the church. He knocked twice on the door, then opened it, stepping aside so Anthony could walk inside.

The door closed behind him, clicking a sound of finality and entrapment. The first—and only—time Anthony had visited this room, his heart had practically pounded right out of his chest. He'd been shocked to see that a criminal moneylender conducted business from a small, unassuming office beneath a church. But then he supposed he should have expected the location at least, since the man was called the Vicar.

A single window high on the ceiling at street level provided a modicum of light, but a pair of sconces also flickered on the wall on either side of the window. A narrow hearth stood to the left, while a simple desk sat to the right.

On Anthony's previous visit, the Vicar had sat

behind the desk. Today, however, he was situated in a plush, velvet-covered high-backed chair near the hearth. Surprisingly youthful in appearance, with an athletic build and shining blond hair, the Vicar wouldn't have looked like a criminal if not for the nasty scar that cut across his chin and into his lower lip.

He surveyed Anthony with piercing blue eyes, one of which was marred with an odd orange spot, that seemed to see into one's very soul. When Anthony had met him, he'd assumed the man had read every one of his vices. And given the knowledge he'd possessed about Anthony's misdeeds, he had to think he was right.

"Lord Colton, I'm surprised to see you."

Anthony's neck pricked. "Last time I came, you were expecting me."

"I was. You'd been referred to me, if you recall." His mouth curled into a half smile. "In addition, I was aware of your debts, some of which were already owed to me." Because he owned two of the hells where Anthony had left IOUs.

"You truly have no idea why I'm here today?"

"Sit." The Vicar gestured to the other chair in front of the hearth. It was not high-backed, nor was it covered in velvet. It was simple wood, and not finely made either. "If you please," he added with a hint of warmth.

Anthony took the chair and waited for the Vicar to respond to his question.

"I don't know why you are here today. I don't usually take meetings in this instance, but since we are acquainted and you paid your debt in full, plus interest, I wanted to extend you a courtesy."

Though fury raged inside him, Anthony knew he was looking at a dangerous criminal. "It's the least you can do after killing my parents." He was proud of himself for keeping his tone even.

The Vicar's icy eyes narrowed briefly as his nostrils flared. "Did you come here to accuse me of something? Be very careful, my lord."

The absurdity of the polite address accompanying the threat nearly made Anthony laugh. But there was nothing humorous about this situation. "I did not. However, I don't see the point in hiding the truth. You had my parents killed when I wasn't able to repay you fast enough."

"Who told you that?" the Vicar asked softly.

"The man who killed them. He sent me a note saying the same would happen to my sister if I didn't pay."

The Vicar turned his head to the hearth, frowning deeply. When he looked back to Anthony, there was a surprising sympathy in his gaze. "I am sorry he did that. He wasn't supposed to kill them at all."

Anthony felt as if the world around him had spun completely sideways. He blinked to bring things back to normal, but couldn't seem to cut through a haze that had descended upon him. "They weren't supposed to die?" His heart, which had slowed after he'd entered the office, picked up speed again, his blood thundering in his ears.

"No. I don't murder people, Lord Colton. I loan money. I collect money. Occasionally, people need to be reminded to repay their debt when they have the means to do so. You had possessions to sell, so you had the means. Consequently, you were supposed to be encouraged to settle what you owed. I was told you would be on that road that day, not your parents."

That was true. Anthony was supposed to have been the one to go.

The Vicar exhaled. "I regret that sometimes my information is not as accurate as I expect, though it doesn't happen very often. And never with such unfortunate results."

Anthony nearly launched out of the chair. He gripped the arms, the wood biting into his fingers and palms. "My parents' deaths were a bit more than 'unfortunate.'"

"Yes, of course. And I understand you have struggled, though I see you haven't resorted to gambling again. Your restraint is commendable." Was that a note of respect?

"I don't want your fucking esteem." Anthony curled his lip. "I want to know why you're extorting money from me after I've already paid you."

The Vicar leaned slightly forward, but kept his voice soft yet dangerous, like silk soaked in poison. "I'll remind you to be careful about accusing me of things. I am more sorry about your parents than you can imagine, but there is nothing I can do to bring them back or change what happened. The man responsible has paid the ultimate price. You must find solace and satisfaction in that. Or not. It's your choice as to how you wish to live your life."

Anthony stared at him. He had no idea what to do with this man's counsel. "I didn't ask for, nor do I need your advice. Are you saying you aren't extorting me?" The Vicar hadn't said any such thing, but twice now, he'd cautioned Anthony about making accusations.

"I don't extort anyone." His steely tone conveyed a deep sincerity. "I am simply a businessman, and extortion is not one of my many enterprises. Why would you think it was me?"

Because he was a criminal? Anthony bit back the retort before it leapt from his mouth. "Because you're the only person who knows of my transgressions.

The note I received said they would all be made public in embarrassing detail: the extent of my gambling, the fact that I had debts, drinking, womanizing…murder." He glanced away and swallowed.

The Vicar scoffed. "You didn't commit murder any more than I did. The rest, however, are quite true. And doesn't everyone know about the drinking and womanizing? You are hardly discreet."

No, he hadn't been about those. "I was about the debts, and no one knows how bad they were or that I had to borrow money from you—which led to my parents' murder."

"Your father knew about the debts, but that's immaterial." The Vicar waved his hand. "The man who referred you to me also knew. How else would he have known you needed help?"

Gilbert Chamberlain—whom Anthony had known since Oxford and with whom he'd often gambled. Chamberlain had money to burn and the luck of the devil. Anthony had stopped seeking his company because it always left him the poorer for it.

"Chamberlain wouldn't have any need to extort me. He doesn't want for funds."

The Vicar chuckled. "You think I have need for funds?"

Anthony lifted a shoulder. "You were insistent I repay you—with interest—by a certain date and threatened me when I wasn't able to do so. It certainly seems like you needed funds."

The Vicar's hands curled around the arms of his chair, his muscles briefly tensing. "As I told you, I'm a businessman. A debt must be repaid, preferably on time. It is the honorable and right thing to do. How can I run a business if people think they can steal from me? I take what is owed, and I never take what I haven't earned." He relaxed, flexing his hands before raising one to support his scarred chin while he rested his elbow on the arm of the chair. "If Chamberlain doesn't need money, perhaps there is another reason he'd extort from you."

Anthony searched his mind. "We were friends. I can't imagine why he would do such a thing."

"Then it must be the money, regardless of what you think. Would you like me to look into his financial situation? Perhaps he isn't as secure as you think."

The Vicar was offering to do him a favor? That was even less believable than Chamberlain extorting him. "How much will that cost me?"

The Vicar grinned and lowered his forearm. "I like you, Colton. As it happens, I am in need of a favor myself."

Anthony steeled himself. He'd been relieved to conclude his business with this man and didn't particularly wish to enter into another arrangement, even if it didn't involve money. "What sort of favor?"

"Nothing terrible, I assure you. I would like to attend a Society event where I can survey certain people. I would provide you with a guest list. You could invite more than that, of course, but those would be the particular people I would want you to invite."

What an utterly bizarre request. Anthony wanted to ask why, but felt certain the enigmatic man wouldn't tell him. "And how am I to introduce you? People will notice you—a man they don't recognize from their circles—and wonder who you are and why you're there."

"If you agree and when you decide to host the party, I will provide that information. Rest assured, I will not embarrass you, and everyone I meet will be charmed." His lips curved into a smile, and despite the garish scar, Anthony believed that would probably be the case. Hell, he'd arrived believing this man had killed his parents, and now he was contemplating hosting a party for the blackguard.

Was it really worth it, however, when Anthony didn't believe Chamberlain could be the culprit? "I just don't think Chamberlain's behind this. Furthermore, I can't host a party without a hostess. My sister is in the country."

"Perhaps you could convince your friend Ripley to host it. Maybe at Brixton Park? I'd love to see the maze."

Was there anything this man didn't know about Anthony? "I don't know that I'm comfortable asking that."

"Then I'll wait until you wed Miss Pemberton. That should be soon, shouldn't it?"

No, there was apparently nothing this man didn't know. "How is it you know all this about me, and you have no idea I was being extorted or who was doing it?"

"That is a very good question, and one I don't have an answer to." He frowned again. "Which is a position I don't like to be in. I'll find out who it is. However, if you want me to share that information with you, I'll need that favor."

"So if it's not Chamberlain—which it won't be— you'll still find out who it is?"

"I will. Do we have a deal?"

Bloody hell. Anthony wanted to turn his back on the devil, but he had to put a stop to this madness. "I'm due to make another payment tomorrow evening. Can you find out before then?"

"Probably. I'll be in touch as soon as possible." He rose, slowly unfolding his legs and rising to a formidable height. He extended his hand.

Anthony stood, staring at the man's hand. If he took it, there was no going back. He'd be in bed with the devil—again.

Clasping the Vicar's hand, Anthony shook it. "I'll look forward to hearing from you." He let go, then turned and walked to the door.

"I am sorry about your parents, Colton. Truly. If I could change what happened, I would."

With his hand on the latch, Anthony turned his head. "That means I would be dead, then."

The Vicar gave him a slight nod. "Perhaps."

Until recently, Anthony would have been just fine with that. But lately, he'd begun to wonder if life didn't have more in store for him, if it wasn't, in fact, worth living. That had to be why he was fighting now, why he'd accepted a deal with the notorious Vicar.

Anthony left the office, eager for the Vicar's information, which he would then provide to Bow Street. The extortionist, whoever it was, wouldn't be able to expose Anthony.

That couldn't happen—not for Anthony's sake, but for those around him, especially Sarah. Jane had convinced him that she didn't need to know, and he would do anything to keep her from finding out. For her own peace of mind.

Especially knowing what he knew now, that his parents' murder truly wasn't supposed to happen, that in some way it was random, that if not for the sheer malevolence of their killer, they'd be alive today.

Or he'd be dead.

Either one of those was better than this. And yet *this* was all he had.

The memory of Jane's touch, of her scent, assailed him. Maybe this wasn't as bad as he thought. It was certainly better than he deserved.

CHAPTER 14

*J*ane sat in bed and tried to read a book, but after staring at the same page for ten minutes, she closed it and set it on the bedside table. She'd hoped Anthony would come to the garden room door after dinner as he had the other night, but he hadn't. After waiting up later than usual, she'd finally come up to bed.

The Spitfire Society meeting had been a success. Lady Gresham had spoken about the Magdalen Hospital for reformed prostitutes, and Lady Satterfield had actually suggested they take a tour! When Jane had voiced her concern about what people would say, Lady Satterfield had waved her hand and said she didn't care, that helping those who were working to help themselves was an admirable endeavor. They'd all agreed.

Suddenly, her bedroom door opened, startling her so she gasped.

Anthony closed the door and moved toward the bed.

"You're late," Jane said, sitting up from the pillows she'd stacked behind her against the headboard for reading.

"You were expecting me?" he asked, dropping his hat and gloves onto the chair by the hearth.

"I'd hoped you would come," she admitted.

He smiled, but gave her a pointed stare. "Best not to see this as a regular occurrence."

"I'm fine with taking turns. I'll come back to your house next."

He finished pulling off his boots, then came around to her side of the bed and kissed her, drawing briefly on her lower lip. "Minx."

She glanced down at his stockinged feet. "Did I invite you to disrobe? To stay?"

"You said you were waiting for me. Were you hoping to play backgammon?" He removed his coat, clearly not believing that she didn't want him there. Or that she preferred him dressed.

Jane grinned, then knelt on the bed in front of him to remove his cravat. "Fine. Disrobe. Stay. Do whatever you like."

He waggled his brows as he unbuttoned his waistcoat. "Whatever?"

"Actually, I think it's time I do whatever *I* like." She stripped his neckcloth away and tossed it to the floor, then pushed his waistcoat over his shoulders so that it fell in the same direction.

"Is that so?" he asked, pulling his shirt over his head.

She plucked open his breeches and slipped her hand inside to cup his shaft. "Mmm-hmm." She slid off the bed and pushed him onto the mattress. "Lie down."

He arched his brows, but wordlessly complied. He started to remove his stockings, but she moved his hands away. "Put those somewhere else. Over your head, perhaps."

Keeping his dark gaze fixed on her, he stretched

his arms up over his head and clasped the headboard. "Better?"

She removed his stockings and tossed them over the end of the bed, then crawled up over him and pulled his breeches down over his hips. His cock bobbed free, arcing out toward her.

After sending his breeches the same way as his stockings, she braced her hands on his thighs and pushed his legs apart so she could kneel between them.

"Jane, what it is you plan to do?"

Taking her finger, she traced it up his thigh and then over to one of his testicles. He drew in a sharp breath. "Jane."

"Since you've used your mouth to excellent effect, I wondered if I might do the same." She trailed her finger up over his sac and then along the underside of his cock. His flesh twitched as she reached the head, then she pushed back the foreskin and watched as moisture coated the tip.

Leaning down, she licked him, surprised at how salty he tasted. "Do you mind?" she asked, looking up his abdomen.

His head was elevated on the pillows she'd stacked. He gazed down at her, his cobalt eyes slitted with desire. "Never. Put me in your mouth and do what you do with your hand, only with your lips and tongue. The deeper you take me, the better it will feel."

Jane's sex throbbed in response. She'd never imagined being so aroused by just talking about what she could do to him. She credited the dark, seductive timbre of his voice and the haze of sexual anticipation he exuded. His hips moved, rising slightly off the mattress in silent plea.

Licking the tip again, she kept eye contact as she swirled her tongue over and around him. He groaned and grabbed her plait, urging her head down. She tore her gaze from his and sucked him into her mouth, sliding his cock along her tongue, taking him deeper and deeper until he nearly touched her throat.

Afraid she might gag, she released him, slowly, using her tongue along him and closing her lips tightly around his flesh. She didn't release him entirely, but took him in again, feeling more confident. Over and over, she sucked him, curling her hand around the root of his shaft to gain more control. Yes, this was better.

"Move your hand too. Up with your mouth." His words inflamed her, and she did as he described, following her lips with her hand as she traversed her way back to the tip. Then she took him in once more, no longer afraid of discomfort. She moved faster, finding a rhythm with her tongue and hand. His hips urged her on, moving in time with her.

He tugged on her plait as he arched up into her mouth. "Jane, I'm going to come." The words were an animalistic growl. She'd reduced him to a beast. Feminine pride burst inside her.

She knew what that meant, of course, and what would happen. Sliding up his cock, she held him while she took her mouth away briefly. "Then come."

She dove down on him, moving at a frenzied pace now as she recalled how fast he moved his fingers on and in her when he brought her to orgasm. He moved with her, crying out as his cock tensed and his seed shot into her mouth.

Unsure of what to do, Jane swallowed until there was nothing left. Then she pulled away and sat back, gingerly wiping her mouth.

Anthony opened his eyes and stared at her. "Good God."

Jane froze, horrified. "Was that bad?"

"Uh, no. Not ever. That was one of the best sexual experiences of my life."

Relief poured through her, along with that female pride again. "Only *one* of the best?"

"I can't elevate it above the gift of your virginity or, honestly, yesterday."

At his house when they'd finally had a bed beneath them. Twice, they'd coupled, and both had been intensely wonderful. Emotional, even.

She knew with sudden clarity and terrifying fear that she was in love with him. She climbed over his leg and went to pour herself a glass of water on the other side of the room.

The bed creaked, and she heard him pad across the carpet, sensing precisely when he stood behind her. She took a drink of water before turning to face him.

"Jane, is everything all right?" He looked at her with grave concern. "Should I have stopped you from—"

"No." He was worried about her reaction to what they'd just done. "I just wanted a drink, that's all. You're rather salty."

He chuckled. "So I've heard."

She thought of where he may have heard that—other women who'd done that to him—and the jealousy burning inside her made her take another drink of water. Feeling foolish, she set the glass down next to the ewer.

"Jane, that was a jest." Had he read her mind? "Come back to bed so I can return the favor," he said with a smile.

She blinked at him. "It wasn't a favor, Anthony. I don't expect anything in return." Except maybe she did. If she didn't expect it, she certainly wanted it—his love. But he'd been very clear that wasn't an option. Wanting his love was madness. It was also incredibly painful.

He took her hand and stroked his thumb along her wrist. "I know you don't expect anything. That's why this affair is so perfect." His words carved a hole into her chest.

He shook his head. "I almost forgot to tell you— because I was incredibly distracted the moment I arrived. Your beauty takes my breath away." He tucked a curl behind her ear and kissed her.

She pulled back. "What did you want to tell me?"

"See? I was distracted again. I know who was trying to extort me."

Jane was surprised he'd been diverted from that important revelation. "You went to Bow Street?"

"No, but I will in the morning. I just received a note tonight about the extortionist. It's the man who sent me to the Vicar for money in the first place. I never imagined he would extort me because he has no need of money. Plus, I thought we were friends." His jaw tightened. "I was mistaken."

"That's awful. Why did he do it if he didn't need money?"

"Apparently, he *is* in need of funds—to buy a new house."

"I don't understand."

"He's a greedy blackguard, which is maybe worse than if he'd actually needed the money."

Jane scoffed. "It's all terrible. Who is this miscreant?"

"Gilbert Chamberlain. I knew him at Oxford. As I said, we've been friends."

Everything seemed to stop, including Jane's heart for a moment. "Gilbert Chamberlain?" Her voice sounded as if it were coming from very far away.

"Yes, do you know him?"

"He's marrying my sister."

"Bloody hell," Anthony breathed.

"We have to stop the wedding."

"When is it?"

"The day after tomorrow." Jane walked past him, going to the bed where she grasped the bedpost. "I'll go see Anne and my parents in the morning." The thought of seeing her mother and father, especially to tell them the wedding they'd been dreaming of for years couldn't happen filled her with dread.

"What will you say?"

Jane turned, dropping her hand to her side. She opened her mouth, but nothing came out. What *would* she tell them? That Anne's betrothed was an extortionist, and she knew this because her lover was currently being extorted by him?

Anthony went to pick up his shirt and pulled it over his head. Then he came to stand in front of her. "Don't tell them anything. Let Bow Street handle it, and the wedding won't happen."

Jane exhaled, then nodded. "I should still go and tell Anne. I can be vague. I don't need to give her the specifics." That the man Chamberlain was extorting was Anthony or that he was her lover. She looked up at Anthony. "How did you find out it was Chamberlain? You said you received a note. It wasn't from Bow Street?" How could it be when he said he hadn't gone to see them?

"I paid a visit to the Vicar today. He offered to find the extortionist, and he did so in an amazingly short time. He seems to know everything."

"How can you be so sure?" Wasn't the Vicar a criminal? Or at least unsavory? "Is this really a man you can trust?"

"Normally, I would say no, but in this case, I think I can." He turned away from her and went to pick up his breeches, but didn't put them on.

"Why? I can't believe you would trust him after what he did."

"Murder my parents, you mean?" He said the words with only the barest inflection. Maybe he truly was healing. "He wasn't responsible. The man who did it was only supposed to threaten them—not even them, actually, but me. I was meant to be on the road to Oaklands."

Jane still wasn't sure if she'd trust such a man, but then why would he lie? "You're certain the Vicar isn't behind all this and trying to blame my sister's be-trothed?"

"I am. The Vicar insists he is a businessman, and that he's not in the business of taking money for nothing. He makes loans, and he collects them. To him, extortion is not an honorable transaction."

Jane snorted softly. "He spoke to you about honor?"

Anthony stared at her a moment. "Do you just not want to believe that Chamberlain is the culprit? That your sister would betroth herself to such a man?"

Jane realized that was part of it—surely Anne would have known better. But then she thought of Phoebe, who'd become betrothed to someone terrible and had luckily discovered that before it was too late and they were wed. Jane couldn't let that happen to Anne, even if there was a chance none of this was true.

"I suppose I think it would be easier for everyone if it wasn't Chamberlain."

"Life is seldom easy," he said with a chill as he drew on his breeches.

"I know." She hated that he was growing upset. Moving around the bed, she touched his arm. "If you believe Chamberlain did this, I trust in you."

He paused in buttoning his fall and cupped her cheek. "Thank you."

"You're leaving?" she asked, watching him tuck the hem of his shirt into his breeches.

"Not quite yet, but soon. I want to be at Bow Street early. I'll come by as soon as I know anything."

"Please do."

He moved closer, sliding his hands around her waist and pulling her against him. "Now, I believe it's my turn to pleasure you. If you'd like." He dipped his head and kissed her cheek and jawline. He sucked her flesh, then nipped her gently. "Or I could go—"

Desire sparked in her core, and she put her arms around his neck, digging her fingers into his flesh. "Don't. Stay. Please." She looked up at him with naked need, wondering if he could see the love simmering inside her, begging to be shared and acknowledged.

"Nothing would make me happier." He kissed her then, his lips moving softly over hers before he cupped her backside and opened his mouth to devour her.

Jane moaned, reveling in his every touch and hoping that what he said was true—that nothing made him happier than being with her. And if it was, could she hope that someday he might love her in return?

~

*U*pon arriving at Bow Street the following morning, Anthony was shown to a small office to await the arrival of Harry Sheffield. Anthony had asked to speak with him since he was a good friend of Marcus's.

A few minutes later, Sheffield came in, closing the door behind him. Broad shouldered with a head of thick auburn hair, Sheffield's presence overtook the room. Anthony could see why the man had chosen to be a Runner. He likely intimidated every criminal he pursued.

Good, because Chamberlain deserved nothing less and likely far more.

Sheffield offered his hand to Anthony. "Good morning, my lord."

Anthony shook the man's hand. "Thank you for seeing me."

"Sit, please." Sheffield gestured to a chair, then sat down at the desk. "How can I help?"

"I've come to report a crime against me. Extortion."

Creases cut through Sheffield's wide forehead. "Let us start with what proof you have. Presumably there was a letter?"

Anthony pulled the folded pieces of parchment from his coat and set them on the desk before the Runner. "Two, in fact."

"I take it he wrote again after you failed to reply to the first?"

"Actually, I paid him the first time."

Sheffield brought the parchment closer and unfolded both sheets without looking down. "It sounds as if you might know who this is."

"Gilbert Chamberlain. You must arrest him with haste. He's due to marry tomorrow, and that cannot happen." Anthony gestured toward the letters. "In addition, as you can see, he's demanded payment before this evening."

Sheffield blinked. "Hmm, that does appear to be a reason for urgency. But I think all crimes deserve urgent attention." He gave Anthony a placid smile, then looked down at the letters.

Anthony tensed. "I would prefer not to share those letters with anyone else."

"Mmm, I can see why." Sheffield took another moment before looking up. "Perhaps you should explain the gambling debts and the murder of your parents," he said softly, his voice carrying an edge of steel.

Swallowing, Anthony worked to calm the apprehension racing through him. "I accumulated a rather large sum of debt more than a year ago. I wasn't able to repay them and had to borrow money."

"Your father wouldn't give you the funds?"

Anthony shook his head and tried to tamp down the shame burning inside him. "He also wouldn't give me money when I continued to lose and was then unable to pay the lender."

Sheffield's jaw clenched briefly, and his eyes narrowed for a moment. He flattened his palms on the desk. "I seem to recall your parents were killed by a highwayman, and the highwayman was hanged. Why does Chamberlain think you are a murderer?"

"Because the highwayman was sent to attack me, not them. If not for my failure to repay the loan, they would still be alive." Dammit. He thought he'd been making progress, but the familiar anguish tore at him again, leaving him raw and open.

"How would Chamberlain know this?"

"He was the one who referred me to the lender. He knew all about my debts, and he somehow learned that my parents' death was not a random event."

"You haven't mentioned the lender," Sheffield said slowly. "Are you trying to protect him?"

He wasn't. "I suppose I didn't want to say. This is all very embarrassing."

"Yes, extortion is, by nature of being extortion." Sheffield stacked the letters in front of him. "Was it the Vicar?" He pierced Anthony with a fiery stare, his brown eyes intense.

The man was very good at interrogation, and this was likely nothing compared with his usual tactics. "Yes. I am not trying to protect him."

"Good, he doesn't deserve your protection or anyone else's. You say he arranged to kill your parents because you didn't repay him?"

"No, I didn't say that. He sent the highwayman to scare me—I was supposed to be on the road, not my parents. However, the highwayman killed them. The Vicar was actually very sorry it happened."

"The hell he was," Sheffield muttered, his lip curling. He speared Anthony with another penetrating stare. "Why don't you think the Vicar is behind this extortion?"

"Because he said he's not. He's a businessman, and he doesn't like extortion."

Sheffield grimaced. "How high was the interest on your loan?"

"Excessive," Anthony said grimly.

"And I suppose you paid it. Of course you did."

Anthony ignored the man's critical tone. "If you compare those letters to something Chamberlain wrote, I'm sure you'll find that they match."

"I'll do that." Sheffield pressed his lips together. "But Colton, you understand these are evidence?" He rested his fingertips on the parchment. "Your gambling debts and the story behind your parents' death will become a matter of record. Everyone will know."

The Runner's words chilled Anthony to the bone. Everyone, including his sister and Felix. He fought to take a breath. "There must be another way."

"I would need other proof—a confession or something that would tie Chamberlain to the Stinking Sheep. I can conduct an investigation, and I will, but that will take time. Which you don't have."

No, he didn't. "Can you arrest him now and then

conduct the investigation? He can't be allowed to get married tomorrow."

"I'm afraid without proof, I can't act. Give me these letters, and I can."

Anthony stood and went to the desk. He grasped the edge of the parchment, and Sheffield lifted his hands. Anthony plucked the letters up and refolded them. "I'll find you proof by the end of the day."

"I hope you do. In the meantime, I'll visit the Stinking Sheep." Anthony was glad to hear it, but he intended to go there too. He might even visit the Vicar again. He'd discovered Chamberlain was behind the extortion. Surely the Vicar could provide proof for how he'd done that?

"Thank you. Hopefully, I'll see you by this evening."

"I hope you do." Sheffield sat back in his chair. "And if you change your mind about the letters, I'll go and compare them to Chamberlain's handwriting, probably arrest him straightaway."

Hell, it was so tempting, but then Anthony thought of Sarah—of Sarah's innocent child who'd been deprived of her grandparents—and he couldn't devastate her by allowing the truth to be known. It would be bad enough for Sarah to learn of it, but for her to have to share in his shame? No, it wouldn't be borne.

Without another word, Anthony turned on his heel and left. He strode from the building, intent on going straight to the Stinking Sheep, where hopefully he would find a connection between the money he'd left with the barkeep and Gilbert fucking Chamberlain.

And if he didn't? He shoved the thought away. He'd find the evidence he needed to stop the wedding, to save Jane's sister. He simply had to.

CHAPTER 15

"It's a pleasure to see you, Miss Pemberton," Mullins, Jane's parents' butler, greeted her with a wide smile. His shock of white hair and affectionate expression were a welcome sight. "You look well."

"I am, thank you, as do you. I imagine things are busy preparing for Anne's wedding tomorrow." Jane glanced around the familiar hall with more than a bit of anxiety. She never imagined returning home while her parents were still not speaking to her and certainly not for the purpose of telling them Anne couldn't get married.

Home. Jane didn't feel a rush of warmth or comfort. Just apprehension and dread.

"I'd like to see my parents. And Anne," she said.

"If you'll wait in the salon, I'll let them know you're here." Mullins left the hall, leaving Jane to make her way into the salon.

This was the main room on the ground floor besides the dining room and was typically where the family congregated. Looking around, Jane recalled happier times spent reading, playing cards, and discussing topics as varied as politics and horti-culture, which was of particular interest to her father. In truth, the more she thought about it, the more she realized there hadn't been enough of those times.

"Jane." Her mother's tone was flat as she walked into the salon. "I'm surprised to see you."

"Disappointed is a better description," Papa said coldly as he followed her into the room.

They both wore matching expressions of distaste. Jane had expected this reaction, but she'd also hoped for maybe a bare hint of something positive. If not happiness at seeing her, then perhaps just less…animosity?

"Coming here to implore us to allow you to attend the wedding tomorrow won't work," Papa said, moving to lean against the mantel where he crossed his arms.

Jane had hoped they might sit and converse pleasantly, but clearly, that was not going to happen. Mama stayed near the door, her face pinched beneath the severity of her hairstyle—her blond curls had been tamed into a tight chignon. Meanwhile, Papa looked as if he might have lost a bit more of his brown hair. And perhaps gained several lines around his eyes and mouth.

"That's not why I came," Jane said evenly, hating that the actual reason would upset them even more. "Where's Anne? She should hear this too."

"Your sister is too busy to join us," Mama said crisply. "Just tell us why you've come and then be on your way."

Jane wanted to insist Anne come downstairs, but determined it was pointless. Her parents were utterly immovable. Her faint hope that she'd be able to persuade them to call off the wedding dwindled. Nonetheless, she took a deep breath and plunged forward. She had to.

"Anne can't marry Mr. Chamberlain. It's come to

my attention that he associates with known criminals and is an extortionist."

Papa dropped his arms to his sides and took a step toward her. "That's a serious accusation. It's also preposterous. What proof do you have of any of that?"

"I realize it sounds unbelievable, but trust me, it's not. I have personal knowledge of his extortion."

"Why, because he's extorting you?" Mama shook her head, her eyes sad. "What embarrassing thing have you done now? Am I going to read the paper and see that you're embroiled in some tawdry affair?"

Jane sucked in a breath that made her cough. "Pardon me. *No.*"

God, she hoped not. She hadn't thought to ask if that could happen. If Chamberlain knew Anthony's worst secrets, wouldn't he know about them too? Not necessarily, but she should ask.

"This isn't about me. He's extorting someone I know."

"Probably someone who deserves it. There's no telling whom you associate with now," Mama said derisively.

Jane stared at her, disbelieving her mother could be so callous. "Who would deserve to be extorted, Mama? What an awful thing to say. And if you'd care to know who I'm associating with now, perhaps you'll ask Lady Satterfield—the newest member of the Spitfire Society—next time you see her." Jane cocked her head to the side. "Or perhaps not. I don't think you know her all that well." As soon as the gibe was out of Jane's mouth, she regretted it. She didn't want to quarrel with them.

"You're just trying to ruin your sister," Papa said, his eyes blazing. "You weren't successful, and you don't want her to be either."

Jane's insides crumbled, and she began to shake.

"How can you say that? I love Anne. I want nothing more than her happiness, which is why I can't stand by and watch her marry a man as horrid as Chamberlain."

"But you have no proof he's horrid," Mama said. "He's absolutely charming—and wealthy into the bargain. Goodness, Jane, we've known him for years. Since your first Season, in fact. Are you jealous he never courted you?" She shook her head sadly.

It was as if Jane was sinking into a mire from which she couldn't escape. No matter what she did, she was sucked deeper and deeper into a dark—and lonely—abyss. She struggled to find words. "No," she said softly. How could she be jealous of Anne, especially with regard to Mr. Chamberlain when her heart belonged completely to Anthony?

She remembered where he was this morning and couldn't believe she hadn't mentioned it sooner. She'd been too nervous and then too upset to think clearly. "It's very likely that Bow Street will arrest Mr. Chamberlain today. I presume when that happens, the wedding won't happen."

Papa's brows shot up, and he and Mama exchanged a look of concern. Jane felt a modicum of relief at last.

"Do you know for sure that's happening?" Papa asked sternly.

No, but she believed it would. How could it not? "I don't know when, but I would expect it at any time."

Mama inhaled and schooled her features into a serene expression. "Then we shall wait and see."

Shocked at their refusal to accept the seriousness of the situation, Jane looked from her mother to her father. "Is there really nothing I can say to convince you I am earnest and that my motives are pure?"

"Pure is not a word you should use," Papa said.

For a brief moment, Jane wondered if he'd somehow heard the old rumor about her and that he…believed it? She wanted to ask, but couldn't. No, on second thought, she didn't want to know. It seemed her connection to this family was over. Or at least to her parents. She wouldn't give up on Anne, especially with regard to her marriage. The moment she heard that Chamberlain would be arrested, she'd inform Anne. And her parents couldn't stop her.

"Please excuse me," Jane said through the emotion clogging her throat. She turned and left, cutting a wide berth around her mother on her way out.

By the time Jane arrived in Cavendish Square, she'd talked herself into feeling better. Anthony had gone to Bow Street, and even now, a Runner might be arresting Chamberlain.

She saw Anthony's coach at the end of the square, and her heart picked up speed. Her vehicle barely came to a stop before she opened the door and waited impatiently for the coachman to lower the step.

Dashing up the steps, she reached the door just as Culpepper opened it. "Is he in the garden room?" she asked, untying her bonnet and handing it to the butler.

"Yes, miss."

Jane hurried to the garden room, ripping her gloves off on the way. She deposited them on a table as she stepped inside. Anthony stood before the garden doors, his tall, sculpted form taking her breath away. He pivoted slowly, and she knew immediately that something wasn't right.

Taking small steps, she moved toward him, stopping a few feet away. "What's happened?"

"I went to Bow Street."

Jane's entire body tensed. "They aren't arresting Chamberlain, are they?"

"Not yet." He turned his head back toward the garden, where the sun shone brightly on the roses and shrubs in full bloom. "Sheffield—the Runner—is investigating."

"Why isn't he just arresting him?"

"Because they require evidence."

"But don't they have that from you?" She tried to think—was his testimony not enough? Even if it wasn't, he had the letters. "You have the letters he wrote you. Surely that's evidence. Or does he need to prove the letters came from Chamberlain since he didn't sign his name?"

"It's not that simple." Anthony's face creased with anguish, and he couldn't seem to maintain eye contact with her. "We need time to find more proof. Besides the letters. Did you visit Anne?"

"I wasn't able to see her. My parents wouldn't allow it." Jane didn't hide her bitter disappointment.

"Are they going to cancel the wedding?"

"No. They accused me of trying to steal Anne's success." Her heart twisted anew as she tried to comprehend how they could think so very little of her. "I told them Chamberlain would likely be arrested by Bow Street today, and they preferred to just wait and see what happens." She took another step closer to him. "But now you're saying he may not be arrested today. I don't understand why they need more proof. Surely the letters he sent you are enough."

"They aren't!" His voice exploded in the room. He closed his eyes briefly and took a deep breath. Then he faced her, his eyes a torrent of emotion. "If they use the letters as evidence, everyone will know about my debts and about my parents' death. It will be, as Sheffield put it, a matter of record."

Jane's breath left her lungs in a rush. Her knees wobbled. "There's no other way?"

"Not unless Sheffield can find more proof. However, it doesn't look good. I went to the Stinking Sheep, where I paid the money he demanded the first time. The barkeep gave the money to an urchin, and he knows no more now than he did when I paid the money. There's no finding the lad, no way to connect my money to Chamberlain. Sheffield may investigate other clues, but I doubt he will make an arrest today." He stared at her in anguish. "Jane, you must convince your sister to cry off."

"She won't." Though Jane hadn't spoken to Anne, she didn't think her sister would agree. And her parents certainly wouldn't allow her to. "Not without proof of Chamberlain's crimes. There has to be some way."

"I also went to see the Vicar, but he wasn't taking appointments today, whatever the hell that means. I'm hopeful he can help provide other evidence, since he traced the extortion to Chamberlain."

He moved toward her, stopping just a breath away. "I can't allow the letters to be evidence. You understand that, don't you? You're the one who convinced me that I needed to protect Sarah from the truth. Think of her and her family."

Jane did understand, just as she understood the need to protect *her* sister. "You'd sacrifice my sister to a criminal in marriage to keep your sister from finding out about your past transgressions?" The question hung heavy between them, a horrible weight of torment and division.

"No." His voice broke, and he looked away again. "I just need more time."

"We are out of that." Her mind tried to scramble, but again, the mire pulled her down, suffocating her.

"I'm sorry, Jane." His dark whisper smashed the last pieces of her heart into bits.

She stared past him at the bright garden, a vision

of beauty that didn't remotely permeate the shadows engulfing her. The sound of his departing footsteps echoed in her brain.

Eventually, she blinked. She looked around the empty room. An overwhelming sense of loneliness swept over her. She'd chosen that when she'd chosen this new life. She'd known she'd be alone—she'd welcomed it. What she hadn't expected was that people she loved would turn their backs on her. That was true loneliness. That was despair.

That was her future.

~

*B*y the time Anthony made his way into White's that evening, he was gratifyingly drunk. The familiar numbness had taken over, and he could almost smile. Almost.

Unfortunately, he could still see the hurt and defeat in Jane's eyes. It nearly tore him in two. And it would have if not for the copious amounts of brandy he'd poured down his throat.

He'd told her she deserved better than him. Hadn't he told her that? Hell, it was bloody obvious. She was everything he wasn't—generous, kind, caring. He'd absolutely defiled her with his presence, and she would be far better off without him.

He didn't have time for such maudlin thoughts. There'd be time enough for that for the rest of his miserable life. Now, he needed to find Chamberlain and put a stop to this wedding. He owed that much to Jane.

After several passes around the club, Anthony finally ran Chamberlain to ground in one of the smaller salons. He weaved his way to where the man sat talking with another gentleman.

"Chamberlain," Anthony said, trying to put on an affable front. "Might I have a word?"

"Colton, it's been too long. Why not sit with us?" He gestured to an open chair next to his.

Anthony glanced toward the other man before fixing Chamberlain with a direct stare. "I'm afraid I need to have a private conversation."

"I see." Chamberlain nodded, then looked over at the other gentleman. "Would you mind excusing us?"

"Not at all." The man, a few years younger than Chamberlain and Anthony, stood and inclined his head before leaving the salon.

Anthony looked back and watched him depart as well as took stock of who remained in the salon. Just a few gentlemen clustered together in a seating area on the other side of the room.

Dropping into the chair, Anthony perched on the edge and angled himself toward Chamberlain. "I came to call you out."

Chamberlain's brown eyes widened. "You want to duel?"

Hell, that hadn't come out right. "No, but I would hate for it to come to that." He looked toward the clock on the mantel. "You will notice I didn't pay your extortion demand before the deadline. Tell me, what do you plan to do?"

"What the hell are you going on about?" Chamberlain whispered urgently, looking wildly around the room before settling a dark glower on Anthony. "You're drunk."

"Yes, I often am. It's a preferable way to navigate life, I've found, particularly when one is being extorted."

"I'm not extorting you." Chamberlain's voice was low and insistent, his gaze darting nervously about.

Anthony waved his hand and shook his head.

"No, no, let's not pretend. You led me to the Vicar, and the Vicar has led me to you. I know you're behind the extortion letters I received."

Chamberlain's nostrils flared, and his jaw clenched. "Prove it."

"I'm working on that, but you could save me the trouble by simply admitting it. I've shown the letters to Bow Street."

Chamberlain swore, then ran his hand through his hair, his gaze furious. Anthony took a small bit of satisfaction in his discomfort.

"So you paid the money for no reason?" Chamberlain asked. "You're just going to let your misdeeds become public?" He looked at Anthony with pity.

Anthony curled his hand around the arm of his chair and squeezed until he couldn't feel his fingers. "*Confess.*"

Lifting a shoulder, Chamberlain picked up his glass of brandy from the table beside his chair and took a long sip. "I think you should just pay me the three hundred pounds. All this will go away."

Anthony gritted his teeth and worked to keep himself in check. He longed to put his fist through Chamberlain's jaw. "Until the next time you want money."

"I promise never to bother you again. Do we have a deal?" He waited, and when Anthony didn't immediately respond, he added, "No one need know about your debts or your parents."

"Why do you want the money anyway? You've plenty. Even for a new house."

"Consider it a wedding gift." He laughed softly, then took another drink.

"I *should* call you out," Anthony growled.

"I'm quite good with a pistol," Chamberlain said with cool confidence. "How are you?"

"Good enough, and I'm sure my second—Ripley

—will ensure I'm at peak performance." Marcus was well known for his accuracy with a pistol.

Chamberlain's façade cracked a bit, his brow darkening. "Just pay the money and be done with it."

It was a disgustingly appealing invitation. That Anthony was tempted only increased his self-loathing a thousandfold. He would've done it if not for Jane's sister. In fact, he would've paid more if Chamberlain also agreed to call off the wedding. But if he cried off, it would hurt Anne more than it would him. Her reputation would suffer, and Anthony couldn't do that to her. Not after everything Jane had endured regarding her own reputation. The only way to preserve Anne's reputation was to ensure Chamberlain's crimes were known. Or that he was arrested. Preferably both.

Finishing his brandy, Chamberlain set his glass down, then stood. He tugged his waistcoat over his thickening middle and straightened his coat, looking down at Anthony with repugnance. "Think about it. I'll give you until tomorrow to make up your mind. Then it *will* be a wedding gift." He clapped his hand on Anthony's shoulder.

Anthony shot to his feet, violently shrugging off the smaller man's touch. He towered over Chamberlain with menace, his hands fisted, ready for battle. "Touch me again, and there really will be no wedding tomorrow. You won't be able to speak, let alone consummate the marriage with your bride."

"Do you really want to fight here?" He looked around. "Think twice before you completely ruin yourself, Colton."

Anthony turned, throwing his shoulder against Chamberlain and knocking him off-balance before striding from the salon. He passed a footman bearing a tray with drinks and plucked one off the salver. Tossing the port down his gullet, Anthony deposited the empty glass on a table before he made his way outside.

The cool evening air rushed over his heated face. He briefly closed his eyes, trying to dissipate some of the anger and helplessness. The self-loathing, however, remained. It would always be there. He wouldn't even try to expel it.

Wiping his hand over his face, he turned up St. James's and nearly walked straight into Marcus.

"Ho there, Anthony," he said. "What were you doing at White's?"

Brooks's was their preferred club. "I needed to see someone."

Marcus frowned, but there was concern in his gaze, illuminated by the streetlamp. "Harry Sheffield came to see me. He said you might need a friend. Looking at you, it seems he's right."

"I don't deserve friends." Anthony pushed past him and started up the pavement.

"Does that include Jane?" Marcus followed him, keeping pace beside him.

Anthony scowled, keeping his gaze focused in front of him. "Leave her out of it."

Marcus snagged Anthony's elbow, drawing him to stop. "I can't. Phoebe and I care about her. We won't allow you to break her heart."

Oh God. What did they know? Anthony swung around to face him, shaking off Marcus's grip. "Why would you think I'd do that? Have you and Phoebe discussed this?"

"Yes. Jane told her about your affair."

Anthony felt as though everything was falling apart. He'd been barely holding it all together as it was—he'd been happy for what felt like an impossibly short span. But then he'd known it wouldn't last, because he didn't deserve happiness. He hadn't, however, known that Jane would go back on her word and tell Phoebe about him.

And why the hell did any of this involve Jane's heart? Anthony had told her from the start that he wouldn't fall in love with her.

"Don't be angry," Marcus said.

"Don't tell me what to be. And don't follow me. I mean it, Marcus." Anthony turned from him and started walking.

A light drizzle started a few minutes later, but Anthony didn't quicken his pace. He wasn't even sure where he was going. And so it was with some surprise that he found himself in Cavendish Square.

He didn't go to her door, but made his way through the mews to her garden. He wasn't sure of the time, but estimated it to be after dinner. Sure enough, she was in the garden room when he reached the door.

Trying the latch and finding it unlocked, Anthony let himself in. She rose from the chair near the hearth without a flicker of surprise. He walked by her and picked up her glass of port, draining it before setting it back down on the small table beside her chair.

He pivoted to face her. "You went back on your word."

Her gaze was steady. "So did you."

"How so?"

She surveyed him slowly, thoroughly, her mouth pulled tight. "You're drunk."

"I never said I wouldn't get drunk. I said I wouldn't drink while I was your guest."

"Then perhaps you should leave."

He leaned toward her. "Do you really care that I'm inebriated?"

"I care that you dislike yourself enough to drink

this much on a seemingly regular basis. I suppose I should be happy you aren't bruised and bloody."

"In fact, you should. That was definitely an option tonight. Might still be yet." He positively ached to do serious damage to Chamberlain.

"How did I go back on my word?" she asked, drawing him back to the start.

"You told Phoebe about me. After I specifically asked you not to."

"Actually, you asked me not to tell Marcus. You also asked that I not tell him about the fight you were in. I didn't tell him anything, and I didn't tell Phoebe about the fight. Whom I tell about our affair is my business."

"It's also mine, Jane. Your reputation isn't the only one at stake."

Her eyes widened, and she let out a sharp laugh. "You mean to tell me you care what people think about your sexual partners *now*?"

"Fucking prostitutes is not the same as carrying on with a respectable lady like you, and you know it." He cringed inwardly at his coarse language.

She stared at him, then nodded. "You're right. And you did try to refuse me. Repeatedly."

He hated the hollow pitch of her voice, the pain in her eyes. "I'm sorry, Jane. I *don't* care about my reputation. I'm an utter reprobate—everyone knows it, including you. I saw Chamberlain tonight. It didn't go well." He turned from her, taking his hat off and running his fingers through his hair. Where the hell had he left his gloves?

"What happened?"

He faced her again and saw the concern creasing her face. Guilt tore through him. "He promised that if I paid him, he wouldn't bother me again."

She paled, her breath snaking in with a sharp gasp. "You're considering it. What about Anne?"

"She can cry off." A chill settled over Anthony, and he knew in that moment that whatever happened, he couldn't return from this place, this utter despair. "I don't care about my reputation—I told you that—but I can't subject Sarah to any of this. You convinced me of that."

"I wish I never had," she said softly. "Sarah is stronger than you think. She would understand why you had to do this. For *my* sister. And her reputation."

"I'm not going to ask her to do that. I can't." Anthony's voice broke, and he looked past her toward the dark garden, his body rife with a tension that threatened to shatter him into pieces.

"I never realized you were a coward."

He pinned his gaze to hers. "You should have seen that the moment you scooped me off your front step. I told you from the start exactly who I am and what to expect."

Her eyes turned to ice, and Anthony didn't think he'd ever find warmth again. "You left out the part where you were a coldhearted scoundrel."

There was only one thing he could say, and he wasn't even sure he believed it was true. "Sarah is all I have left."

Her eyes widened slightly before turning frigid once more. "And here I'd hoped you knew you had more than that. You had me."

Holding her head high, she swept past him and quit the room. He stood there, his body frozen, until he felt something nudge his leg.

He looked down and saw the kittens attacking his foot. Maybe he did have more than he realized. Or he had, anyway.

Squatting down, he petted them both. When he stood, he looked around the room, his heart squeezing and his throat burning. He made his way to the door and gave the kittens a small smile. "If you could talk, I would tell you to tell her that I love her." He exhaled raggedly. "It's probably best that you don't."

He turned and left, certain that Jane now possessed whatever had remained of his heart.

CHAPTER 16

*J*f Jane had slept an hour, she would have been surprised. Tormented by Anthony's rejection and absolute self-destruction, she'd almost gone to his house to make sure he was all right. To tell him he *would* be all right, that he had to be. Because even if they weren't going to be together, she loved him. Even if he was so trapped in his own despair that he couldn't do what he ought, she loved him.

But he didn't want her love. Maybe that was why he'd chosen to break her heart instead.

Jane's coach stopped in front of the church. Rain streamed like tears down the windows, and Jane was glad to find her eyes were dry after last night's bout of crying.

Taking a deep, fortifying breath, she waited for the coachman to open the door. He held up an umbrella for her until she passed between two of the tall Corinthian columns and into the covered portico of St. George's Church.

"I'll wait for you here, miss," the coachman said.

Jane nodded and moved into the vestibule. Finding it empty, she moved into the sanctuary. Her parents and Anne stood a little way down the center aisle.

"Jane!" Papa strode toward her, his brows pitched into an angry V. "We told you not to come."

"You've told me to do many things, and as you've noted, I've decided I prefer my own counsel." She looked past him to her sister. "Anne, I must speak with you."

"No, you may not," Mama said, moving to stand in front of Anne.

Anne veered around their mother and came toward Jane. She threw an irritated look at their parents. "Leave Jane be. I want her to be here. She *should* be here."

Tears sprang to Jane's eyes as she beheld her sister. Adorned in a pale blue dress trimmed in tiny pearls and embroidered flowers, her blond curls entwined with pearls and blue and white ribbon, she was breathtaking. "You look beautiful."

Anne's gaze softened, and she took Jane's hand. "Thank you. I'm so glad you're here."

An older woman with ruddy cheeks and a pleasant smile approached them. "Come, let's move to the back. The guests are beginning to arrive." She led them down the center aisle and into a room on the right side. Giving Anne a gentle pat on the arm, she said, "It won't be long now." Then she returned to the sanctuary.

Spurred into action, Jane tightened her grip on her sister's hand and turned toward her. "Listen to me, Anne. You can't marry Mr. Chamberlain."

"Stop it this instant," Mama cried. "You will not ruin your sister as you ruined yourself. This is an excellent match—one you should have made years ago. Your jealousy is horrendous."

Jane cast her a beleaguered glance. "I'm not jealous, Mama. I wouldn't want Chamberlain if he were the last man alive."

"Why not?" Anne asked cautiously.

"Because he's an extortionist. And he associates with criminals. He's an awful person, Anne."

"Listen to her."

Jane swung her head to the doorway. Anthony stood just inside, garbed in stark black, his face pale, his hair brushed back from his forehead. Despite her anger and hurt, her pulse thrummed at the sight of him.

"Lord Colton?" her father asked, having turned toward his voice just as Jane had—and as her mother and Anne had too.

Anthony came farther into the room. He didn't look at Jane, but kept his gaze on her father. "You must listen to your daughter. Chamberlain is an extortionist, and he does associate with criminals. I know this because he sent me to an underworld moneylender so that I could borrow money to repay my substantial gambling debts and has been extorting me with that scandalous information."

"That's absurd," Papa spat.

Anthony arched a brow at him. "Are you calling me a liar, sir?"

Papa's jaw worked. He tipped his head briefly toward the floor. "No. But why would Chamberlain do such a thing?"

"I'm not entirely sure, but it scarcely matters. Perhaps he just likes to wield power over people—he certainly didn't need the two hundred pounds I paid him or the three hundred he demanded I give him today as a wedding gift." He sent a sympathetic look toward Anne. "I'm sorry."

Jane squeezed her sister's hand in support as she stared at Anthony in disbelief.

"I'd hoped Bow Street would arrive to arrest

Chamberlain, but I was unable to find a Runner this morning. I did leave word, however. Along with the evidence—letters Chamberlain sent me outlining my transgressions and his demand for payment to keep them secret."

The older woman came in again, her features creased in a clearly agitated state. "I'm sorry to disturb you, but there seems to be a problem in the sanctuary. A Bow Street Runner has arrived."

Papa strode past Anthony and the older woman. Anne let go of Jane's hand and followed him, and Mama was fast on her heels.

Jane went to Anthony and stood before him. "Why?" It was all she could think to say.

"I couldn't let her marry him—no matter the cost."

"Unhand him!" Jane's father's voice carried from the sanctuary.

Jane picked up her skirts and hurried from the room. She heard Anthony moving behind her.

In the center aisle, two men flanked Chamberlain, whose face was a dark, mottled red. His gaze snapped to Anthony. "You!"

Several guests had arrived. They stood farther back in the center aisle, their attention rapt on the shocking scene before them.

"You can't arrest him at his own wedding," Papa said angrily.

Jane gaped at him. "You'd rather he marry Anne?"

"This is what he wrote to me." Anthony's voice rang out clear in the church. "'I know what you did, how you killed your parents. Unless you want everyone to know your sins, I require two hundred pounds, delivered to the barkeep at The Stinking Sheep in Blackfriars. You must deliver the funds personally on the seventeenth of May, or everyone in

London will know *the embarrassing and tawdry details* of your transgressions—gambling, debt, drinking, womanizing, *but most of all,* murder.'" He turned to Jane's father. "You want your daughter to marry the author of that?"

Papa's face turned to ash, and in that moment, Jane felt sorry for him. But her pride in and love for Anthony outshone that and every other emotion fighting within her.

"He can't marry your daughter anyhow," one of the Runners announced. "We're taking him to Bow Street."

Chamberlain sneered at Anthony. "You've just ruined yourself. There's no coming back from this."

"There was no coming back from it anyway," Anthony murmured. "I was already lost."

Jane's heart, broken after the previous night, swelled as she looked at him. He turned his head, and their eyes connected. His lips curved into a small smile. "I'm so sorry, Jane. My deepest regret will always be how I treated you."

Then he turned and cut over to the side aisle. She watched him go, desperate to follow him, but rooted to the floor as everything crumbled around her. Mama had started to cry, and Papa came toward Jane.

"Colton was your friend who was being extorted? I can well imagine what sort of 'friend' he was."

A horrible awareness bloomed inside her. "You knew about the rumor," Jane said, certain now. "And you *believed* it."

Anne came to her side. "*That* rumor?"

Jane barely nodded. "That I was a wanton, and that no respectable young man should wed me." Tears stung her eyes. "It was a lie, Papa. Started by God knows who."

"It was started by him."

Everyone turned to look at who had spoken. It was Lord Rockbourne—Chamberlain's brother-in-law. His wife, Dorothea, Lady Rockbourne, rushed to his side and urgently whispered something to him.

Lord Rockbourne raised his hand and cast her a dark frown. He looked to Jane with an apologetic stare. "I should have known it wasn't true. You were such a charming and intelligent young lady, so lively. I was quite taken with you."

Anne stalked toward her betrothed. "Is this true? Did you start that vile, disgusting rumor about my sister?"

Chamberlain jerked his head toward his sister, Lady Rockbourne. "She begged me to do it. She wanted Rockbourne and feared he was about to formally enter into a courtship with your sister."

"So you ruined Jane?" Anne's voice climbed, echoing in the sanctuary. Then she did the most alarming, shocking, wonderful thing: she hit her betrothed in the nose.

Chamberlain's head snapped back, and he yowled in pain.

"I wouldn't marry you if there was a pistol to my head, and I don't give a fig if that ruins me. If Society would rather I wed a lying, extorting, filthy piece of rubbish, I would prefer to be cast out, thank you." Anne marched back to Jane and took her hand.

The Runners dragged Chamberlain down the aisle. All the guests that had arrived and gathered moved aside, their mouths agape. Oh, this was going to set the tongues wagging for *quite* some time.

Jane beamed at her sister. Then she sent a glare of pure loathing toward Lady Rockbourne, who was appropriately crestfallen. Rockbourne, on the other hand, looked positively livid. He left her and walked down the aisle to where Jane stood with Anne.

"My deepest apologies," he said, bowing to Jane.

"When I think of what was stolen from you, from us…"

Jane nodded as a tangle of emotions gathered in her throat. But then just one overruled them all. She smiled at Lord Rockbourne. "As it happens, I think I was given a gift—one that took a few years to come to fruition, but one that is greater than anything I could have hoped for." Indeed, she felt sorrier for Rockbourne and his current situation than she ever could for herself.

The viscount turned and went back to his wife. Taking her arm, he escorted her from the church with alacrity.

Papa put his arm around Mama, and they returned to the room at the back of the sanctuary, leaving Jane and Anne to deal with the repercussions of what had just occurred.

Anne lifted her voice. "Clearly, there will be no wedding. Nor will there be a wedding breakfast." She glanced at Jane, then added, smiling at everyone, "Thank you for coming."

Jane nearly laughed at the absurdity of her last statement. Then she realized she wanted to say something too. Addressing the guests, she said, "I trust none of you will hold this against my sister. Miss Anne Pemberton is blameless in all this—her reputation must not be maligned."

"And neither must Jane's," Anne said, sliding a mischievous look toward Jane. "Society owes her an apology for believing a vicious lie."

"Hear, hear!" someone called, and Jane realized it was Phoebe. She stood at the back of the sanctuary with her husband.

Jane laughed softly, lifting her hand to cover her mouth as tears began to streak down her cheeks. Anne put her arm around her. "Don't cry, Jane. This has all turned out marvelously. For both of us."

Jane turned to her sister, wiping her cheeks. "Don't you see? It hasn't turned out well at all. The man I love has ruined himself. Worse than that, he's faced his demons, and no one is there to keep him safe and whole." Heart racing, Jane hugged her sister hard and fast. "I have to go."

Anne nodded. "I hope he knows what he has in you."

"I hope so too."

~

*A*rriving home from St. George's, Anthony went straight to his study, intent on pouring a glass of whatever he grabbed first. Before he could get there, Purcell intercepted him with a letter. "This just arrived for you, my lord."

Sarah's handwriting leapt out at Anthony from the missive. He went into the study and sat down near the hearth. Tearing open the parchment, he read the contents slowly, and even smiled at one point. The end, however, chilled him to his core.

I do hope you'll come visit. I am desperate for you to meet Marianne. Won't you be going to Oaklands soon? Please write when you can.

Anthony hadn't been home to Oaklands since last summer. The journey had nearly broken him. Just taking the road on which his parents had been murdered had sent him into a spiral of abject sorrow and anger. He honestly didn't know when he would return.

He could visit Sarah and Felix and meet Marianne at Stag's Court. While it was somewhat near Oaklands, he could get there via an alternate route. It would take longer, but that was a small—and per-haps necessary—price to pay.

Why not take that route to Oaklands?

Anthony wanted to rail at the voice in his head. Stag's Court didn't remind him of his parents, nor were they buried there.

His mind did the unthinkable—it traveled the route his parents had taken. He imagined them in their coach, which he'd had destroyed after their deaths, enjoying their journey. Or not. Perhaps they'd spent the ride from London discussing their chagrin with Anthony. From his gambling debts to his failure to take a wife to his refusal to go to Oak-lands to deal with estate matters, he'd utterly disap-pointed them.

What had they done when the highwayman had overtaken them? The villain had shot the coachman, rendering him unconscious but not dead, and the poor man hadn't remembered a thing about the event. Anthony had sent him into retirement with a hefty purse.

Closing his eyes, Anthony let his imagination take over as he hadn't done in quite some time. He thought of his mother, with her blue-gray eyes that could be cool and exacting, but then warm and car-ing. And his father, with features that were very near Anthony's own. Sometimes, when he looked in the glass, he saw his father. In those moments, he never failed to look away.

Had the highwayman told them why he was there? That his purpose was to intimidate Anthony into paying his debt? His father had been aware of it, because he'd refused to give Anthony the funds to cover it. When Anthony thought of what must have gone through his father's mind in those moments...

Had he been shot first or had it been his mother? He hoped it was her, because he didn't like to think of her horror if she'd seen her husband shot first. But then he thought of his father witnessing his wife's death—if she'd died immediately—and pain seared through Anthony's midsection.

What if they hadn't died right away? Or what if one had and the other's life had slowly slipped away? What if one had held the other as they passed? The scenarios played over and over in his mind until he feared he would go mad. If he wasn't already.

With an anguished cry, he crumpled his sister's letter and threw it into the hearth. His body shaking, he stood and violently shoved everything off the mantel. Then he went to his desk and did the same. Chest heaving, he looked at the sideboard and battled with whether to break everything on it or drink every last drop. While the former would be most satisfying at present, the latter was the smarter decision. He hadn't plunged himself this deep into hell in a long time—because he'd kept himself numb. And that was far preferable to this.

He stalked to the sideboard and reached for a decanter.

"Anthony, don't."

Her voice was a balm that should have soothed him. But after what had happened at the church— no, after what he'd done to her before that—her presence only drove him deeper into despair.

He turned, his hand on the decanter. "You shouldn't be here." His voice was low and raw, and just looking at her beauty in the den of his own ugliness hurt.

Jane came into the study, closing the door behind her. She slowly removed her hat and then her gloves, setting them on the chair he'd vacated. She looked around at the mess he'd made, but didn't say a word. At least not about that.

She inclined her head toward the sideboard. "Do

you want to be numb, or do you want to feel? I prefer feeling, because if I didn't, I wouldn't love you, and that is absolutely unconscionable to me."

The storm inside him crested. "You can't love me. I told you not to."

"Actually, you said you wouldn't love me." Her tone was even, not at all what he wanted. He wanted her anger, her disappointment, her hatred. Didn't he deserve all that? Hadn't he *earned* it? "I never promised not to fall in love with you."

Anthony gripped the decanter but didn't lift it. "Numbness is easier."

She sauntered toward him, her head dipping gently to the right. "That is probably true, but is it better than feeling? It certainly isn't better than love."

He let go of the decanter and pivoted to face her, lunging toward her as rage poured through him. "Love comes with pain and disappointment! It is the ultimate misery. I don't want any part of it, Jane. I can't." He collapsed, and he had to reach behind him to grasp the sideboard to keep from falling. "*I can't.*"

She rushed forward, putting one hand on his waist and the other against his cheek. Her touch blistered him, reminding him that he *did* feel, even if he didn't want to. "Yes, love can hurt, but isn't it worth the pain? It is to me," she said softly.

Unable to hold himself up any longer, he dropped to his knees before her. He put his hand over hers on his cheek and clasped her hip. He stared up at her as emotion flooded him.

"Yes, I would rather feel," he rasped. "I can't seem to *stop* feeling. And it's all because of you. For you." His fingers dug into her. "I love you so damned much."

She smiled down at him, and with her thumb, wiped away a tear snaking down his cheek. "I thought you might. I *hoped* you might."

"I didn't want to. At all. And I really don't want you to love me." He pulled her hand from his face and clutched it tightly. "I don't deserve you, Jane."

"I disagree, and anyway, love is not about what we deserve. We don't choose whom we love, or maybe we do, because I choose you." She squeezed his hand, her gaze warm with love. "We agreed to move forward *together*, and I'm still here, ready to do that. You and me."

The light she always brought to him seemed brighter suddenly, or the darkness less. The pain inside him contracted, leaving a tightness in its wake. But also a thread of hope.

He kissed her hand and let her go. Rising to his feet, he wiped his hands over his face. The tears had stopped, and he felt a steadying calm.

"I want that," he said quietly. "I want *you*. But, I need to be sure I'm worth it. I'm not—not yet."

"I'll wait," she said simply, her mouth pulling into a small smile.

He nodded. "I'll try not to make it too long."

"However long it takes, I'm not going anywhere." She turned and went to fetch her accessories. "You know where to find me."

Then she left.

Anthony drew a deep, shuddering breath. He glanced toward the sideboard, but didn't move. The calm she'd brought to him remained.

He began to tidy the room, replacing the things he'd knocked down and arranging them neatly. When he was finished, he sat at his desk and pulled out a piece of parchment.

Inking a quill, he thought for a moment. Then he began to write to his sister, to tell her everything she needed to know. It would have been better to do it in person. Better still if he'd told her long ago. She deserved the truth, and Jane was right—Sarah was strong. Far stronger than he was.

As the quill scratched across the page, emotion drained from him. When he was finished, he sat back, feeling better than he had in some time.

He wasn't whole—not by a great measure—but for the first time, he imagined it was possible.

CHAPTER 17

The sun beat warm on Jane's shoulders as she sat in the garden. Lemonade and a stack of correspondence sat on a small table to her left. She watched Daffodil and Fern chase insects and bat at flowers, but not even their antics could lift her spirits.

It had been a week since Anne's aborted wedding and since she'd seen Anthony. He hadn't said how long he needed, and while she didn't want to press him, the longer he took, the more worried she became.

Was he all right? Had he spiraled back into self-loathing? Was he even in London?

He hadn't been seen—that much had been noted. Society was abuzz with the events of Anne's wedding: Anthony's revelations, Chamberlain's arrest, the old rumor about Jane.

In fact, Jane had received several notes of support regarding the rumor. Only a few had contained actual apologies, and slightly more were actual invitations. Still, Jane wasn't sure if the latter were due to awareness that she'd been the victim of a false rumor or because Lady Satterfield had made it clear she was a staunch supporter of Jane's. She'd called the day after the wedding, *and* she'd invited Jane to call, which Jane had done two days prior.

After Chamberlain was arrested, several other people had come forward to say he'd also extorted them over the years. It even looked as though he would be transported to Australia for his crimes. Jane thought it a fitting sentence.

As for Anthony, she missed him dreadfully. It took every fiber of strength she possessed not to go to his house, if only to inquire after his welfare. She hadn't even sent a note.

Oh, she'd written several. They sat in a stack on her desk in the sitting room outside her bedchamber. Perhaps today, she'd send one.

Daffodil leapt after a butterfly and crashed into her sister, who had done the same. They fell to the ground and rolled over each other in playful abandon. Jane couldn't help but chuckle.

"Now, that is the sweetest sound I've ever heard."

Jane turned toward the house. Anthony stood leaning nonchalantly against the doorframe leading to the garden room. He looked exceptionally handsome in a crisp white cravat and a rich green waistcoat. His navy coat and buff breeches clung to his familiar frame. She nearly sighed with want.

"How long have you been standing there?" she asked.

He pushed away from the doorframe and came toward her. "Too long, probably. I couldn't resist the view." He sat down in the chair on the other side of the table and sipped from Jane's glass of lemonade.

"That's just lemonade," she said.

He gave her a wry look. "Good."

The kittens ran to greet him, and he laughed down at them. "Has anyone told you that you aren't dogs?" He looked over at Jane. "Have you ever seen cats rush to meet someone?"

She shook her head, overcome with joy at how good he looked and sounded, at how happy she was to see him. "No. But then they've always done that with you. You're special." She held her breath, waiting for him to argue that he wasn't.

He leaned down to scratch them both behind the ears. "It seems so," he murmured.

"You look well," Jane said, devouring him with her eyes.

"I feel well," he said. "As well as when I stayed here with you." He sat up, leaving the cats to frolic once more. "That was the best week of my life." His gaze met hers, and her heart skipped.

Then she realized what he'd said. "But I wasn't with you the past week."

"No, and I'm glad for that. It wasn't very pretty, and not just because I stopped drinking spirits entirely—I did that when I was with you too."

"Then why?"

"I allowed my mind to go where it needed, to be angry, to be sad, to grieve." He grimaced. "I wish I could say I'm done."

"I wouldn't expect you to be."

"Well, it has been a year. Almost," he added softly.

"A year of pushing it all to the side. There is no time limit on grief—or recovery," she said, feeling bad that she'd been so impatient for him to come. But also glad that he was finally here.

"Yes, and I want to be honest with you. I tried to be, but it's hard when you aren't honest with yourself," he said dryly, cracking a smile that lit her entire world. It faded before he added, "I still don't like myself very much."

"Oh, Anthony." She stood and went to his chair. "I like you enough for both of us."

He laughed, then clasped her hand and tugged

her onto his lap. "That is the very best news, for I quite love you." He leaned forward, encircling his arms around her waist, and kissed her, his lips so soft and familiar against hers.

She curled her arms around his neck. "I love you too."

He pulled back and looked into her eyes. "Enough to marry me?"

Her breath caught. She'd hoped they would get to that—eventually. She never imagined he would ask so soon. "Are you sure?" she asked, wanting him more than anything, but not wanting to push him too far too fast.

"Never more. I am still healing, but I wager I'll make even more progress if the greatest nurse in London is at my side."

She laughed, unable to stop grinning. "I was hardly that."

He grew serious. "You gave me succor and support when I needed it most—physically, mentally, emotionally. I would be lost without you. Of that I am certain. If you have the patience to continue to suffer my madness, I would be honored to make you my wife."

"As it happens, I do." She cupped his face, her heart bursting with love. "And you're not mad."

"I'm mad about you." He winked at her. "Oh good, it still works."

She kissed him with wild abandon, twining her fingers in his hair.

"Ahem."

They broke apart, and Anthony lifted her while he rose from the chair.

The Marquess of Ripley stood in the doorway to the garden room. "I feared if I didn't interrupt, this would just continue."

Anthony grinned. "Probably." He turned to Jane

and took her hands. "Just to confirm, you consent to be my wife?"

She held tightly on to him. "Yes. Yes. *Yes.*"

"Oh, good. If you're amenable, we can wed right now." Anthony inclined his head toward Ripley, who led a procession of people into the garden: Phoebe, Anne, Anthony's butler and another gentleman, and Jane's entire household.

"How?" was all Jane could manage to ask.

"Special license, my love," Anthony said. "And a great deal of help. It turns out when you ask people for that, they are delighted to give it."

Jane felt as if her heart was going to burst with joy. Phoebe brought her a sprig of flowers and hugged her.

"You knew about this?" Jane asked.

Phoebe nodded. "I thought it was a brilliant idea."

Jane did too. She couldn't quite believe it.

Anne joined her. "I'm going to stand as your witness, unless you'd prefer Lady Ripley."

"No." Jane hugged her sister tightly. "I'm so glad you're here." She stepped back and asked the question she wasn't sure she wanted an answer to. "Do Mama and Papa know?"

Anne shook her head. "I didn't want to give them the satisfaction of knowing until it was done." She leaned in and whispered, "I wanted to make sure you were going to say yes!"

Jane smiled and nodded in understanding. "Thank you. You'll tell them?"

"When I get home. They think I'm shopping with Mrs. Hammond." Anne looked toward the house, where Mrs. Hammond stood in the doorway to the garden room. She smiled and waved.

"Come out and join us," Jane invited before

turning her attention back to Anne. "Are Mama and Papa still planning on leaving London?"

"Yes." Anne had sent Jane a note about that the other day. "But I'm not going with them. I'd prefer to move in with my sister, Lady Colton."

"Oh yes!" Jane hugged her again. "Of course you will."

Anthony came to interrupt them, his gaze settling on Jane. "The rector is ready." He offered Jane his arm, and they walked to the center of the garden where the rector stood.

Anne joined them, standing near Jane, and Ripley moved next to Anthony.

"I'm so pleased to marry at least one Miss Pemberton today," the rector said with a smile, clearly referencing the wedding that wasn't last week.

"Not as pleased as I am." Jane beamed up at her soon-to-be husband as the rector started the ceremony.

And then, in the presence of those she loved most, with kittens running around the rector's feet, all of Jane's dreams came true.

*S*arah Havers, Countess of Ware, laid the cornflowers on the ground between the graves of their parents, then stood back to join Anthony. Their arms touched as they looked down together.

"I'm glad you decided to come," Sarah said softly.

Anthony slid a glance toward his sister. "Well, you wouldn't let up."

She smiled. "Once you married Jane, you must have realized there was no stopping the both of us."

He laughed. "No, but then I'd already told you I would come *before* I married her."

"I suppose that's true. I'm just sorry I missed the wedding."

He turned to her. "I know, but we agreed there would be no more regrets. Actually, I think that was your insistence."

She faced him, her familiar blue eyes warm with love. "Yes. When I think of all that you've endured...*alone.*" She shook her head.

After he'd sent her the letter detailing his failures, she'd responded with a vehement admonition that he stop blaming himself. It was a response he'd never expected—and had taken time to feel he deserved. Thankfully, Jane had helped.

"I'm not alone anymore."

"You never were." She swatted his arm. "Men are so frustrating."

He smirked. "We can be, yes."

Sarah looked back at the headstones of their parents. "They'd be proud of you."

"I'll spend every day trying to ensure that's true."

"Mama would be absolutely *delighted* to know you married Jane. She always liked her."

"Mama would have been delighted if I'd married a shrubbery."

Sarah laughed. "Perhaps. I'm glad it was Jane—she's been exceptionally good for you."

"She has been everything." It was a simple and completely unavoidable truth. She was the reason he woke up every day, the love in his heart, and the very air he breathed.

With a final look at the graves, they turned back toward the house. Sarah looped her arm through Anthony's. "How is it with Jane's sister living with you?"

"It's fine. She's very busy with the Spitfire Society project."

"The ladies-only workhouse? Such a marvelous undertaking. I can't wait to help. I'm going to teach them to sew and, if they like, to make hats."

"You're going to do that personally?" Anthony asked.

"When I can."

"You are an exceptionally enterprising woman," he noted. Wife, mother, owner of a millinery shop in London. He realized just how unengaged he'd been the past year. But no more. He'd already taken on two committees in the House of Lords and looked forward to returning to work when Parliament was back in session.

They returned to the house, where Jane was holding Marianne. Felix met them at the door and bussed his wife's cheek.

"She woke up?" Sarah went to take her daughter from Jane.

"Yes, but she's been quite happy," Jane said, smiling as she delivered her niece to Sarah.

Her niece. He loved that Jane was now a part of his family. He looked over at Felix, his oldest and dearest friend, who gazed at his wife and child with such open adoration, it would have made most gentlemen in London roll their eyes.

"I never imagined you as a smitten father," Anthony teased.

"Yes, well, I never imagined you would be such a pain in my ass for more than a year." Felix sent him a sardonic look.

Anthony knew he was joking. Felix had greeted him with such fierce affection the day before, almost moving him to tears. But then they shared a bond that was almost brotherly, and Felix had known Anthony's parents nearly as well as Anthony had. It was a connection Anthony would cherish forever.

"Nearly sorted, though?" Felix asked.

Anthony wasn't sure about nearly, but things were getting better every day. "Still some dark spots, but overall, there's improvement." He'd started having nightmares every once in a while. He awakened Jane with his thrashing and crying out, and she invariably soothed him, lulling him back to a place where he knew all was right—or would be.

His gaze settled on his wife of almost two months, and his heart nearly burst with pride and love. He still didn't know how he'd ended up on her doorstep that morning, but he would be eternally grateful.

As if she could feel his attention, Jane looked

over at him, her eyes narrowing slightly as a secret smile teased her lips. His breath caught, thinking he was the luckiest man in the entire world to have her look at him like that.

Later that night, when they climbed into bed, Anthony didn't falter as he had the night before. This had been his parents' chamber, and he wasn't sure he could sleep there. But then Jane had taken him into her arms and held him until he'd surrendered to a dreamless slumber.

Tonight, however, he had other plans.

As soon as she was beneath the coverlet, he rolled on top of her and kissed her thoroughly. She drove her hands into his hair, kissing him back and rising up off the bed to press her breasts into his chest.

He pulled her night rail up to her waist. "Why are you wearing this?"

"I wasn't sure you wanted to—"

He kissed her again. "I want to."

She wriggled her hips. "Good, because I want to too."

Together, they worked to discard the garment, and Jane pulled him back down for another kiss. Several minutes later, he licked down her throat as she clasped his head.

"Sarah assured me that we could do this without any problems while I'm carrying a babe."

Anthony froze just before he took her nipple into his mouth. He looked up at her. "You're with child?"

"I think so. I haven't had my courses in… Well, since you came to stay with me. I think that day at your house, when we got carried away and you didn't—"

He claimed her mouth again as joy swept through him. He looked down at her with more happiness than he'd ever thought possible. Then darkness washed over him.

She reached up and touched his jaw. "What is it?"

"What if I'm a terrible father?"

"You won't be. I have only to look at you with the kittens. Oh, I miss them."

"You think because Daffodil and Fern adore me, I'll be a good father?" He let out a soft laugh. "Kittens are not children."

She chuckled, stroking his face. "No, but you are sensitive and kind and absolutely charming. Plus, you make me feel like the most wonderful person in the world. I've no doubt you will make our child feel the same."

Anthony kissed her again, bearing her down onto the mattress and settling himself between her legs. She curled herself around him, welcoming him into her, and for some time, he was quite blissfully lost.

Later, when he rolled to the side, he gathered her against him. She snuggled into him and stroked his chest.

"Why did you fall in love with me?" he asked. "I specifically told you I wasn't going to love you."

"Or marry me," she said. "And look at us now." She traced her finger around his nipple. "It was when you came to stay with me. In fact, I think it was when the kittens decided you were their favorite person."

"You were jealous?"

She laughed. "Maybe."

"I can't imagine why you would have loved me then. I wasn't remotely worthy. And, God, I looked atrocious."

"You were also incredibly vulnerable. And sweet. And charming. I didn't realize it, but I was lonely, and I felt as if *I* wasn't worthy of having people around me. You showed me I was wrong."

He turned to face her. "You're the worthiest woman I know. I'll spend my life proving it to you."

She caressed his face, bringing her lips to his. "You already have."

Want to read about Lady Gresham and her mysterious past when she tangles with Bow Street Runner Harry Sheffield? They'll sizzle the pages in the first book of The Pretenders trilogy, **A Secret Surrender**, coming August 2020!

Then stay tuned for a truly shocking partnership between newly widowed Lord Rockbourne and Miss Whitford when she sees something she shouldn't have in **A Scandalous Bargain**!

Finally, find out how Rafe Blackwell became the Vicar and the many ways in which he's had to pretend in order to survive, and see if Anne Pemberton may be the one to heal his soul in **A Rogue to Ruin**!

Thank you so much for reading A Duke Will Never Do! It's the third book in The Spitfire Society series. I hope you enjoyed it!

Would you like to know when my next book is available and to hear about sales and deals? Sign up for my VIP newsletter at https://www.darcyburke.com/readergroup, follow me on social media:

Facebook: https://facebook.com/DarcyBurkeFans
Twitter at @darcyburke
Instagram at darcyburkeauthor
Pinterest at darcyburkewrite

And follow me on Bookbub to receive updates on pre-orders, new releases, and deals!

Want to read about some of the characters in this book such as Felix and Sarah, the Earl and Countess of Ware? Or Marcus and Phoebe, the Marquess and Marchioness of Ripley? Grab The Duke of Distraction (especially for Anthony's "origin story") and A Duke is Never Enough! Then stay tuned for my next heart-stopping Regency series, **The Pretenders**, featuring Lady Gresham and Beatrix Whitford, Anne Pemberton, Harry Sheffield, Lord Rockbourne (yes!), and…the Vicar. I'm so excited and hope you are too!

Need more Regency romance? Check out my other historical series:

The Untouchables - Swoon over twelve of Society's most eligible and elusive bachelor peers and the bluestockings, wallflowers, and outcasts who bring them to their knees!

Wicked Dukes Club - six books written by me and my BFF, NYT Bestselling Author Erica Ridley. Meet the unforgettable men of London's most notorious tavern, The Wicked Duke. Seductively handsome, with charm and wit to spare, one night with these rakes and rogues will never be enough…

Love is All Around - heartwarming Regency-set retellings of classic Christmas stories (written after the Regency!) featuring a cozy village, three siblings, and the best gift of all: love.

Secrets and Scandals - six epic stories set in London's glittering ballrooms and England's lush countryside.

Legendary Rogues - Four intrepid heroines and adventurous heroes embark on exciting quests across Regency England and Wales!

If you like contemporary romance, I hope you'll check out my **Ribbon Ridge** series available from

Avon Impulse, and the continuation of Ribbon Ridge in **So Hot**.

I hope you'll consider leaving a review at your favorite online vendor or networking site!

I appreciate my readers so much. Thank you, thank you, *thank you*.

Love is All Around
(A Regency Holiday Trilogy)

The Red Hot Earl
The Gift of the Marquess
Joy to the Duke

Wicked Dukes Club

One Night for Seduction by Erica Ridley
One Night of Surrender by Darcy Burke
One Night of Passion by Erica Ridley
One Night of Scandal by Darcy Burke
One Night to Remember by Erica Ridley
One Night of Temptation by Darcy Burke

Secrets and Scandals

Her Wicked Ways
His Wicked Heart
To Seduce a Scoundrel
To Love a Thief (a novella)
Never Love a Scoundrel
Scoundrel Ever After

Legendary Rogues

Lady of Desire
Romancing the Earl
Lord of Fortune
Captivating the Scoundrel

Contemporary Romance

Ribbon Ridge

Where the Heart Is (a prequel novella)
Only in My Dreams
Yours to Hold
When Love Happens
The Idea of You
When We Kiss
You're Still the One

Ribbon Ridge: So Hot

So Good
So Right
So Wrong

THE UNTOUCHABLES SERIES

THE FORBIDDEN DUKE

"I LOVED this story!!" 5 Stars

-Historical Romance Lover

"This is a wonderful read and I can't wait to see what comes next in this amazing series..." 5 Stars

-Teatime and Books

THE DUKE of DARING

"You will not be able to put it down once you start. Such a good read."

-Books Need TLC

"An unconventional beauty set on life as a spinster meets the one man who might change her mind, only to find his painful past makes it impossible to love. A wonderfully emotional journey from attraction, to friendship, to a love that conquers all."

-Bronwen Evans, *USA Today* Bestselling Author

THE DUKE of DECEPTION

"...an enjoyable, well-paced story ... Ned and Aquilla are an engaging, well-matched couple – strong, caring and compassionate; and ...it's easy to believe that they will continue to be happy together long after the book is ended."

"This is my favorite so far in the series! They had chemistry from the moment they met...their passion leaps off the pages."

THE DUKE of DESIRE

"Masterfully written with great characterization...with a flourish toward characters, secrets, and romance... Must read addition to "The Untouchables" series!"

"If you are looking for a truly endearing story about two people who take the path least travelled to find the other, with a side of 'YAH THAT'S HOT!' then this book is absolutely for you!"

THE DUKE of DEFIANCE

"This story was so beautifully written, and it hooked me from page one. I couldn't put the book down and just had to read it in one sitting even though it meant reading into the wee hours of the morning."

"I loved the Duke of Defiance! This is the kind of book you hate when it is over and I had to make myself stop reading just so I wouldn't have to leave the fun of Knighton's (aka Bran) and Joanna's story!"

-Behind Closed Doors Book Review

THE DUKE of DANGER

"The sparks fly between them right from the start... the HEA is certainly very hard-won, and well-deserved."

-All About Romance

"Another book hangover by Darcy! Every time I pick a favorite in this series, she tops it. The ending was perfect and made me want more."

-Sassy Book Lover

THE DUKE of ICE

"Each book gets better and better, and this novel was no exception. I think this one may be my fave yet! 5 out 5 for this reader!"

-Front Porch Romance

"An incredibly emotional story...I dare anyone to stop reading once the second half gets under way because this is intense!"

-Buried Under Romance

THE DUKE of RUIN

"This is a fast paced novel that held me until the last page."

" ...everything I could ask for in a historical romance... impossible to stop reading."

THE DUKE of LIES

"THE DUKE OF LIES is a work of genius! The characters are wonderfully complex, engaging; there is much mystery, and so many, many lies from so many people; I couldn't wait to see it all uncovered."

"..the epitome of romantic [with]...a bit of danger/action. The main characters are mature, fierce, passionate, and full of surprises. If you are a hopeless romantic and you love reading stories that'll leave you feeling like you're walking on clouds then you need to read this book or maybe even this entire series."

THE DUKE of SEDUCTION

"There were tears in my eyes for much of the last 10% of this book. So good!"

"An absolute joy to read... I always recommend
Darcy!"

-Brittany and Elizabeth's Book Boutique

THE DUKE of KISSES

"Don't miss this magnificent read. It has some
comedic fun, heartfelt relationships, heartbreaking
moments, and horrifying danger."

-The Reading Café

"...my favorite story in the series. Fans of Regency
romances will definitely enjoy this book."

-Two Ends of the Pen

THE DUKE of DISTRACTION

"Count on Burke to break a heart as only she can.
This couple will get under the skin before they steal
your heart."

-Hopeless Romantic

"Darcy Burke never disappoints. Her storytelling is
just so magical and filled with passion. You will fall
in love with the characters and the world she
creates!"

-Teatime and Books

SECRETS & SCANDALS SERIES

HER WICKED WAYS

"A bad girl heroine steals both the show and a high-wayman's heart in Darcy Burke's deliciously wicked debut."

–Courtney Milan, *NYT* Bestselling Author

"…fast paced, very sexy, with engaging characters."

–*Smexybooks*

HIS WICKED HEART

"Intense and intriguing. Cinderella meets *Fight Club* in a historical romance packed with passion, action and secrets."

–Anna Campbell, *Seven Nights in a Rogue's Bed*

"A romance...to make you smile and sigh…a wonderful read!"

–*Rogues Under the Covers*

TO SEDUCE a SCOUNDREL

"Darcy Burke pulls no punches with this sexy, romantic page-turner. Sevrin and Philippa's story grabs you from the first scene and doesn't let go. *To Seduce a Scoundrel* is simply delicious!"

–Tessa Dare, *NYT* Bestselling Author

"I was captivated on the first page and didn't let go until this glorious book was finished!"

–*Romancing the Book*

TO LOVE a THIEF

"With refreshing circumstances surrounding both the hero and the heroine, a nice little mystery, and a touch of heat, this novella was a perfect way to pass the day."

—The Romanceaholic

"A refreshing read with a dash of danger and a little heat. For fans of honorable heroes and fun heroines who know what they want and take it."

-The Luv NV

NEVER LOVE a SCOUNDREL

"I loved the story of these two misfits thumbing their noses at society and finding love." Five stars.

—A Lust for Reading

"A nice mix of intrigue and passion...wonderfully complex characters, with flaws and quirks that will draw you in and steal your heart."

—BookTrib

SCOUNDREL EVER AFTER

"There is something so delicious about a bad boy, no matter what era he is from, and Ethan was definitely delicious."

-A Lust for Reading

"I loved the chemistry between the two main characters...Jagger/Ethan is not what he seems at all and neither is sweet society Miss Audrey. They are believably compatible."

-Confessions of a College Angel

LEGENDARY ROGUES SERIES

LADY of DESIRE

"A fast-paced mixture of adventure and romance, very much in the mould of *Romancing the Stone* or *Indiana Jones*."

-*All About Romance*

"...gave me such a book hangover! ...addictive...one of the most entertaining stories I've read this year!"

-*Adria's Romance Reviews*

ROMANCING the EARL

"Once again Darcy Burke takes an interesting story and...turns it into magic. An exceptionally well-written book."

-*Bodice Rippers, Femme Fatale, and Fantasy*

"...A fast paced story that was exciting and interesting. This is a definite must add to your book lists!"

-*Kilts and Swords*

LORD of FORTUNE

"I don't think I know enough superlatives to describe this book! It is wonderfully, magically delicious. It sucked me in from the very first sentence and didn't turn me loose—not even at the end ..."

"If you love a deep, passionate romance with a bit of mystery, then this is the book for you!"
    -Teatime and Books

CAPTIVATING the SCOUNDREL

"I am in absolute awe of this story. Gideon and Daphne stole all of my heart and then some. This book was such a delight to read."

"Darcy knows how to end a series with a bang! Daphne and Gideon are a mix of enemies and allies turned lovers that will have you on the edge of your seat at every turn."

Contemporary Romance

RIBBON RIDGE SERIES

A contemporary family saga featuring the Archer family of sextuplets who return to their small Oregon wine country town to confront tragedy and find love...

The "multilayered plot keeps readers invested in the story line, and the explicit sensuality adds to the excitement that will have readers craving the next Ribbon Ridge offering."

-*Library Journal* Starred Review on YOURS TO HOLD

"Darcy Burke writes a uniquely touching and heart-warming series about the love, pain, and joys of family as well as the love that feeds your soul when you meet "the one.""

-*The Many Faces of Romance*

I can't tell you how much I love this series. Each book gets better and better.

-*Romancing the Readers*

"Darcy Burke's Ribbon Ridge series is one of my all-time favorites. Fall in love with the Archer family, I know I did."

-*Forever Book Lover*

RIBBON RIDGE: SO HOT

SO GOOD

" ...worth the read with its well-written words, beautiful descriptions, and likeable characters...they are flirty, sexy and a match made in wine heaven."

-*Harlequin Junkie* Top Pick

"I absolutely love the characters in this book and the families. I honestly could not put it down and finished it in a day."

SO RIGHT

"This is another great story by Darcy Burke. Painting pictures with her words that make you want to sit and stare at them for hours. I love the banter between the characters and the general sense of fun and friendliness."

-The Ardent Reader

" ...the romance is emotional; the characters are spirited and passionate... "

-The Reading Café

SO WRONG

"As usual, Ms. Burke brings you fun characters and witty banter in this sweet hometown series. I loved the dance between Crystal and Jamie as they fought their attraction."

-The Many Faces of Romance

"I really love both this series and the Ribbon Ridge series from Darcy Burke. She has this way of taking your heart and ripping it right out of your chest one second and then the next you are laughing at something the characters are doing."

-Romancing the Readers

ABOUT THE AUTHOR

Darcy Burke is the USA Today Bestselling Author of sexy, emotional historical and contemporary romance. Darcy wrote her first book at age 11, a happily ever after about a swan addicted to magic and the female swan who loved him, with exceedingly poor illustrations. Join her Reader Club newsletter at http://www.darcyburke.com/readerclub.

A native Oregonian, Darcy lives on the edge of wine country with her guitar-strumming husband, their two hilarious kids who seem to have inherited the writing gene. They're a crazy cat family with two Bengal cats, a small, fame-seeking cat named after a fruit, and an older rescue Maine Coon who is the master of chill and five a.m. serenading. In her "spare" time Darcy is a serial volunteer enrolled in a 12-step program where one learns to say "no," but she keeps having to start over. Her happy places are Disneyland and Labor Day weekend at the Gorge. Visit Darcy online at http://www.darcyburke.com and follow her on social media.

facebook.com/DarcyBurkeFans

twitter.com/darcyburke

instagram.com/darcyburkeauthor

pinterest.com/darcyburkewrites

goodreads.com/darcyburke

bookbub.com/authors/darcy-burke

amazon.com/author/darcyburke

CPSIA information can be obtained
at www.ICGtesting.com
Printed in the USA
LVHW090432140621
690153LV00015B/332

9 781944 576752